# Shadow, Spell & Spell: Expert

CHICAGO & TORONTO

# Credits

Written by Richard Iorio II

Additional Material by James Maliszewski and Gabriel Brouillard

Line Editor John M. Kahane

Proof Reading by Michael Wolf, Gabriel Brouillard, Brendan Davis, Rebecca Moss, Kathryn Peterson, Dominic Hu, Zachary Houghton, Daniel Perez, Jae Walker, Anthony Ragan, James Maliszewski and Ariana Fisch

Art Direction by Richard Iorio II

Layout and Pre-Press by Richard Iorio II

Art by Bradley K. McDevitt, Alfredo Lopez Jr., Jeff Preston, Gabriel Brouillard, V Shane, Maciej Zagorski, Pawel Dobosz, LeCire, Steve Robertson, ©iStockphoto.com/natashika, ©iStockphoto.com/jpa1999, ©iStock- photo.com/laurien, ©iStockphoto.com/Thomas51471, and ©iStockphoto.com/ IgorZakowski, Jordan Mallon

Playtesting by Kathy Bauer, Steve Bauer, Nick Roberts, Tom Robinson, Joanne Clarke, Angela Marsh, Steven Ross, Tammy Powers, John M. Kahane, Rebecca Moss, Kathryn Peterson, Dominic Hu, Henry Sanders, Frederick

**Shadow, Sword & Spell** logo by Jeremy Simmons

To my friends who inspire me, my teachers who influence me, and my enemies who motivate me.



ISBN 978-0-9796361-9-6

Published by **Rogue Games, Inc.**

**Rogue Games'** Rogues are Richard Iorio II and James Maliszewski



Visit the **Rogue's** on the web: www.rogue-games.net

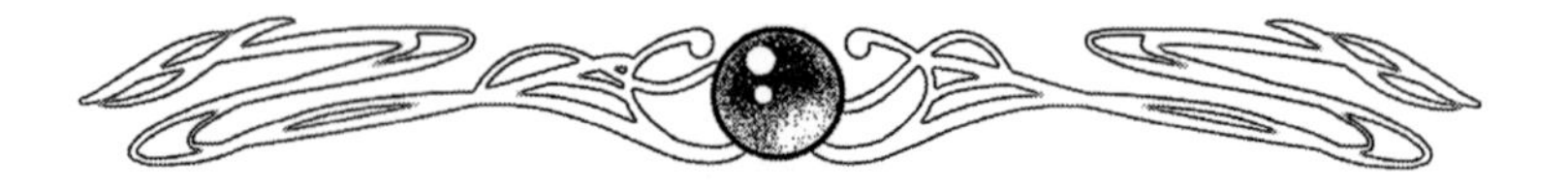

# Table of Contents

## Table of Contents

## Table of Contents

## Table of Contents

## Table of Contents

## Table of Contents

## Table of Contents



**List of Tables**

## Table of Contents

# Introduction

As long as fantasy games have existed, players and Gamemasters have looked for the endgame. For roleplaying games, especially fantasy ones, the concept of the endgame has been there since the hobby's beginnings. After all, when playing your hero, they grow in stature as well as power and influence. It is only a natural desire for a player to want their character to lead mercenary companies, sit on thrones, and work their influence within merchant circles. Many attempts to define the endgame have occurred in the roleplaying game industry, some of these attempts divorcing the slow build and growth of the hero, and instead focusing on the immediate. Two ready examples of this are TSR's *Birthright* setting, and *REIGN*. Both of these games center on rulership, and are great at what they set out to accomplish. However, what has always been difficult is to find games that contain rules or advice centered on taking your own hero and having them rule their own domains, band of cut throats, or... well you get the point.

> **endgame |'en(d),gām| (also end game)**
>
> noun
>
> the final stage of a game such as chess or bridge, when few pieces or cards remain: the knight was trapped in the endgame | figurative the retaliatory endgame of nuclear warfare.

**Shadow Sword & Spell: Expert** builds upon the rules found in **Basic**. In Basic, you created your character. You have braved numerous dangers, made many enemies, and probably killed a few of your foes as well. You have gone

from not having any or little influence or prestige, to now being a person of renown or infamy. You have survived the trials and ordeals before you.

Through your wits, guile, and fortitude, you have fought back the hordes of unholy terror. You have saved countless men and women from the bonds of slavery. You have discovered hidden treasures, long forgotten tombs, and tomes of arcane knowledge. You have become a hero, an outlaw, even a thorn in the side of the powers that be. Your trials have prepared you, and now, you are ready to inscribe your name in the rolls of history. The world will feel your justice. Your enemies will know your vengeance. Those with the power will now have no choice but to share it with you. You will be a king, and the dynasty you found will endure for centuries.

**Shadow Sword & Spell: Expert** answers the question: What's next? Your hero has grown in power, and now they are ready to tame the world. Building upon the rules found in **Basic, Expert** adds new opportunities for your game. What you will find here are new options and rules that you can use to expand your current **Shadow, Sword & Spell** game, as well as allow you to run games grander in scope.

**Shadow Sword & Spell** is a game influenced by The Three – H.P. Lovecraft, Clark Ashton Smith and Robert E. Howard – and the game works as an homage to, and to pay respect to them. **Expert**, perhaps more than **Basic**, is heavily influenced by Howard's (*By this axe I Rule*) and the later stories of Conan as king. Howard, more than the others, had a firm grasp of showing the possibilities offered in this vein by heroes who rule kingdoms. In his stories, even though the hero is a leader, they still have just as many dangers to face. The stakes become even higher when you have to fight to protect your throne. In addition, **Expert** focuses on other type of characters who might not be warriors, and instead make a living through thievery.

What if you are not ready to run a game centered on politics? Have no fear, **Expert** contains items that are easily added to **Basic**. New magic, relics, monsters, and the like, are all found here. Think of **Expert** as your inspiration. Take from it what you want, and ignore areas you are not ready for; this is your game after all, and make of it what you will.

# 1

# Skills & Schemes

## Character Creation Options

In **Shadow, Sword & Spell: Basic** we presented one way to create a character. That method, as you remember, is to assign 35 points between each of the five Abilities, and to assign 45 points into various Skills. This method is perfectly fine, and creates somewhat capable characters. Some players and Gamemasters (GMs) might crave other options which provide a little more variety. The methods detailed below are just some of the possibilities. GMs are advised and encouraged to create their own variants on these rules.

### Option One: Gygaxian & Arnesonian Method

Using this optional method, the character's starting Abilities are determined randomly, and not via the expenditure of points. In this method, you simply roll a d12 once for each Ability, and the results are assigned in order to each Ability. Using this option, characters have a wider range for their Abilities, including the possibilities of having Ability scores of 1 or 12. This option is a trade-off however, and is a way to handle character creation in a manner similar to how it is handled in such classics as *Dungeons & Dragons*, *Advanced Dungeons & Dragons*, *Traveller*, *Chivalry & Sorcery* and *RuneQuest*.

## Option Two: Dice Pool

Another method of character creation available for use combines the current point buy method found in **SHADOW, SWORD & SPELL: BASIC** with the randomness of dice rolling. In this method, you roll 5d12, and this gives you the number of points usable in purchasing Abilities for the character. No Ability can be below 3, nor can an Ability go above 12.

## Option Three: More Powerful Heroes

Sometimes you will want to create a Hero who is either more powerful or weaker. This is easy to do, and all that needs to be done is to adjust the starting points. This method, if taken to the extreme, allows for characters to have more Ability Points than usual. Depending on the Power Level you wish your game to have, the maximum for an Ability ranges between 12 and 24. In addition, the weaker you wish to make a character, the lower the maximum Ability range. The table below is a quick reference to use for the creation of weaker or stronger characters. Pick the Power Level, and then find the number of Ability Points, Skill Points, as well as the Maximum value an Ability can have, as well as the Maximum Rank for a Skill.

Note that characters can exceed the limits at each level during the course of a campaign.

**TABLE 1:1 POWER LEVELS**

| Power Level | Ability Points | Skill Points | Max Ability | Skill Rank |
|---|---|---|---|---|
| Infirm | 15 | 25 | 4 | +8 |
| Feeble | 20 | 30 | 6 | +10 |
| Weak | 25 | 35 | 8 | +10 |
| Below Average | 30 | 40 | 10 | +12 |
| Average | 35 | 45 | 12 | +12 |
| Above Average | 45 | 50 | 14 | +14 |
| Experienced | 55 | 55 | 16 | +14 |
| Seasoned | 65 | 60 | 18 | +18 |
| Veteran | 75 | 65 | 20 | +18 |
| Legendary | 85 | 70 | 22 | +20 |
| Mythic | 95 | 75 | 24 | +20 |

# Skills

In **SHADOW, SWORD & SPELL: BASIC,** we listed a number of Skills which fit the genre of pulp fantasy. With **EXPERT** there is a need for a few more Skills, and this section has them. In addition, you will find a few additions and modifications to the current Skills, and these additions are about bringing the background of **SHADOW, SWORD & SPELL**'s setting (known as The World, see **Chapter 9** for more details) into more focus with these skills.

## Skill Additions

### Languages in The World

With the introduction of The World (see **Chapter 9**), there needs to be further discussion of the languages found in the game and its associated world. The following are all the Languages available to characters in the game, in addition to the Language you also start with if the language is verbal, as well as if it is a written tongue. Fluency in a Language means that your character does not need to make any Skill Test in order to read, write or speak the language in question, usually one's Native Language. Note that characters who are Fluent in their Native Language do not need to make any tests to read or write their native language.

**Ancient** (Verbal, Read/Write): Rumors abound that this is the language of Atlantis and Ku'Kku. This language is popular among scholars, sages, and those who practice the magical Arts.

**Bargon** (Verbal, Read/Write): The language of Bærgøstēn. The written form is runic base.

**Beidhan – Commoner** (Verbal): The language of Beidha spoken by the lower class.

**Beidhan – Courtly** (Verbal, Read/Write): The language of Beidha only used by the nobility.

**Cal'athar** (Verbal, Read/Write): The language of Cal'athar.

**Cantonin** (Verbal, Read/Write): The language of the League of Cantons.

**Catharian** (Verbal, Read/Write): The language of Cathar.

**Elder Tongue** (Verbal, Read/Write): No one knows where this language comes from, as it dates back to an ancient time. Those who know it, keep their knowledge a secret.

**Imperial** (Verbal, Read/Write): The language of The City-States of Döârn.

**Karelian** (Verbal, Read/Write): The language of Karelia.

**Old Tongue** (Verbal, Read/Write): The Language of The Merchant League, the League of Cantons, and The City States of Döârn.

**Nipuran** (Verbal, Read/Write): The language of Nipur.

**Nogotian** (Verbal, Read/Write): The language of Nogoton.

**Noric** (Verbal, Read/Write): The language of Noricum, the written form is runic base.

**Runic** (Read/Write): A written language based on runes and favored by barbarians.

**Trader** (Verbal, Read/Write): The language of not only The Merchant League, but all traders and merchants.

**Tribal** (Verbal): This is a catch-all for all of the tribes found not only in Moarn but other tribal groups as well. There is no way to catalogue all of the different versions of this language. There are no known written languages.

**TABLE 1:2 DIALECTS OF THE TRADE TONGUE FOUND IN THE MERCHANT LEAGUE**

| Dialect | Location |
|---|---|
| Amberian | Region of the Amber Petals including Fox Point |
| Canal | The City of Gravina |
| Coastal | Coast of the League of Merchants |
| Daven | Davenport |
| Northie | Wall |
| The Cant | Bluff |
| Vint | The Vintage including Crossroads |

## Dialects

Some languages have dialects. Dialects are linguistic varieties differing in pronunciation, vocabulary, and grammar. Dialects are really just a sub-form of a language which are typically still comprehensible. Different speakers use their own local words for everyday objects or actions, or have a regional accent. These dialects are typically understood by native speakers, but for those who are not native speakers, they tend to be a little difficult to understand. The combination of differences in pronunciation and the use of local words may make some dialects

| TABLE 1:3 MORAN TRIBAL DIALECTS |
|---|
| Coastal Tribes |
| Eastern Tribes |
| Hill Folk |
| Lake Folk |
| Mountain People |
| Northern Jungles |
| River Folk |
| Southern Region |

almost unintelligible from one region to another.

Dialects come into play for languages such as Tribal and Trade Tongue. These languages, though sharing a common structure, have differences that make them harder to understand. Like Skills, Language Dialects can be taken as a Specialization (see **Chapter 3, SS&S BASIC**).

## Performance

Found throughout The World, there are a number of performance arts that are practiced, as well as used to earn a living. The following list covers some specializations that can be added to the Performance Skill found in **SS&S: BASIC Chapter 3.**

**Performance Emphasis:** Acrobat, Clown Contortionist, Escape Artist, Fire-Eater, Harpist, Jester, Juggler, Mimic, Mime, Prestidigitator, Puppeteer, Storyteller, Sword-Swallower and Tumbler

## Professions

There are a number of professions found in The World. This list is a small sampling of the ones that are available. These professions should be used in conjunction with the Profession skill (see **SS&S: BASIC Chapter 3**).

**Profession Emphasis:** Baker, Barber, Beekeeper, Boatman, Bookbinder, Bookkeeper, Butcher, Carpetmaker, Cheese maker, Cook, Dyer, Farmer, Fisherman, Gardener, Jeweler, Joiner, Mason, Miller, Porter, Printer, Rope maker, Scribe, Shoemaker, Tailor

# Schemes and the Art of Scheming

As characters gain power, fame and prestige, threats against them take on a different meaning. When beginning her career, a Hero might have been a simple sell-sword, wandering priestess or a petty thief. Though she might have plots and plans she wants to act on, she does not always have the resources to do so. As she gains in power, the access to resources the hero has allows her to scheme, plot or set her own plans into motion. For many, schemes and plots are easily dealt with via roleplaying or by working with the Gamemaster. Some players, however, might want more structure to their scheming. These rules, then, help provide structure to whatever plots the player might want to come up with.

Influence is never a sure thing. Events inexorably head in the direction where forces are greater than the resistances encountered. These rules expand the use of certain Skills to create an underlying force intended to shape social events and the reaction of the masses. These rules bring game story elements that, while not for everyone, add color to any game. Moreover, aside from Success and Failure, the possible outcomes to a character's schemes are limited to the player's perception of the Gamemaster's opinion. What these rules allow is for a defined array of predictability, and for a social "domino effect" preconceived by the player. With this structure in place, players can allow their character to take advantage of a situation.

Initiating a scheme requires certain steps that necessitate the character assess the power at her disposal, compare it to the target's own power, choose a means of action, and finally sustain the effort long enough for the desired results to occur.

Before undertaking a scheme, the player must undertake one important step: state clearly the objectives of the scheme and the expected reactions from the target. This is vital, the reason being that it aids the Gamemaster to determine the outcome of the scheme, as well as prepare for the adventure possibilities such a scheme provides.

## Step One: Establishing the Scope

Scope is an abstract measure of the power at the character's disposal. Ultimately, all power comes from the desire of people to follow the steps proposed (and undertaken) by the instigator to reach her aims, and is established by the number of people directly or indirectly contributing to the scheme. More importantly, if the individuals the character is using have their own resources available to them, the character benefits from that. As for the scope, all schemes fall under four broad categories. Approximate the instigator and their target in the following tables, and take note of their Scope Level.

Scope is crucial because it sets the minimum number of people the character must use to not only put their scheme into action, but the minimum number of people needed for it to succeed.

**Table 1:4 Establishing Scope**

| Level | Equivalent amount of people | Level | Faith/Adoration Scope |
|---|---|---|---|
| 1 | 1 person | 1 | |
| 2 | 10 people | 2 | |
| 3 | 15 people | 3 | |
| 4 | 20 people | 4 | Small local sect |
| 5 | 100 people | 5 | Regional belief |
| 6 | 1,000 people | 6 | City celebrity, superstition |
| 7 | A small town | 7 | Cultural belief or tradition |
| 8 | A small city | 8 | Religion well established in a region |
| 9 | A large city | 9 | Region-wide celebrity |
| 10 | A region | 10 | Religion spread across the kingdom |
| 11 | A kingdom | 11 | |
| 12 | The entire world | 12 | |

| Level | Political Scope | Level | Military Scope |
|---|---|---|---|
| 1 | | 1 | Solider |
| 2 | | 2 | Sergeant |
| 3 | Local activists | 3 | |
| 4 | A neighborhood | 4 | Unit (5 soldiers + Sergeant) |
| 5 | An assembly | 5 | |
| 6 | A crowd of supporters | 6 | Platoon |
| 7 | City mayor | 7 | |
| 8 | City-wide popular movement | 8 | Division |
| 9 | A Domain | 9 | |
| 10 | Government Official | 10 | Battalion |
| 11 | King | 11 | |
| 12 | The Emperor | 12 | Army |

| Level | Business Scope |
|---|---|
| 1 | |
| 2 | Kiosk, street corner stand |
| 3 | Small boutique, family business |
| 4 | Standard shop |
| 5 | Average franchised member |
| 6 | Local factory or office |
| 7 | |
| 8 | |
| 9 | |
| 10 | |
| 11 | |
| 12 | |

More importantly, an instigator does not benefit from her usual Scope Level when it comes to lower level goals. For example: a leader of a band of thieves found in a small city (Scope Level 8) can easily overpower lesser rivals with ease when using the resources at her disposal to do so. However, the band is too large to deal with something as trivial as the same leader trying to exert her parental authority and reform her undisciplined son into a model child. Thus, the situation has reduced her Scope Level to one. Each scheme demands a re-evaluation of one's Scope Level.

**Table 1:5 Scope Difference**

| Static Culture | Dynamic Culture | Time for Effect |
|---|---|---|
| N/A | +11 | Instantaneous |
| N/A | +10 | Instantaneous |
| N/A | +9 | Instantaneous |
| +11 | +8 | Instantaneous |
| +10 | +7 | Instantaneous |
| +9 | +6 | Instantaneous |
| +8 | +5 | Instantaneous |
| +7 | +4 | Instantaneous |
| +6 | +3 | 1 hour |
| +5 | +2 | 1 day |
| +4 | +1 | 1 week |
| +3 | Even | 1 month |
| +2 | -1 | 3 months |
| +1 | -2 | 6 month |
| Even | -3 | 1 year |
| -1 | -4 | 2 years |
| -2 | -5 | 5 Years |
| -3 | -6 | 10 years |
| -4 | -7 | 25 years |
| -5 | -8 | 50 years |
| -6 | -9 | 100 Years |
| -7 | -10 | 200 years |
| -8 | -11 | 500 years |
| -9 | N/A | 1,000 years |
| -10 | N/A | 2,500 years |
| -11 | N/A | 5,000 years |

### Dynamic or Static?

Each Scope Level the instigator has above or below the level of the target modifies the base required time by one on the scale shown below. Having the advantage of Scope reduces the time before the results appear and having the disadvantage increases this period of time.

## Step Two: Choosing the Means

Once the Scope of a scheme is determined, the second step is to establish the Method the character will employ to affect the target. Method is nothing more than the character's material assets, the contacts and Skills they can use to put their plans into motion. Also, instigating the process sets a Proximity Level between the instigator and the target, the type of Social Approach undertaken, and the instigator's Exposure.

## Proximity

This expresses both the distance put between the instigator and the target as well as how the said target is reached. This distance is determined by the Scope Level in question.

**Examples of Proximity:** Direct Contact, Indirect Contact, Posting Campaign, Ministerial Songs and Satire

## Social Approach

The Social Approach is a measure of the general ethical acceptance of the object or context of the influence. The identity of the instigator also comes into play in regard to this acceptance. For some situations, a scheme may be more efficient with a less ethical Social Approach to the Method.

**Examples of Social Approach:** Denial, Legal, Illegal, Violent and Armed

## Exposition

The Exposition Factor is the level of attention the instigator has put to conceal her own identity and the attention paid to the presence of strings attached to other people. It may seem like a good idea to retain maximum secrecy for each scheme, but often this is at the expense of the overall effectiveness of the attempt.

Certain combinations of Methods and Factors are counterproductive. It is, for example, more than unlikely that a character could plant a rumor by shooting a crossbow bolt at the people close to the target of the scheme. In such a case, the only rumor likely to spread is that the instigator has blown her cover, and the brutalized target will turn on the instigator the first chance she gets instead of lending her voice to further the scheme.

**Examples of Exposition:** Known agent, Unknown agent, Fence agent and Cell activists

## In Theory...

The player must devise a plan to affect the target in the desired manner by anticipating the reactions of all parties. The Character's understanding of these reactions is based on the appropriate Skill coupled with the Will Ability. Skills such as Bargain, Bureaucracy, Diplomacy, Empathy, Intimidation, Socialize, Streetwise, and Tactics (if the Test is successful) can be used to discover an exploitable advantage or a weakness on which the scheme can be based.

The Gamemaster can adjust the Situation Modifier if the Character takes her time to study the potential target, or if the target has taken steps to protect themselves from such scrutiny. By researching her target and making a successful Skill Test, the Character can discover a weakness or exploitable weakness or exploitable advantage in the target. A Dramatic Success reveals two different weaknesses that are exploitable, which are can be employed for running parallel schemes that aim for the same results.

Failure reveals nothing the Character can employ against her target. A new Test can be permitted if the Character's Skill is increased, if the target's situation has sufficiently changed by itself, or simply if the GM estimates that enough time has elapsed. Dramatic Failure gives the Character false information, which not only causes the influence to fail, but also worsens the Collateral Effects.

To ensure that the player does not unconsciously meta-game her Character's decision to accept or refuse to commit herself based on the result of the roll, it is strongly recommended the GM makes the roll in secret. In any case, the GM must take note of the Degree of Success or Failure, which will be of use in determining the Collateral Effects.

## In Practice...

Once a weak point has been found that makes the target react according to the Character's desires, she must decide on the approach to take to exploit the advantage and execute the plan. To help both the player and GM, the six methods that can be employed for this purpose are described below. Players and GMs can use these, or use them as examples to create their own methods.

## Lies and Manipulation

Though some would think this is the easiest method to employ, in practice it is not. It seems easy to Lie, but that requires a character to be able to lie convincingly, as well as to remember what the lie is. Lying can be something as simple as saying that the character did lock the door, to something as elaborate as forging physical evidence. Unlike lying, Manipulation is the ability to make a person perform a task, or reveal information, because they are compelled to do so. Manipulation allows the Character to have others either agree with her, or to allow no argumentative options because of an exterior factor such as a time limit, the embarrassing presence of someone else, or employing their own words against them.

**TABLE 1:6 LIES AND MANIPULATION**

| | Lies and Manipulation | Collateral Modifier |
|---|---|---|
| **Proximity** | | |
| Direct contact | +2 | 0 |
| Indirect contact | -1 | -1 |
| Posting campaign | -2 | 0 |
| Ministerial Songs | -1 | +1 |
| Satire | +0 | +2 |
| **Opposition Modifier** | -1 | |
| **Social Approach** | | |
| Denial | +1 | +1 |
| Legal | +0 | +2 |
| Illegal | -2 | -1 |
| Violent | -1 | -2 |
| Armed | -3 | -3 |
| **Support Modifier** | -1 | |
| **Exposition** | | |
| Known agent | -1 | -3 |
| Unknown agent | +1 | 0 |
| Fence agent | -2 | +1 |
| Cell activists | -3 | +2 |
| **Secrecy Modifier** | -1 | |

## Rumors

A Rumor is the manner and fashion in which the information is spread. While Lies and Manipulations require sustaining them in order to take effect, Rumors spreads due to the efforts and credibility of others. This makes it more difficult to link a potentially harmful element of the rumor to its instigator, but also exposes the message to random alterations and permits for the chance of it dying out completely.

**Table 1:7 Rumors**

| | Rumors | Collateral Modifier |
|---|---|---|
| **Proximity** | | |
| Direct contact | +0 | 0 |
| Indirect contact | -1 | -1 |
| Posting campaign | -1 | 0 |
| Ministerial Songs | +1 | +1 |
| Satire | +2 | +2 |
| **Opposition Modifier** | **+0** | |
| **Social Approach** | | |
| Denial | +1 | +1 |
| Legal | -2 | +2 |
| Illegal | +0 | -1 |
| Violent | N/A | -2 |
| Armed | N/A | -3 |
| **Support Modifier** | **+1** | |
| **Exposition** | | |
| Known agent | -2 | -3 |
| Unknown agent | +0 | 0 |
| Fence agent | -1 | +1 |
| Cell activists | +3 | +2 |
| **Secrecy Modifier** | **+2** | |

A Rumor need not be true, but it must meet a certain level of credibility and authenticity for it to survive long enough to have an effect. An alternate form of rumor is an unsaid or an undefined fact. By casually neglecting to mention certain facts, refusing to comment on an issue, or denying something with too much zeal, others can be led to speculate on the missing information.

### Bribes and Rewards

The response to the offer of a Bribe or some sort of Reward varies depending on the motivations of the target. Something of interest to the target has to be offered to tempt them into acting in accordance with the parameters set for them. What is offered, and the manner in which it is brought to the target, will determine how this Influence is handled. Offers are usually of a material, social, sentimental, or carnal nature.

### Blackmail and Humiliation

The threat of revealing an embarrassing truth or a damaging situation harmful to guilty parties is another means that can be employed. Making sure the target is aware of the negative consequences of exposure is called

Blackmailing. It is the opposite of Bribes and Rewards in the sense that instead of a gain, the target is promised a loss.

The key to blackmailing someone is to totally convince them you have something dangerous, and that you are willing to use it at the first opportunity if your conditions for not using it aren't met.

If the Character does not have the reputation, or the background, to induce fear, or the element of truth itself held is not dangerous enough, then the target's perception of danger may be amplified. A good way of countering this is to take or fake the steps necessary to expose the truth and falsely link other events to it that appear to be the instigation of the consequences. The target may either believe that the Character holds more than they suspect, or that they have not assessed the true extent of their victim's guilt.

TABLE 1:8 BRIBERY & BLACKMAIL

| | Bribe and Reward | Blackmail | Collateral Modifier |
|---|---|---|---|
| **Proximity** | | | |
| Direct contact | +0 | +1 | 0 |
| Indirect contact | -2 | +0 | -1 |
| Posting campaign | N/A | -2 | 0 |
| Ministerial Songs | N/A | -1 | +1 |
| Satire | N/A | +0 | +2 |
| **Opposition Modifier** | **+0** | **-3** | |
| **Social Approach** | | | |
| Denial | +0 | +0 | +1 |
| Legal | +0 | +2 | +2 |
| Illegal | -2 | -2 | -1 |
| Violent | N/A | N/A | -2 |
| Armed | N/A | N/A | -3 |
| **Support Modifier** | **+1** | **-2** | |
| **Exposition** | | | |
| Known agent | +0 | +0 | -3 |
| Unknown agent | -3 | -1 | 0 |
| Fence agent | -1 | -1 | +1 |
| Cell activists | -2 | -2 | +2 |
| **Secrecy Modifier** | **+1** | **+1** | |

## Leadership and Authority

While it can often be attributed to circumstances, the emergence of a Leader has a lot to do with the virtues of the intended target. A character may assume a similar role because she was entrusted with responsibilities, and is acknowledged for them.

The difference between pure leadership and the exercise of authority is obvious. A Leader is followed for what she can stir up or create in the people near her. With eloquence, inspiration or by serving as an example, this character can become a leader and create influences using leadership methods to shift people toward her desired results and outcomes.

Someone occupying a position of authority has been put in place by a system, and others react to her in accordance with their support of the system. While a character working high within a chain of command is not necessarily void of all sense of leadership, she is not presenting her own attributes to influence a target, but rather is using the system of rules, regulations, laws, and ethics to do so. Thus, the character is borrowing the power of a social structure, rather than using her attributes and skills.

**Table 1:9 Leadership & Intimidation**

| | Leadership and Authority | Intimidation | Collateral Modifier |
|---|---|---|---|
| | Proximity | | |
| Direct contact | +1 | +1 | 0 |
| Indirect contact | -1 | -1 | -1 |
| Posting campaign | -3 | -4 | 0 |
| Ministerial Songs | -2 | -3 | +1 |
| Satire | +0 | +1 | +2 |
| **Opposition Modifier** | **+1** | **-2** | |
| | Social Approach | | |
| Denial | +0 | N/A | +1 |
| Legal | +1 | +1 | +2 |
| Illegal | -1 | 0 | -1 |
| Violent | -2 | +1 | -2 |
| Armed | -3 | +2 | -3 |
| **Support Modifier** | **+1** | **-1** | |
| | Exposition | | |
| Known agent | +1 | +1 | -3 |
| Unknown agent | -4 | -1 | 0 |
| Fence agent | -2 | +0 | +1 |
| Cell activists | -3 | +1 | +2 |
| **Secrecy Modifier** | **-3** | **-2** | |

### Intimidation

Intimidation is typically used to coerce someone into compliance, and implies that the instigator displays and demonstrates sufficient means to act upon their threat of harm.

There is a subtle way to intimidate; if one induces fear through the eventuality of the same mistreatment, then identical results may be achieved. This often takes the form of an ultimatum, a bargain, or an exemplary assassination. The target has to feel insecure enough so that their actions will be directed towards the goal as determined by the Character.

The player's description of the Character's scheme helps determine the three Factors of Influence: the Proximity, the Social Approach and the Exposition. All three serve to broaden the results beyond success or failure and translate into collateral effects, which can then become story elements.

## Step Three: Applying Skills

Now that the instigator has perceived her target's weakness, devised a plan, and put it into effect, the GM must determine the scheme's outcome. After the time period indicated by the difference of Scope Levels has elapsed, and everything from the target's reaction to the appearance of possible collateral effects has been resolved, it is time to see if the scheme succeeds.

So how is the Situation Modifier determined? Easy. The chart below sets the Situation Modifier for the appropriate Skill Test. Cross reference the Method column with one of the three Factor rows. This gives you three numbers, which must be added together to get the Situation Modifier. Playing people is never easy, and in many cases the Situation Modifiers will be negative.

Once you have the Situation Modifier, the GM again makes a Skill Roll using one of the Skills previously mentioned (Bargain, Bureaucracy, Diplomacy, Empathy, Intimidation or Socialize) best suited to the situation. The Skill need not be the same. Again the Gamemaster must take note of the Degree of Success or Failure for the eventual Collateral Effects.

Some schemes might be complicated, and require numerous smaller actions in order for the larger scheme to succeed and achieve its goals. For example, the Character must dispose of someone, steal something, or persuade an ally to lend their support (lend her Scope); all of these actions must be performed, and they offer the Gamemaster new adventure possibilities as well. The GM is encouraged to add additional elements to the Collateral Effects in the case of a Dramatic Success or a Dramatic Failure on this second roll.

## Step Four: Interpreting the Results

Have both Skill Tests been successful? If so then the instigator's plan has made the target react as anticipated and desired, and the story and life continue around all that this implies. All that's left is to check for possible Collateral Effects.

If the initial assumption of weakness provided with the initial Skill Test was wrong, and the instigator still went through with her plan, regardless of its execution, the primary objective is not attained. Furthermore, it is quite likely that unfavorable Collateral Effects occur. If the execution was faulty, as revealed by the result of the second Skill Test, then the Character failed in terms of the scheme's primary objective. That character is also exposed to Collateral Effects, but will generally fare better than one who executed a flawed plan.

### Collateral Effects

Notice that in the previous table additional columns and rows are grayed out. These are the figures to employ for Collateral Effects previously mentioned. Take note of the Opposition, Support and Secrecy Modifiers from under the Method employed and, to each, add its own Collateral Modifier provided by the types of Proximity, Social Approach and Exposition.

At this point, you should have three numbers plus the Degrees of Success or Failure from the two Skill Rolls from before. You need to add the two Degrees of Success or Failure to each of the three Modifiers. You now have three values, which must be looked up in **Table 1:10**.

#### Opposition

The target of the scheme may be staggered as a consequence of it. On the opposite side of the spectrum, the recent ordeal may have prepared the target against further attempts by the instigator. In game terms, the target may lose or gain a Scope Level concerning the instigator, or similar schemes, for a period of time. The target doesn't really change their Scope Level, but being more alert, cautious and less trusting has similar consequences and repercussions as a change of her Scope Level would. If somebody else initiates a scheme of a totally different nature, then the modification to the Scope Level is not taken into account.

**Table 1:10 Collateral Effects**

| Opposition | | |
|---|---|---|
| **Roll result** | **Effect** | **Recovery time** |
| 17 and 18 | Target loses a relative Scope Level. | Permanent |
| 14 to 16 | Target loses a relative Scope Level. | 5 years |
| 9 to 13 | Target loses a relative Scope Level. | 1 year |
| 1 to 8 | No Opposition Collateral Effect. | None |
| -4 to 0 | Target gains a relative Scope Level. | 1 year |
| - 7 to -5 | Target gains a relative Scope Level. | 5 years |
| -20 or worse | Target gains a relative Scope Level. | Permanent |

| Support | | |
|---|---|---|
| **Roll result** | **Effect** | **Recovery time** |
| 20 or better | Perpetrator gains support or sympathy. | Permanent |
| 19 to 14 | Perpetrator gains support or sympathy. | 5 years |
| 13 to 8 | Perpetrator gains support or sympathy. | 1 year |
| 7 to -7 | No Support Collateral Effect. | None |
| -8 to -13 | Perpetrator makes new enemies. | 1 year |
| -14 to -19 | Perpetrator makes new enemies. | 5 years |
| -20 or worse | Perpetrator makes new enemies. | Permanent |

| Exposure | | |
|---|---|---|
| **Roll result** | **Effect** | **Recovery time** |
| 10 or better | Other Influence works and currents are discovered. | Permanent |
| 9 to -3 | No Exposition Collateral Effect. | None |
| -4 to -11 | Perpetrator OR scheme, even if successful, is exposed. | Permanent |
| -12 or worse | Perpetrator AND scheme, even if successful, are exposed. | Permanent |

## Support

The actions of the instigator may have attracted the attention of potential allies or enemies that are ready to push toward the same goal. While this does not mean that the instigator has gained or lost a Scope Level, she may benefit from the Skills or assets of others. In the case where the instigator has remained unknown to all, these potential sympathizers might manifest themselves publicly, or be contacted by the instigator so she can "collect" their help.

The same is true if the influence has generated enemies for the instigator. The new opponents will instead try to identify and oppose her. The GM decides on the nature of these new allies or enemies as well as their capabilities.

### Exposure

The Exposure is the measure of success an instigator has achieved at remaining unknown. By distancing herself enough from her target, the instigator may have perceived other influences at play, as well as social, economic or cultural tendencies. This information can lead an instigator to "the man behind the throne," new markets, or important discoveries about the truth behind a past event. The GM should provide a means for the Character to gain access to secret knowledge.

If the instigator was not acting with any secrecy (related to Proximity and Exposition Factors seen and determined earlier) and openly made herself known, then she may not necessarily suffer from certain outcomes. Depending on the situation, a scheme or an instigator or both may be revealed to the target. If the instigator or target has high Scopes Levels involved in the scheme, then any revelation may lead to other organizations, the public, etc.

In the situation where a would-be instigator went ahead with a scheme based on a false weakness provided as a result of a Dramatic Failure (the first Skill Roll), then her intentions are automatically compromised. The Character receives a -4 on all three types of Collateral Effects Tests noted in the previous table.

### Recovery Time

Collateral Effects will be in effect for a period of time as indicated in the rightmost column of **Table 1:10.** If the GM is running a "dynamic Universe," she may choose to adjust non-permanent periods in accordance. In such a case, 1 year becomes 1 month and 5 years becomes 6 months.

# 2

# Gear

In SHADOW, SWORD & SPELL: BASIC, the number of weapons and gear available are somewhat limited on purpose. The reason for this is due to desired page count for the game, as well as the scope of that game's rulebook. BASIC is about starting out, and the amount of money, as well as the type of gear that is available, is limited. In EXPERT, since the scope is much bigger, the options for weapons and gear is greater still. This chapter presents more weapons, armor, gear, and services which the Gamemaster (GM) can make available to his players.

## Option: Adjustable Prices

In EXPERT, the world is bigger. For this reason, the prices for gear and services vary somewhat. This variation is due to the proximity to or the distance from urban sources. GMs wishing to have prices fluctuate based on the location can set different prices. The three locations are: Urban, Rural, and Wild. How are these three region types defined? Read on.

### Urban

Urban generally relates to a settlement ranging in size from a hamlet (between 50 and 250 people), village (200-1,000 people), town (500-1,000 people), and city (1,000 or more people).

### Rural

Rural areas pertain to the countryside, rather than to cites. Their populations usually include no more than 50 people, and rural areas typically tend to be farming communities, small outposts, and similar social structures. All the gear found in **Shadow, Sword & Spell** uses this price as the default price.

## Wild

Wild areas are those unsettled by many people. These are the regions that have not seen the touch of civilization yet, there might be small pockets of what passes for civilization in these places.

## Price Fluctuations

With these three different locations, the price of goods changes depending on where they are bought. See **Table 2:1**, below, for how prices are affected by the type of area. For example, your character buys a knife which normally has a price of 2 SC. This is the price for the knife found in Rural areas. The same knife, if bought in an Urban area, has a price reduction of 10%. Thus if the knife is bought in an Urban area, the listed prices is reduced by 10%, or 1 SC. The same knife, if bought in a Wild area, would have a new price of 3 SC.

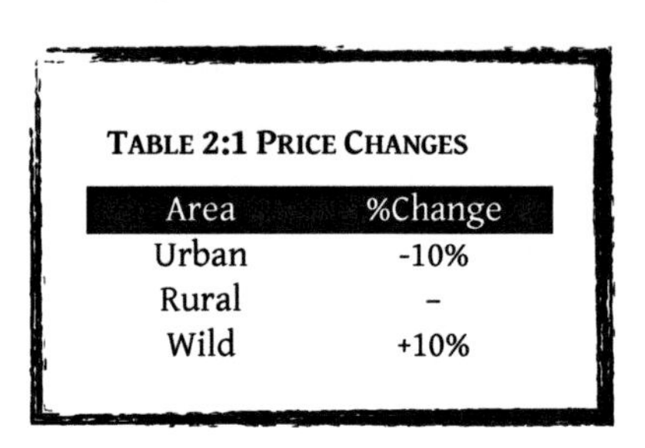

**Table 2:1 Price Changes**

| Area | %Change |
|---|---|
| Urban | -10% |
| Rural | - |
| Wild | +10% |

**Table 2:2 Weapons**

| Type | DV | Min | D | R | RoF | Sz | Cost |
|---|---|---|---|---|---|---|---|
| Ahir | 4(75) | - | - | - | - | 1H | 16 |
| Blackjack | 2(25) | - | - | - | - | 1H | 5 |
| Blowgun | - | - | - | 5/10/15 | 1/1 | 2H | 3 |
| Blowgun Dart | 1(15) | - | - | - | - | - | 5 IC/dart |
| Broadsword | 8(90) | - | - | - | - | 1H | 12 |
| Cestus | 1(25) | - | - | - | - | 1H | 5 |
| Cudgel | 2(35) | - | - | - | | 1H | 2 |
| Falchion | 6(90) | - | - | - | - | 1H | 14 |
| Knife | 2(35) | - | - | - | - | 1H | 2 |
| Kris | 2(40) | - | - | - | - | 1H | 4 |
| Main Gauche | 1(30) | - | +1 | - | - | 1H | 20 |
| Maul | 5(70) | 9 Brawn | -1 | - | - | 2H | 7 |
| Net | Special | - | +1 | 5 | 1/1 | 2H | 4 |
| Poniard | 3(35) | - | - | - | - | 1H | 5 |
| Rapier | 5(65) | - | +2 | - | - | 1H | 12 |
| Scimitar | 5 (75) | - | - | - | - | 1H | 13 |
| Seax | 4(40) | - | - | - | - | 1H | 4 |
| Scythe | 5(60) | - | - | - | - | 2H | 7 |
| Tulwar | 5(90) | - | +1 | - | - | 1H | 18 |

**Notes:**
DV – Damage Value
Min – Minimum Attribute needed to wield
D – Defend
R – Range
RoF – Range of Fire
Sz – Size

# New Gear

## Weapons

### Descriptions

**Ahir:** Found mainly in Beidha, this sword has a heavy, thick blade with a curve greater than a scimitar. The heavy blade allows the wielder to inflict deeper cuts on his opponents.

**Blackjack:** A blackjack is a small, leather club favored by muggers.

**Blowgun:** Blowguns are tubes 2'-4' in length which are breathed through at one end, and fire darts which are blown out of the other end. Darts do little

damage on their own, but are often coated with poison. This is a weapon favored by many tribes as well as assassins, who look for a way to silently kill their prey.

**Broadsword:** Heavier, and with a blade a little wider than a longsword, broadswords tend to be favored by northern barbarian tribes.

**Cestus:** A spiked, metal gauntlet worn either around the hand or built into a glove.

**Club:** A club is a crude blunt weapon — little more than a roughly shaped piece of wood — that can be used in one hand. Unlike a cudgel, clubs tend to be weighted due to bands of iron welded around it.

**Cudgel:** A small club, usually carved from a tree root, or from a piece of wood with a rounded knot.

**Falchion:** Favored in the Cantons and City-States, this is a one-handed sword with a wide curved blade, resembling an oversized cleaver.

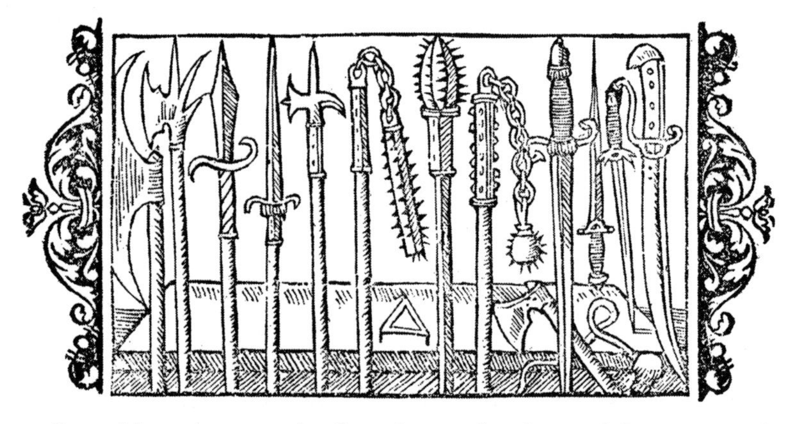

**Knife:** Unlike a dagger, a knife is designed to be used for cutting, slicing, and as a backup weapon. Unlike a dagger, which can be thrown, a knife is not as effective when used as a missile.

**Kris:** This dagger is found in Nipur and Beidha, but is also found in more civilized areas of The World as well. This dagger's blade is wavy and designed to cause more damage due to the weapon's jagged edge.

**Main Gauche:** This is a fencing dagger with a double edge and two parallel prongs jutting out from the handle which are designed to catch an opponent's sword. Those skilled with this weapon (via Specialization) do not suffer the off-hand weapon penalty when using it.

**Maul:** This is a larger version of a warhammer, and is used two-handed. A heavy weapon, it is favored by those who are strong, who want to sacrifice speed for the ability to cause as much damage as possible.

**Net:** Nets designed to be used in combat, typically some 6' to 9' in diameter. They are designed to knock an opponent off their feet, as well as entangle them, thus making it hard for them to move. Successfully hitting a target with a net requires the target to make a Quickness Test, with failure resulting in their losing their balance and falling to the ground. They remain entangled until they succeed at a Quickness Test. While entangled, they suffer a -2 to all Tests due to their loss of balance and lack of mobility.

**Poniard:** A thin, bladed dagger designed to puncture armor.

**Rapier:** The favorite weapon in the Cantons, this sword is flexible and designed to be used mainly for thrusting, as well as quickly parrying attacks.

**Scimitar:** This curving blade sword is as lengthy as a longsword, and is favored by the nomadic tribes of the Shimmering Sands.

**Seax:** This is a large single edge weapon that falls in size between a knife and a short sword.

**Scythe:** Scythes are long, inward curving blades mounted on a shaft six to eight feet long.

**Tulwar:** Used by the warriors in Beidha, this is a thin curved blade used for slicing, and also makes for a good parrying weapon.

# Armor

## Descriptions

**Brigandine Armor:** A cloth garment, typically canvas or leather, lined with small oblong steel plates that are riveted to the fabric.

**Quilt Armor:** Due to the heat of Beidha, metal armor is not practical, nor is it favored. Quilt armor consists of two layers of a thick heavy fabric with thick cotton sandwiched between them.

**Table 2:3 Armor**

| Type | AV | Cost |
|---|---|---|
| Quilt Armor | 10 | 20 |
| Brigandine | 15 | 25 |
| Ring Armor | 20 | 23 |
| Studded Armor | 25 | 25 |

**Notes:**
AV – Armor Value

**Ring Armor:** Constructed as a series of metallic rings sewn to a fabric or leather foundation, Ring Armor is often wrongly referred to as chain mail.

**Studded Armor:** This is a more protective version of leather armor, and has small leather rings sewn across it that offer more protection against slashing weapons.

# Shields

## Descriptions

**Buckler:** This is a small metal disc, no more than 2 feet in diameter. The shield is used as a parrying aid, and due to its size, the buckler give a +1 bonus to Defend Tests. Because of its size, heroes can use a buckler in conjunction with a dagger, knife, poniard or kris.

**Kite Shield:** This shield is typically 6 feet long, and is made out of wood reinforced with metal. The shield is favored by the warriors in the Northern regions of The World, and is often employed as a movable wall, allowing bowmen to fire from behind a shield bearer.

**Table 2:4 Shields**

| Type | Defend | Cost |
|---|---|---|
| Buckler | +1 | 2 |
| Kite Shield | +3 | 20 |

# Barding

Barding is much like the armor worn by warriors, but it is designed to be worn by horses.

## Descriptions

**Chain Barding:** This type of barding is constructed out of small, interlocked metal rings which offer more flexible protection to a horse.

**Leather Barding:** This type of barding is made from leather strips, sewn together to offer limited protection to a horse.

**Plate Barding:** The heaviest type of barding, this is made out of small metal plates which are linked with chain. Very heavy, and only the strongest of horses can easily wear this.

**Scale Barding:** Constructed from plates of leather with metal plates sewn to them, this offers better protection than leather barding.

**Table 2:5 Barding**

| Type | AV | Cost |
|---|---|---|
| Leather | 20 | 40 |
| Scale | 30 | 75 |
| Chain | 35 | 150 |
| Plate | 45 | 500 |

# Transportation – Land Based

## Descriptions

**Camel:** Found only in the Shimmering Sands, camels are the primary mode of transportation for the nomads, as well as residents of the oases.

**Cart:** Carts are two-wheeled vehicles which are able to be pulled by one or two horses. As an option, carts can have a bench attached to allow for a driver.

**Horse, Draft:** Powerful horses, draft horses are known for their ability to not only carry heavy loads, but work with a team of such animals and pull heavy loads for long

**Table 2:6 Transportation – Land Based**

| Type | Cost |
|---|---|
| Camel | 1 GC |
| Cart, 1 Horse | 100 |
| Cart, 2 Horses | 150 |
| Horse, Draft | 40 |
| Horse, Riding | 75 |
| Horse, War | 250 |
| Pony | 35 |
| Saddle and tack | 25 |
| Saddle Bag | 5 |
| Wagon, 2 Horses | 200 |
| Wagon, 4 Horses | 250 |

distances.

**Horse, Riding:** The most common horse found throughout The World.

**Horse, War:** Smaller than a draft horse, but larger than a riding horse, war horses are trained for combat.

**Pony:** A young horse.

**Saddle and Tack:** Including a saddle, blanket, bridle, and reins, this is everything you need to ride a horse.

**Saddle Bags:** Nothing more than a pair of sacks sewn together and slung over a horse's saddle in order to distribute the weight evenly.

**Wagon:** A large four-wheeled vehicle, pulled by either a 2-horse team or a 4-horse team, wagons are used for transporting not only cargo, but can also be converted to carry passengers, as well as to serve as a mobile house.

**Table 2:7 Transportation – Water Based**

| Type | Cost | Crew | Passengers | Miles/Day |
|---|---|---|---|---|
| Barge | 500 | 2/8 Rowers | 2 | 36 |
| Canoe | 30 | 2 | - | 18 |
| Caravel | 30,000 | 40 | 20 | 80 |
| Galley | 25,000 | 10/50 Rowers | 100 | 90 |
| Longboat | 15,000 | 75 | 150 | 85 |
| Outrigger | 75 | 10 | – | 18 |
| Rowing Boat | 1,000 | 1 | 6 | 18 |
| Skiff | 100 | 1 | – | 72 |
| Sloop | 3,000 | 10 | 10 | 72 |

# Transportation – Water Based

## Descriptions

Ships and boats need a skilled crew to man them, while some need unskilled rowers as well. If more than five crew are required, there must be a captain, and if more than fifteen crew are required, not only must there be a captain, but there must be a first mate as well.

**Barge:** A flat-bottomed boat that has no sail, and that typically ranges between 20'-30' long and 10' wide, a barge is used not only for moving cargo, but can also serve as a ferry as well.

**Canoe:** This small boat is typically no more than 15 feet in length and 3 feet in width. Canoes are typically made from waterproof leather or cloth which is stretched over a wooden frame. Canoes can also be constructed from a dug out tree, as well as bark overlapping a wooden frame. Canoes have either one or two seats, and are meant to be used on rivers, swamps, lakes, and ponds.

**Caravel:** Either a two- or three-masted ship, caravels are typically 70 feet in length and about 20 feet wide. Caravels have two decks, as well as multiple levels at the fore and aft of the ship.

**Galley:** A galley is an ocean-going ship between 60'-100' in length and 10'-15' in width. Galleys are not only able to sail oceans, but are capable of sailing rivers that are wide enough to accommodate them.

**Longboat:** A longship is a single-masted boat between 60'-80' in length and 10'-15' in width. Longships are designed for trade as well as to move troops along rivers and coasts. The 75 crew normally act as both rowers and warriors. This boat is favored by the tribes in the north.

**Outrigger:** Nothing more than a canoe which has a hull running parallel with the boat attached to one side. Outriggers are able to have one or two hulls attached. A single-hull outrigger is perfectly suited for coastal waters, while two-hulled outriggers are able to brave the deepest oceans and seas.

**Rowing Boat:** A small boat no more than 20 feet in length and 5 feet in width, rowing boats are typically used to move people and goods between ship and shore. They are often used as lifeboats on larger vessels as well.

**Skiff:** A skiff is a single-masted boat between 15'-45' in length and 5'-15' in width. Designed for lakes and coastal waters, they are also used from time to time for river travel. Skiffs are commonly used as fishing boats.

**Sloop:** A sloop is a one- or two-masted ocean going ship ranging between 60'-80' in length and 20'- 30' in width.

## Building & Construction

Prices for buildings have the cost of the unskilled and/or semi-skilled labor required for building construction already included. Prices do not include the cost of hiring an architect, foremen, and engineers (all of whom are vital in the construction of any structure). It takes 500/day to build a structure, as well as requiring the presence of one engineer. This cost is based on the assumption that construction takes place in a remote, yet accessible, location. If it is being built in an inaccessible place – a mountain top, the middle of a raging river, on an island only accessible at low tide – the cost is doubled. If building in a more civilized location – such as the edge of town or even in a town – the costs are half.

**Table 2:8 Building & Construction**

| Item | Cost |
|---|---|
| Arrow Slit | 10 |
| Barbican | 37,000 |
| Battlement (50') | 250 |
| Building, Stone | 3,000 |
| Building, Wood | 1,500 |
| Corridor, Dungeon | 500 |
| Door, Secret | Cost x5 |
| Door, Exterior (Iron/Stone) | 100 |
| Door, Interior (Iron/Stone) | 50 |
| Door, Interior (Reinforced) | 20 |
| Door, Interior (Wood) | 10 |
| Drawbridge | 250 |
| Floor, Flagstone | 100 |
| Floor, Marble | 150 |
| Floor, Tile | 100 |
| Floor, Wood | 40 |
| Gate, Wooden | 1,000 |
| Gate, Metal | 2,000 |
| Gatehouse | 6,500 |
| Keep, Round | 100,000 |
| Keep, Square | 75,000 |
| Moat, Filled | 800 |
| Moat, Unfilled | 400 |

### Descriptions

**Arrow Slit:** A narrow window slit designed to let defenders shoot out whilst not exposing them to return fire.

**Barbican:** Two 30' x 20' towers that flank a 20' square gatehouse, with a built-in iron portcullis. This is a single unit.

**Battlement (50'):** This is 50' of wall with a parapet behind it. Price includes crenelations and parapet, not the wall that the battlement is on.

**Building, Stone:** This is a two-story stone building.

**Building, Wood:** A two-story wooden building.

**Corridor, Dungeon:** A 10' x 10' x 10' section excavated from rock. Depending on the depth of the dungeon – in multiples of 50'– digging a 10' x 10' x 10' section at a depth of 150' will cost triple the listed price.

**Door, Secret:** A door disguised and hidden so it is unnoticeable unless searched for.

**Door, Exterior (Iron/ Stone):** Measuring 7' in height and 6' in width, this is a heavy double door.

**Door, Interior (Iron/ Stone):** Measuring 7' in height and 3' in width, this is a heavy double door.

**Door, Interior (Reinforced):** A wooden internal door reinforced with iron bands.

**Table 2:8 Building & Construction (cont.)**

| Item | Cost |
|---|---|
| Shutters, Window | 5 |
| Staircase, Stone | 60 |
| Staircase, Wood | 20 |
| Tower, Bastion | 9,000 |
| Tower, Round Large | 30,000 |
| Tower, Round Small | 15,000 |
| Trap Door | Cost x2 |
| Wall, Stone | 5,000 |
| Wall, Wood | 1,000 |
| Window, Barred | 20 |
| Window, Open | 10 |

**Door, Interior (Wood):** A standard wooden internal door.

**Drawbridge:** A 10' wide, 20' long reinforced wooden bridge that is raised or lowered to allow access to a fortified area.

**Floor, Flagstone:** Section of floor covered in flagstones, measuring 10' x 10'.

**Floor, Marble:** Section of floor covered in marble, measuring 10' x 10'.

**Floor, Tile:** Section of floor covered in tiles, measuring 10' x 10'.

**Floor, Wood:** A floor covered in polished fitted wood, measuring 10' x 10'.

**Gate, Metal:** A 20' tall by 10' wide gate, suitable for putting in a stockade wall.

**Gate, Wooden:** A 20' tall by 10' wide gate, suitable for putting in a stockade wall.

**Gatehouse:** A 30' high building portcullis.

**Keep, Round:** A heavily reinforced area.

**Keep, Square:** A heavily reinforced area.

**Moat, Filled:** Nothing more than a wide canal with each section measuring 100' long, 10' deep and 20' wide. To surround a castle, keep or other structure sections need to be dug and linked together, otherwise, you simply have a trench. Monsters and alligators are not included in the price.

**Moat, Unfilled:** Nothing more than a wide canal with each section measuring 100' long, 10' deep and 20' wide. To surround a castle, keep or other structure, sections need to be dug and linked together, otherwise, you simply have a trench. Monsters and alligators are not included in the price.

**Shutters, Window:** Window shutters provide no defense, but do protect against bad weather.

**Staircase, Stone:** A stone staircase.

**Staircase, Wood:** A wooden staircase.

**Tower, Bastion:** A half-circle tower that measures 30' in height and 30' in diameter.

**Tower, Round Large:** A 30' tall, 30' in diameter round tower.

**Tower, Round Small:** A 30' tall, 20' in diameter round tower.

**Trap Door:** This is nothing more than a 5' x 5' section of floor with an opening mechanism allowing for anyone to drop through a hole in the floor.

**Wall, Stone:** 100' in length, some 20' tall and 5' thick reinforced stone wall, with a walkway and battlements on the top.

**Wall, Wood:** 100' in length, some 20' tall and 5' thick reinforced wooden wall, with a walkway on the top.

**Window, Barred:** A 3' x 1' window with bars preventing anyone from entering.

**Window, Open:** A 3' x 1' open window.

# Hirelings, Services & Specialists – Mercenaries

## Descriptions

Unless noted, assume all mercenaries wear normal, standard clothing.

**Archer:** Armed with a short bow and sword, and wearing leather armor.

**Cavalry:** The typical cavalryman is armed with a sword and lance, and wears leather armor, while their horse sports leather barding. Other types of cavalry wear either plate or chain mail, while their horses wear either plate or chain barding.

**Crossbowman:** Armed with a crossbow, they wear chain mail.

**Footman:** Armed with sword and shield, they often wear either chain or leather armor. They are often called Sell-swords by many as well.

**Longbowman:** Armed with longbow and a short sword, they typically wear breast plates.

**Militia:** Commoners armed with spears, and wearing a helmet.

**Table 2:9 Hirelings, Services & Specialists – Mercenaries**

| Type | Cost |
|---|---|
| Archer | 5/month |
| Cavalry | 15/month |
| Crossbowman | 4/month |
| Footman | 3/month |
| Longbowman | 10/month |
| Militiaman | 1/month |

# Hirelings, Services & Specialists – Specialists

## Descriptions

**Animal Trainer:** Animal trainers domesticate and train animals.

**Armorer:** Armorers create and repair armor, and you need one for every 50 soldiers, regardless of whether the troops are conscripted or mercenaries.

**Artillerist:** An artillerist is in charge of the placement, maintenance, and operation of siege weapons.

**Bailiff:** The Bailiff is an official looking after a portion of an entire castle, making sure that the stronghold is in good repair.

**Blacksmith:** A blacksmith makes simple metal goods.

**Castellan:** A castellan oversees all military aspects of a stronghold.

**Chamberlain:** A person overseeing the management of a stronghold's cleaning and cooking staff.

**Craftsman:** This a catch-all category, and covers such occupations as cobblers, coopers, bakers, candle makers, butchers, milliners, and so forth.

**Engineer:** An engineer oversees the design and construction of buildings, roads, bridges, and other large scale structures. One engineer is needed per 100,000 cost of a building project.

**Table 2:10 Hirelings, Services & Specialists – Specialists**

| Type | Cost |
|---|---|
| Alchemist | 4000/month |
| Animal Trainer | 500/month |
| Armorer | 100/month |
| Artillerist | 750/month |
| Bailiff | 5/month |
| Blacksmith | 25/month |
| Castellan | 2000/month |
| Chamberlain | 5/month |
| Craftsman | 15/month |
| Engineer | 750/month |
| Healer | 40/month |
| Herbalist | 50/month |
| Lawyer | 500/month |
| Magistrate | 2000/month |
| Marshal | 5/month |
| Rower | 2/month |
| Sage | 2000/month |
| Sailor | 10/month |
| Scribe | 2,000/month |
| Sheriff | 8/month |
| Ship's Captain | 250/month |
| Ship's Navigator | 150/month |
| Sorcerer | 5000/month |
| Stableman | 5/month |
| Steward | 1,000/month |
| Warden | 5/month |

**Guard Captain:** A guard captain is in charge of not only the ruler's personal guard but the guarding of the entire stronghold.

**Healer:** Skilled in the art of medicine and healing, they are handy to have around when you have a bone to set, wound to heal or sickness to cure.

**Herald:** A herald makes announcements, and is also in charge of maintaining up-to-date news on the rulers of nearby lands.

**Herbalist:** Skilled in the art of plants and their use.

**Lawyer:** Someone skilled in the law, and serving as your legal representative in all legal matters.

**Magistrate:** In charge of administering all justice within a Domain, and also overseeing the common magistrates and sheriffs.

**Marshal:** A marshal oversees the recruiting and training of troops.

**Rower:** A rower is someone who rows in a galley.

**Sage:** A sage is someone who specialize in history and lore.

**Sailor:** Skilled in the operating and maintaining of ships and boats.

**Scribe:** Is in charge of book-keeping and accounts within a stronghold, in addition to the transcriptions and pen proclamations.

**Sheriff:** Responsible for law enforcement in an area of dominion.

**Ship's Captain:** Is in charge of not only a ship but the entire crew.

**Ship's Navigator:** Navigators ensure a ship does not get lost.

**Steward:** A steward oversees all household affairs, including housekeeping and maintaining food supplies.

**Warden:** A military advisor who reports to a castellan, and is responsible for defending a specific area within the Domain.

# Siege and Artillery

## Descriptions

**Ballista:** A large crossbow which is mounted on a sturdy platform, and fires bolts the size of spears.

**Battering Ram:** A large heavy tree usually banded with iron, and used to break down wooden walls or doors.

**Catapult:** Catapults consists of a frame with a wooden pole that has a basket or bowl at one end. The pole is pulled back, and when released, fires a projectile at a target.

**Trebuchet:** A trebuchet is a long pole with a sling on one end and a heavy weight on the other. When the pole is pulled down, the sling is loaded, then it is released.

**TABLE 2:11 SIEGE AND ARTILLERY**

| Type | Crew | DV | Blast | R | ROF | Cost |
|---|---|---|---|---|---|---|
| Ballista, Light | 1 | 4(40) | – | 10/20/30 | 1/10 | 200 |
| Ballista, Medium | 2 | 5(60) | – | 10/20/30 | 1/16 | 300 |
| Ballista, Heavy | 4 | 7(80) | – | 12/24/36 | 1/20 | 400 |
| Battering Ram | 4 to 8 | 5(60) | – | –/–/– | 1/1 | 250 |
| Catapult, Light | 1 | 4(50) | 10’ | –/–/30 | 1/10 | 250 |
| Catapult, Medium | 3 | 5(60) | 15’ | –/–/35 | 1/16 | 350 |
| Catapult, Heavy | 5 | 6(70) | 20’ | –/–/40 | 1/20 | 500 |
| Trebuchet | 5 | 6(75) | 20’ | –/–/50 | 1/20 | 750 |

**Notes:**
DV – Damage Value
Blast – Some weapons cause damage in a small area. All within that area suffer damage.
Range – Ranges are listed in feet for Small, Medium and Long. Some weapons are not effective at any range but Long.
RoF – Rate of Fire tells you how many rounds it takes between attacks. 1/10 means it is one attack per ten rounds.

# 3

# Followers & Domains

## Henchmen & Hirelings

As characters grow and gain experience, their reputations grow as well. Because of this increased reputation, they might often be asked to undertake missions or perform tasks that are too big for just themselves. Some characters might have their own goals, and in order to accomplish these goals, they might need to hire extra help. Conversely, the character's reputation might have others seek them out in the hopes of joining their cause or swearing allegiance to their banner.

Henchmen and hirelings come from all walks of life and offer characters access to skills that they might not have, or might not have the time to use. Henchmen and hirelings are more than just tools – however, some characters might view them as this – they are trusted confidants, loyal followers or even well-respected friends.

# Henchmen

Exactly when a Hero, or a Villain, attracts followers is left up to the Gamemaster. Acquiring followers is an organic outgrowth that follows on from play and deeds. A rough rule of thumb is that a Hero begins to attract followers once she has made a name for herself. This can be done after numerous adventures, or after performing tasks that bring her prestige.

How many Henchmen can a Hero have? A number equal to the Hero's Resolve. For example, your Hero has a Resolve 40. This means that she can easily lead a group of henchmen that numbers up to 40. Keep in mind that just because your Hero can have Henchmen, it doesn't mean that she acquires them automatically. She must hire them, persuade them to join her cause, or have a reputation which attracts people to her.

**Table 3:1 Leadership Penalty**

| # Over Resolve | Penalty |
|---|---|
| 1-5 | -1 |
| 6-10 | -2 |
| 11-15 | -3 |
| 20-25 | -4 |
| 26-30 | -5 |
| 31+ | -6 |

Let's use an example. Growing up on the mean streets and canals of Gravina, Johanna the Black took to thieving in order to survive. As a young lass she became a pickpocket, and eventually learned the skills enabling her to be a burglar. Over time, her reputation grew, and for this reason one, then two, partners in crime sought her out to join her "gang." Johanna, whose Resolve is 30, soon found herself leading a band of 15 thieves. To keep her band together, Johanna's player constantly sought ways to keep them happy.

So, can you have more Henchmen than your Resolve allows? Yes, but to do so requires the Hero to make a Diplomacy, Tactics, or Intimidation Test every time she wishes to have her henchmen undertake some task. This Test has a penalty depending on how many Henchman over the usual maximum total the Character is leading.

Note that the number of Henchmen your Character has is not the same as the number of families attached to their Domain (see below). Henchmen are a whole different beast when compared to ruling a kingdom. Think of Henchmen as trusted agents, lieutenants, and people who have been with your Hero as she has gained in power and infamy.

Unlike hirelings who get paid (see below), Henchmen are not covered by a set pay rate. That does not mean that Henchmen do not cost anything, or that they work out of gratitude. There is an exception among henchmen that they are to be given a place to live, food to eat, and a chance to gain wealth via a percentage of the spoils. Characters who do not take care of their Henchmen will soon find themselves with Henchmen harder to lead, prone to leaving, or worse still, wanting to mutiny.

As a general rule of thumb, payment for Henchmen can use **Tables 2:9** and **2:10** (see pages 33 & 34) as a rough guideline when it comes to their payment rates.

# Hirelings

Hirelings are those who are loyal to your Hero due to one fact — they are being paid. Hirelings work for the Hero and perform jobs, and it cost a number of Silver Coins per day to employ a hireling (see **Chapter 2**).

# Group Resolve

Followers, Henchmen and Hirelings are collectively known as Retainers, and they have Retainer Resolve, which is a measure of how happy, or angry, they are. Retainer Resolve covers both Henchmen and Hirelings as a means to keeping track of all Retainers morale. The initial Resolve rating is equal to the sum of the Retainers' Resolve multiplied by 5. Whenever a Resolve Check is made, look up the current Resolve rating on the Resolve Level Table which indicates the new Resolve. Remember that although Resolve changes frequently, the Resolve Level only changes when a Resolve Check is made — even if the rating moves into a different range between checks.

## Monthly Resolve Check

At the start of each month, the Gamemaster checks the current Resolve Rating in order to determine the Resolve Level of the henchmen. This Resolve Check may also be required as a result of certain actions by their leader (such as when an expected holiday is canceled) or as a result of a disaster striking the group (an unsuccessful fight leading to the death of a beloved follower).

So how do you check Retainer Resolve? Simply see what the current number is, by finding it on **Table 3:2.** For example, your Retainers have a current Resolve of 153. Looking at **Table 3:2,** you see that 153 means they are Unsteady; this is your current Retainer Resolve.

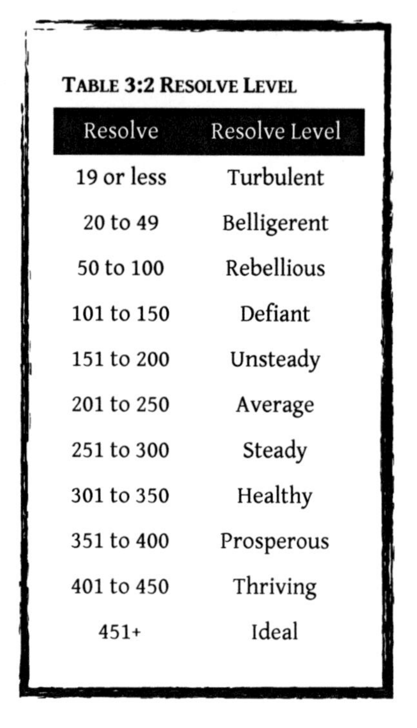

TABLE 3:2 RESOLVE LEVEL

| Resolve | Resolve Level |
|---|---|
| 19 or less | Turbulent |
| 20 to 49 | Belligerent |
| 50 to 100 | Rebellious |
| 101 to 150 | Defiant |
| 151 to 200 | Unsteady |
| 201 to 250 | Average |
| 251 to 300 | Steady |
| 301 to 350 | Healthy |
| 351 to 400 | Prosperous |
| 401 to 450 | Thriving |
| 451+ | Ideal |

Descriptions of the various Resolve Levels and their effects on the group are given below.

### Average

The group is running smoothly. There are no special conditions or effects.

### Belligerent

A –20 penalty is applied to the Retainer Resolve. In addition, a Diplomacy Test [-3] is always required when the Hero orders the Retainers to do something.

### Defiant

A –10 penalty is applied to the Retainer Resolve. In addition, a Diplomacy Test [-1] is always required when the Hero orders the Retainers to do something.

### Healthy

A +10 bonus is applied to the Retainer Resolve. In addition, any Tests the Retainers undertake have a +1 Bonus to their TN.

## Ideal

A +25 bonus is applied to the Retainer Resolve. In addition, any Tests the Retainers undertake have a +3 Bonus to their TN.

## Prosperous

A +15 bonus is applied to the Retainer Resolve. In addition, any Tests the Retainers undertake have a +2 Bonus to their TN.

## Rebellious

A –15 penalty is applied to the Retainer Resolve. In addition, a Diplomacy Test [-2] is always required when the Hero orders the Retainers to do something.

### Steady

A +10 bonus is applied to the Retainer Resolve.

### Thriving

A +20 bonus is applied to the Retainer Resolve. In addition, any Tests the Retainers undertake have a +2 Bonus to their TN.

### Turbulent

A –25 penalty is applied to the Retainer Resolve. In addition, a Diplomacy Test [-3] is always required when the Hero orders the Retainers to do something.

### Unsteady

A –10 penalty is applied to the Retainer Resolve.

## Resolve's Ebb and Flow

Depending on how the Hero treats her Retainers, their Resolve ebbs and flows with their circumstances. This ebb and flow is based on the actions of the Hero, as well as the conditions the Retainers face.

### Event Descriptions

#### Each Day no Pay

Most Retainers are loyal, but loyalty only goes so far if there is no pay. As soon as pay is received, the morale stops dropping.

#### Each Day Off

Call it a holiday, celebration or the like; if a day off work happens, then everyone is happy.

#### Death of a Retainer

Death comes to all, and when a Retainer dies due to either violence or natural causes, this hits everyone hard.

#### Forced to do Something Against Will

This is a broad category which covers such acts as a forced march, doing a job that is beneath one's status, and the like.

#### Miss a Meal

Regular meals are important, Retainers do not like missing one, and each one missed drops their morale more and more.

### Extra Pay

Raising the salary, awarding a bonus; after all, everyone likes extra money.

### Promotion

Be it a cook becoming head chef or a solider being promoted to sergeant, a promotion is always good.

### Gift

A new cloak, a new mount, even a new sword; everyone likes gifts.

### Forced to Work Holiday

From religious observances to traditional celebrations, most do not like working unless they have to. Most holidays are considered to be either days of partial or no work. Being made to work a full day, or worse, longer than normal hours, affects the Resolve.

### Sickness

Being sick is never fun, but when someone cannot work due to illness or worse, and still needs to work despite the illness, this affects morale.

### Sickness in Family

Unlike themselves being sick, when someone is sick in the Henchman's family, this is a situation where many find working is very difficult.

**Table 3:3: Impact of Actions**

| Action | Resolve -/+ |
| --- | --- |
| Each day no pay | -10 |
| Each day off | +10 |
| Death of a Retainer | -20 |
| Forced to do something against their will | -30 |
| Miss a meal | -5/meal missed |
| Extra pay | +15 |
| Promotion | +5 |
| Gift | +5 |
| Forced to work holiday | -35 |
| Sickness | -2 |
| Sickness in family | -4 |
| Suffer defeat | -30 |
| Suffer defeat with ¼ casualties | -60 |
| Suffer defeat with ½ casualties | -90 |
| Suffer defeat with ¾ casualties | -120 |
| Victory | +75 |
| Victory, Minor | +25 |
| Victory, Major | +100 |

### Suffer Defeat

From a barroom brawl to a skirmish with bandits, losing stinks.

### Suffer Defeat with ¼ Casualties

This is the same as suffering a defeat, but there are a minimum of 1d12 casualties.

### Suffer Defeat with ½ Casualties

Not only did you lose, but you lost half of your men. Maybe you should hire a better general.

### Suffer Defeat with ¾ Casualties

You lost, and lost big. It is time to rethink your military tactics and outlook.

### Victory

Winning a skirmish or competition, because everyone likes to win.

### Victory, Minor

Not only did you win, but you beat the odds.

### Victory, Major

You beat the impossible.

## Domains

When characters come to the attention of rulers through the performance of deeds that only Heroes can manage, they may be granted titles of nobility and grants of land. This will vary from campaign to campaign, depending on the preferences of the players and the Gamemaster.

The area of land ruled by a noble (whether a player character or otherwise) is called a Domain. This concept of a Domain applies whether or not the noble is given their title by a ruler or if the noble strikes out on their own and simply claims land and assumes a title. A single Domain consists

**Rogue States**

It is possible for a character to ignore hierarchy, and simply lay claim to an area, declaring themselves its ruler, and adopting whatever title they see fit to use. Depending on the location chosen and the title adopted, this may be met with anything from indifference to hostility by other local rulers.

While it may seem attractive to have no obligations, independent Domains are at risk of being invaded by hostile forces wishing to add the Hero's holding(s) to their own.

of a stronghold and all the surrounding land that is ruled from and protected by the stronghold. If a ruler has more than one stronghold (except in the case of it being a garrison), then each one and its surrounding lands is considered a separate dominion.

The following sections assume that the character is awarded a Domain by a ruler. This ruler gives a character land to manage and rule, but it is not free from obligation. They still must swear allegiance to the ruler, still have obligations to meet, and from time to time might have to send troops, or even money, to support the entire kingdom of which the character's small Domain is a part.

## Building a Stronghold

No Domain operates without a Stronghold of some type, which administers the Domain as well as being a place of refuge and safety for the character. Usually, a Domain consists of a single fief, with a stronghold located in the center so that no point within the Domain is too far away for easy access.

Domains range in size from 12 miles in radius up to 24 miles. The only requirement is that the ruler should be able to reach any part of their Domain within a day's travel. If they wish the Domain to be larger, than strongholds must be built to protect the extra portions of their land.

**Tables 3:4 Domain Classification**

| Terrain Classification | Within 144 miles of a city | More than 144 miles from a city | Within 72 miles of a Civilized Domain | Not near a city or Civilized Domain |
|---|---|---|---|---|
| Coastal | Civilized | Civilized | Borderland | Wilderness |
| Barren Lands | Borderlands | Wilderness | Wilderness | Wilderness |
| Clear[1] | Civilized | Borderlands | Borderlands | Wilderness |
| Desert[2] | Borderlands | Wilderness | Wilderness | Wilderness |
| Forest | Civilized | Civilized | Borderland | Wilderness |
| Grasslands | Civilized | Borderlands | Borderlands | Wilderness |
| Hills | Civilized | Borderlands | Borderlands | Wilderness |
| Jungle | Borderlands | Wilderness | Wilderness | Wilderness |
| Mountains | Borderlands | Wilderness | Wilderness | Wilderness |
| River | Civilized | Civilized | Borderland | Wilderness |
| Settled | Civilized | Civilized | Borderlands | Wilderness |
| Swamp | Borderlands | Wilderness | Wilderness | Wilderness |
| Tundra | Wilderness | Wilderness | Borderlands | Borderlands |

1. Strongholds of this type can become Settled if populated by anyone.
2. Strongholds containing oases are considered to be Civilized.

So what is a Stronghold? Any structure, be it a manor house, keep, castle or tower that serves as the central hub of activity for the Domain. From this Stronghold, the ruler governs ensuring her citizens are not only protected, but that they remain productive for the enrichment of the Domain.

In order to build a Stronghold, the surrounding area needs to be cleared of all threats. Once the area is cleared, the Stronghold may be designed and built. The costs for building a Stronghold can be found in **Chapter 2**.

## One Size Fits All?

The rules for Domains are one size fits all. The key assumption to them is that a Kingdom consists of one ruler having a whole bunch of little domains with a series of strongholds. A king, queen or emperor rules this kingdom, and the

Heroes are just one of the many smaller domains that make up this Kingdom. The reason for this assumption is simple: it is easier on the players and the Gamemasters. There are numerous styles of government that exist, and to cover them all, would make the rules needlessly complex. So what do you do if you want to set up a system that falls outside of this assumption? Use the rules are a baseline, and adjust the perspective.

**Table 3:5 Civilization Level**

| Type | Settling Families | Max Families |
|---|---|---|
| Wilderness | 1d12x10 | 1200 |
| Borderlands | 2d12x100 | 2400 |
| Civilized | 3d12x150 | 5400 |

For example, say you want to have something like a Republic. The hero's domain is a manor, and is part of a series of manors which make up a ruling council. The manor is part of a region, which in turn elects a representative to represent the region in a Ruling Council.

# Terrain & Resources

To determine the resources available to a Domain, the terrain needs to be determined. Each Domain is classified as being either Civilized, Borderlands or Wilderness, according to the material found in **Table 3:4 Domain Classification**, and depending on the terrain as well as the proximity to a major city or other civilized Domains. Other civilized Domains do not necessarily need to belong to the same Domain or even the same country. As long as some form of trade links exists, then it is considered civilized.

**Table 3:6 Number of Resources**

| d12 | # Resources |
|---|---|
| 1-2 | 1 |
| 3-4 | 2 |
| 5-6 | 3 |
| 7-8 | 4 |
| 9-10 | 5 |
| 11-12 | 6 |

**Table 3:7 Resource Type**

| d12 | Resource Type |
|---|---|
| 1-4 | Animal |
| 5-8 | Plant |
| 9-12 | Mineral |

A Domain's level of civilization sets two things in place. First, it gives you the number of families that can settle in the Domain once the Stronghold is built. Second, it determines the total number of families the Domain is capable of sustaining.

Now, a few notes. Terrain that is classified as Clear, Forest, Grassland or Hills whose population is greater than 1000 families is also classified as Settled. In addition, if the Domain dips below a population of 1000 (even if it is by only one person), it loses the Settled classification and immediately reverts back to its original Terrain Classification.

Here's an example of this process. Tobara Darkenhand has built her Domain in a Grassland. The Domain is not located near a major city, so the Domain's initial Civilization is Wilderness. Due to her hard work, and her reputation as being a fair ruler, Tobara's Domain's population is 1250 families. These factors mean the Terrain is now considered Settled. After a brutal winter which sees not only sickness but also a band of marauders attack, the population drops to 950 families. As a result of this, the Terrain is no longer considered Settled, and reverts back to the initial designation of Grasslands.

## Resources

Regardless of the Domain's history or terrain classification, all Domains have between one and six Resources that are exploitable for the Domain to generate income. To determine the number of Resources, roll a d12 and consult **Table 3:6.**

**TABLE 3:8 POPULATION CHANGE**

| Number of Families | %Change |
|---|---|
| 1-100 | +1% |
| 101-200 | +2% |
| 201-300 | +4% |
| 301-400 | +6% |
| 401-500 | +8% |
| 501-600 | +12% |
| 601-700 | +16% |
| 701-1000 | +18% |
| 1001+ | +24% |

Once the number of Resources are determined, the next step is to figure out the type of Resources found. In **SHADOW, SWORD & SPELL**, there are three types of Resources: Animal, Plant and Mineral. However, the form these Resources take is left up to the Gamemaster and the player.

For example, Tobara Darkenhand's Domain has 3 Resources. Rolling for the type, she rolls a 2, a 9, and a 12, and gets one Animal and 2 Mineral Resources. The GM and player talk about the Domain, and decide the Animal Resource will take the form of wild sheep which graze in the Domain's ample grasslands. These sheep can be exploited for a multitude of products (meat as well as wool), and represent one of the 3 Resources available. As for the two Mineral Resources, the player suggests that gold and diamonds are found in her Domain. The Gamemaster, feeling that this is far too much wealth, rules that instead of gold, marble is found in the Domain. In addition, instead of diamonds, the GM decides the other mineral found here is flint.

## Rulership

Unlike combat, ruling a Domain in **SHADOW, SWORD & SPELL** employs a different time scale and frame. This scale uses not only months and years, but depending on certain events, even days. Why? It makes it easier on both the GM and the player. A side benefit of this scale is that it is much easier to slip in lots more narratives to the act of ruling. In addition, this allows the Gamemaster to structure adventures that fit within the month-to-month life of a Domain, while still allowing for adventures involving the characters.

Specifically, changes to population and economy are dealt with monthly, and the Resolve of the Domain's population can be handled yearly.

To keep things easier, as well as make the game a bit more streamlined, calendars are left up to the Gamemaster to decide. Even within the The World material (see **Chapter 9**), years and dates are not provided. This is not an example of us being lazy or purposefully vague, this is done to make things easier. In our own games we've employed dating techniques influenced by the real world calendar. Doing this makes the passage of time simpler, and allows the players to not have to memorize different months, seasons, and the like. It is easier to use a month, such as May, then it is to use a month known as Spring-Turn, Hammer Fell, and the like. In the end this is your game, and if you want to create a different calendar, or use different months, go for it.

## Population Change

Every month, the number of families in a Domain will fluctuate for a number of reasons. To keep the mechanics simple, population changes are handled with a single check. For each Domain, the change in population is based on the current population.

In addition to this increase, Domains with less than 250 families must roll 1d12 and consult the following:

1-6 = Lose 1d12 families

7-12 = Gain 1d12 families

What if the Domain has a large population? The small ebbs and flows have no effect, and are considered to be irrelevant in comparisons to normal population growth.

So how does this work? Here's an example involving Tobara Darkenhand. When Tobara built her keep, the Domain was considered to be Wilderness. Thus, it attracted 1d12 x 10 families as the first settlers. You rolled a d12, and got a 7, so 70 families settled.

After a month, you check the population growth, and since there are less than 100 families, there is a 24% increase, making for 94 families. Additionally, because there are less than 250 families in the Domain, you roll a d12 to see what the random fluctuation has been. Rolling a 12 means that there is a further increase in population of 1d12 families. You roll a 2, which means two extra families arrive, giving you a total of 96 families at the start of the second month.

# Resolve

Each dominion has Resolve, which is known as Domain Resolve. This represents the general state of contentment (or discontent!) of the whole Domain. Just as it is with Retainers (see above), there is a single Resolve Test made for the entire Domain.

When a Domain is established, the initial Domain Resolve is set equal to the sum of the character's Resolve multiplied by 100. Besides Resolve, Domains have a Resolve Level which is based on this rating, and periodically a Resolve Check is made. Whenever a Resolve Check needs to be made, look up the current Resolve Rating on **Table 3:9,** which indicates the new Resolve. Remember, although Resolve changes frequently, the Resolve Level only changes when a Resolve Check is made — even if the rating moves into a different range between checks.

**Table 3:9 Resolve Level**

| Resolve | Resolve Level |
|---|---|
| 49 or less | Turbulent |
| 50 to 99 | Belligerent |
| 100 to 149 | Rebellious |
| 150 to 199 | Defiant |
| 200 to 299 | Unsteady |
| 300 to 399 | Average |
| 400 to 499 | Steady |
| 500 to 599 | Healthy |
| 600 to 699 | Prosperous |
| 700 to 799 | Thriving |
| 800+ | Ideal |

## Yearly Resolve Check

At the start of the year, the Gamemaster checks the current Resolve Rating in order to determine the Resolve Level of the Domain. This Resolve Check may also be required as a result of certain actions taken by the ruler (such as when an expected holiday is canceled) or as a result of a disaster striking the dominion.

Descriptions of the various Resolve Levels and their effects on the Domain are given below.

### Average

The dominion is running smoothly, and there are no special conditions or effects.

### Belligerent

If the Domain has fewer troops than one-half the number of families, half the families will form a peasant militia (providing an average of 2 troops per family). In addition, the following conditions exist within the Domain:

- No taxes can be collected.
- 25% of normal service income can be collected in areas without a peasant militia, but none can be collected in areas with a peasant militia.
- A quarter of the normal resource income can be collected in areas without a peasant militia, but none can be collected in areas with a peasant militia.
- A –10 penalty is applied to the Domain Resolve.
- All trade caravans and traveling officials will be attacked by bandits.
- Any of the Domain's troops moving or deploying within the Domain will be attacked by peasant militia, deserters, bandits, or enemy agents.
- At the Gamemaster's discretion, there is a chance that an enemy state will provide the peasant militia with military support and other types of aid.

## Defiant

In Domains with fewer troops than one-third of the number of families, half the families will form a peasant militia (providing an average of 3 troops per family). However,these militia will not attack unless provoked. In addition:

- No taxes can be collected.
- 50% of normal service income can be collected in areas without a peasant militia, but only a third can be collected in areas with a peasant militia.
- 50% of the normal resource income can be collected in areas without a peasant militia, but only a third can be collected in areas with a peasant militia.

## Healthy

The Domain's income is 10% greater than normal. Additionally, there is a chance that any enemy agents working in the Domain will be exposed.

## Ideal

All income is 10% greater than normal. In addition, there is a chance that any enemy agents working in the dominion will be exposed. Typically this is at the Gamemaster's discretion, but you could roll a d12 and if the result is even, the enemy agent(s) are found. If a random check indicates a disaster occurs during the coming year, there is a chance that it will not happen. A +25 bonus is applied to the Domain Resolve, and the Resolve cannot drop below 400 before the next Resolve Check.

## Prosperous

All income is 10% greater than normal. There is a chance that enemy agents working in the Domain will be exposed. Typically this is at the Gamemaster's discretion, but you could roll a d12 and if the result is even, the enemy agent (s) are found. If a random check indicates that a disaster occurs during the coming year, it will not happen.

## Rebellious

The Domain has fewer troops than one-third of the number of the total of families, and half of the families form a peasant militia (providing an average of 2 troops per family). This militia will not attack unless provoked. In addition, the following effects take place:

- No taxes can be collected.
- Only 30% of normal service income can be collected in areas without a peasant militia, but only 25% can be collected in areas with a peasant militia.
- Finally a –10 penalty is applied to the Domain Resolve.

## Steady

There is a chance that enemy agents working in the Domain will be exposed. Typically, this is at the Gamemaster's discretion, but you could roll a d12 and if the result is even, the enemy agent(s) are found.

## Thriving

All Domain income is 10% greater than normal. In addition, roll a d12, and if the result is even, one enemy agent working in the dominion is exposed. If a random check indicates that a disaster will occur during the coming year, roll a d12, and if the result is 1, 2 or 3, it will not happen.

## Turbulent

95% of the Domain's families form a peasant militia (providing an average of 3 troops per family). No income of any kind may be collected, except by force. A –10 penalty is applied to the Resolve rating. The Resolve cannot rise above 100 until the ruler of the Domain is removed, either through assassination or revolt. All trade caravans and traveling officials are attacked by bandits. Any of the dominion ruler's troops moving or deploying within the Domain will be attacked by peasant militia, deserters, bandits or enemy agents. One or more enemy states will provide the peasant militia with military support.

## Unsteady

Roll a d12; if the result is a 1 or 12, a –10 penalty will apply to the Resolve rating.

# The Economy

Each game month, the ruler of the Domain, along with the Gamemaster, needs to check on the Economy and tally up the income and expenditures for the month.

# Income

Monthly income comes from three sources: Resources, Services, and Taxes.

## Resources

Before going going into detail, a couple of things need to be kept in mind. First, the system presented in this chapter is designed so as not to be too detailed. Running a Domain should not be an exercise in extensive book-keeping and require a use of spreadsheets. Second, this system is purposely designed to be more of a broad brush system. This means that price fluctuations and discrepancies between resources are purposely left out. This is done to ease the burden, and make the process much more smooth. That does not mean a Gamemaster cannot add in these details. For the purpose the game, however, a much simpler approach is followed.

Each Domain has between 1 and 6 Resource types, which provide income for the dominion's ruler. The amount of income is:

Animal= 2/family

Plant= 1/family

Mineral= 3/family

Each family works a single Resource within the Domain, and the ruler simply allows the population to split themselves evenly between the available Resources, or may direct the populace to concentrate on exploiting a particular Resource. There are a few limitations to keep in mind.

First, given the infrastructure needed to exploit a particular Resource (animals need breeding, crops need sowing, mines need digging), the ruler can only change the emphasis on the Resources once per year. The ruler must decide what their priorities are to be at the start of each year. The actual changes to these priorities occur at the beginning of the following year. In doing so, it is convenient to assign priorities in terms of the percentages of families rather than in absolute numbers of families, since the total number of families in the Domain changes from month to month.

Second, the population must work all the Resources in the Domain for the local economy to thrive and for the populace to be content. In particular, forcing too much of the population to work, for example, in dangerous and unhealthy mines will make the ruler very unpopular, and could sow the seeds of revolution.

In game terms, each Resource must be worked by at least 20% of the families in the fief. For each 1% below that threshold per year, there is a cumulative –1 penalty to the Domain's Resolve. Similarly, no more than 50% of the families in the fief should be made to exploit mineral wealth. For each 1% above that threshold per year, there is a cumulative –1 penalty to the dominion's Resolve Rating.

Finally, any Domain bringing in monthly revenues of 15,000 Crowns or more attracts corruption, black marketeers, and bandits. Unless that Domain contains a Stronghold (see above) which is the center of the Domain's administration, 1d12 x 5% of the potential resource income is lost to such forces.

### Service

Families in the Domain bring in the equivalent income worth 10 Crowns per month in Service. Services range from building works, growing food, tending animals, trades, and so forth.

Unlike other sources of income, this income does not go to the ruler of the Domain. It can be used to offset expenses such as holidays, tithes, taxes, and the paying of armies (mercenary or otherwise). Any Service income not used for these purposes is wasted, and cannot be put into the coffers for a rainy day.

### Taxes

The families in the Domain normally pay 1 Crown per month per family in taxes. The ruler of the dominion can set higher or lower tax rates, if she so desires. Each extra 1 Silver paid per family incurs a –10 penalty to the Domain's Resolve each year. For each 1 Silver less paid per family, there is a +5 bonus to the Domain's Resolve Rating each year. Additionally, when tax rates increase, there is an instant -25 penalty incurred to the Domain's Resolve Rating, and it forces an immediate Resolve Test. Similarly, decreasing the tax rates gives an instant +10 bonus to the Domain's Resolve Rating.

Example: In the Domain containing her keep, Tobara Darkenhand assigns 25% of the families to work in the marble quarries, 25% of the families to work the flint mine, and 50% of the families to work in sheep herding. Since she has at least 20% of the population working on each resource, and she does not have more than 50% of the population working on mineral resources, there is no effect on her Domain's Resolve.

After a few years of growth (not in real time, but game time), the Domain's population is 447 families, with the following breakdown:

447 × 25% = 112 families mining flint

447 × 25% = 112 families quarrying marble

447 × 50% = 223 families herding sheep

The income from the Resources in the first month of that year is:

(112 × 3) + (112 × 3) + (223 × 1) = 895 Crowns

The Service income of the fief is simply ten times the population, which is:

(10 × 447) = 4,470 Crowns

Tobara has not set taxes higher or lower than the 1 Crown/family, so the Taxes received are:

(1 × 447) = 447 Crowns

Thus, for her Domain, Tobara Darkenhand receives a total of 1,342 Crowns in payment and 4,470 Crowns in services offsetting her expenses.

## Expenditures

### Stronghold Staff and Maintenance

Besides armies, which are always accounted for separately, the costs of a Stronghold staff and routine maintenance are assumed to be covered by the Service income of the Domain. However, extraordinary expenses such as rebuilding in the wake of a raid or a natural disaster needs to be paid for out of the ruler's pocket. Service income may be used to pay for these expenses.

### Troops

It does not matter if it is a full-time standing army, an elite group of adventurers, or a mercenary company; troops must be paid for. Armies and mercenaries can be paid for with Service income, based on their costs (which are found in **Chapter 2**), but adventurers usually only work for cold hard cash. In times of need, a peasant militia can be mobilized from the local population. Up to 10% of the families in a Domain provide "poor" quality peasant militia (an average of 2.5 troops per family). A further 10% of the families in an area can provide "untrained" quality peasant militia (providing an average of 2.5 troops per family). Any called for service are unable to produce income of any type during the months they serve with the militia.

### Tithes

A tenth of all gross income (income before any expenditures) must be given in tithes to the various churches and temples that are have been established throughout the Domain. This tithe is the total given to all temples/churches within the Domain. Tithes may be paid with either Service income or personal wealth, or a combination of the two. Failure to provide the full amount of the tithe results in angering the clergy who make their anger known to the population. The net result of this is that any year in which tithes are not paid in full incurs a −50 penalty to the Domain Resolve.

Not paying, or underpaying, tithes more than one year in a row offers a chance each year that an extra "Disaster" event happens due to the Gods showing their disfavor and anger. If such an event is going to happen, it will be preceded by omens and prophetic dreams. Angering the gods and invoking Their wrath has much potential for the GM. If a second event is to take place, play this up by describing omens as well as prophetic dreams.

## Festivals and Holidays

Throughout the year, there are certain days declared as festivals or holidays. These may have been declared by the ruler of the country, or by one of the major religions of the country, or the ruler of the Domain may declare her own. Overall costs for a holiday are 5 Crowns per family. This represents not only the expenses for the celebrations, but the lost income due to the people not working. This cost may be paid for with either Service income, personal wealth, or a combination of the two.

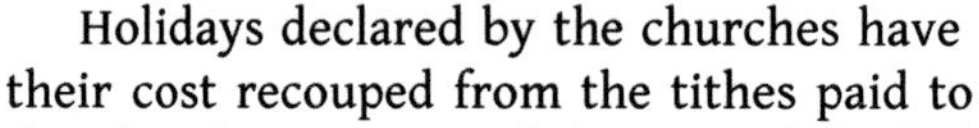

Holidays declared by the churches have their cost recouped from the tithes paid to the church. However, if the cost of the holiday is too much to cover by the tithes or taxes (or if the holiday was declared by the Domain ruler instead of a higher power), the Domain ruler must pay the remaining costs themselves. Each time a regular holiday or festival that the population is expecting is canceled, a –5 penalty is applied to the Domain's Resolve, and an immediate Resolve Check must be made.

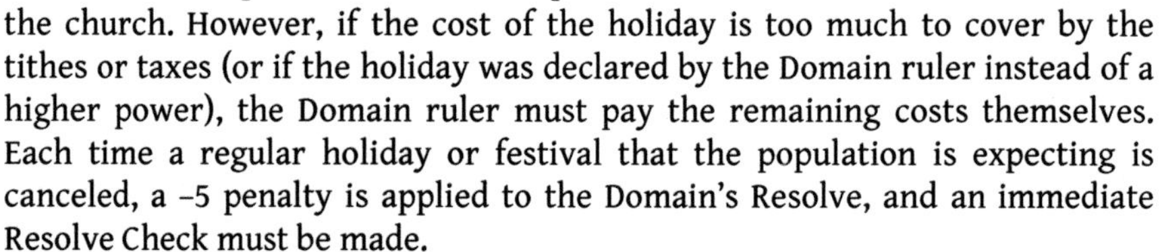

Each time an extraordinary holiday or festival day is announced, a +2 bonus is applied to the Dominion's Resolve (no Resolve check needs to be made until the festival or holidays are over).

## Entertaining Visitors

Etiquette requires that any nobility or royalty visiting the Domain are entertained according to their station.

The following costs apply whenever a noble (and their retinue) visits the Domain:

Knight — No Extra Cost

Baron — 100 Crowns/Day

Viscount — 150 Crowns/Day

Count — 300 Crowns/Day

Marquis — 400 Crowns/Day

Duke — 600 Crowns/Day

Archduke — 700 Crowns/Day

Prince — 1,000 Crowns/Day

King — 1,500 Crowns/Day

Emperor — 2,000 Crowns/Day

**Table 3:10 Number of Events**

| d12 | #Event |
|---|---|
| 1-3 | 1 |
| 4-6 | 2 |
| 7-9 | 3 |
| 10-12 | 4 |

**Table 3:11 Domain Event Table**

| d12 | Event Type |
|---|---|
| 1-2 | Major Positive Event |
| 3-4 | Minor Positive Event |
| 5-6 | An Event |
| 7-8 | Minor Negative Event |
| 9-10 | Major Negative Event |
| 11-12 | Disaster |

## Experience for Income

Characters gain Experience Points due to running their Domain. The Experience Point rewards are based on the monthly income the Domain has. When calculating the Experience Points the ruler gets from their monthly income, two rules must be followed.

First, only cash income (i.e., Resources and Taxes) provide Experience Points. Service income provides none at all.

Second, Experience Points are derived from the gross income (before any expenditures are determined and taken out of the equation). Even if the income is spent due to heavy expenditures and the ruler ends up having a net loss, they still receive Experience Points.

So how do you gain Experience Points? You use the following formula:

**Income Received ÷ 1000 = Experience Gained**

As always, round down.

For example, Tobara Darkenhand receives a total of 1,342 Crowns in cash and 5,390 Crowns in services this month. She gains Experience for all of the cash even though she had to spend some of it, but does not get any Experience for the Services money. Tobara Darkenhand therefore gains 1 XP this month.

## Events

Each year, between 1 and 4 random events happen in the Domain. Due to the huge variety of events that can potentially occur, it is not possible to list

them all here. However, they can be roughly classified into different types of Events. For each Event occurring, roll on the Domain Event Table below.

The table is random, but Gamemasters should be fair to the players, and not have players' Domains wiped out by a few bad rolls indicating disaster after disaster, and if the dice seem to be against the players, the Gamemaster should introduce plot elements or potential adventures into the game that can mitigate the worst situations. Similarly, if the dice are favoring the players and they are getting bored just raking in the money every month without challenge, the Gamemaster should introduce plot elements or adventures that can cause additional problems.

However, in either case the Gamemaster should be careful not to railroad the players and make them feel that the status quo is being forcibly maintained. The Gamemaster should make sure that the players' decisions have a real impact on the way their Domains prosper or struggle.

### Major Positive Event

A Major Positive Event benefits the Domain greatly. It might result in a bonus to Resolve up to +25, a doubling of income for a month, a population increase up to +25%, or any combination thereof. Depending on the nature of the event, the ruler may need to get involved personally to get the best results — but there should be some positive results even if the ruler does nothing.

*Examples*: New resource type found, ancient treasure found, a God decides to become the patron of the Domain.

### Minor Positive Event

A Minor Positive Event benefits the Domain, as well as not harming it. It may take the form of a bonus to the Domain Resolve of up to +15, up to 50% extra income for a month, a population increase up to +15%, or some combination of the above. The ruler might have to get involved personally in order to gain the benefits — but there should be no negative results even if the ruler does nothing.

*Examples*: A new trade route opens, a hostile tribe of barbarians moves away from the Domain, passing adventurers clear out local bandits without needing to be hired to do so.

### An Event

An Event either benefits the Domain or harms it, depending on how it is dealt with. An Event might result in a change to the Domain Resolve of up to +/-10, up to 25% extra or less income for a month, a population change of up to

+/-10%, or some combination of the above. Whether the Event works out positively or negatively depends on how the ruler handles it.

*Examples*: An important visitor arrives unexpectedly, comets or other omens are seen in the sky, heresy is discovered in a local church, a local tribe of barbarians is displaced by a different tribe.

### Minor Negative Event

A Minor Negative Event harms the Domain, or at the least does not benefit it. It may result in a penalty to the Domain Resolve of up to -15, up to 50% less income for a month, a population decrease of up to -15%, or some combination of the above. The ruler might have to get involved personally in order to avoid harm — but there should be no significant positive results no matter how well the ruler handles the situation.

*Examples*: Bandits start raiding merchant caravans, an official is assassinated, a monster arrives in the area, a disease breaks out.

### Major Negative Event

A Major Negative Event harms the Domain greatly. It may result in a penalty to the Domain Resolve of up to -25, up to 50% less income for a month, a population decrease of up to -25%, or some combination of the above. Depending on the nature of the event, the ruler may need to get involved personally in order to get the least bad results — but there should be some negative results no matter how well the ruler handles the situation.

*Examples*: One of the Domain's resources runs out, an epidemic strikes, a powerful monster enters the domain, agents plot a rebellion against the ruler, a major fire breaks out.

### Disaster

A Disaster harms the Domain greatly in a similar way to a Major Negative Event. It may result in a penalty to the Domain Resolve of up to -50, up to 75% less income for a month, a population decrease of up to - 50%, or some combination of the above. It also results in an immediate Resolve Check. Depending on the nature of the event, the ruler may need to get involved personally in order to get the least bad results — but there should be seriously negative results no matter how well the ruler handles the situation.

*Examples*: An extremely powerful monster attacks the Domain, plague strikes, a hurricane, tornado, or avalanche sweeps through the Domain, an earthquake strikes, a God smites the dominion.

## Using Events for Adventure

Besides affecting the Domain, events, especially negative ones, serve as adventure inspirations. GMs should use events as a means to move along any long-term plots of the campaign, as well as introduce new wrinkles into the campaign.

# 4

# Magic

## Common Spells

In **Shadow, Sword & Spell: Basic**, a number of Common Spells were introduced. For players and Gamemasters wanting more variety in these Common Spells, this section is for you.

### Bar

Range: Touch
Vitality Cost: 1
Duration: Instant
Sanity Cost: 0
Perform On: Lock, Door, Gate

This Spell allows a Caster to lock any one mechanical lock, bar or any other means of locking a door, gate or portal. No matter how hard a person tries to open it, the door will not budge. Successfully casting the Spell causes one lock or door to permanently lock, while a Dramatic Success causes any door or lock within 20 feet of the caster to lock up tight. The locking or barring lasts until the Caster will it, but as long as he does not touch the lock after the Spell is cast, the Bar Spell remains in effect. Failing to cast the Spell results in the door or gate not being locked, while a Dramatic Failure results in the lock or door crumbling to dust. The higher the Power Rank in this spell, makes it more difficult for others, such as those with the Open spell, to release the lock.

## Cause Gloom

Range: Feet equal to Will — Vitality Cost: 6

Duration: Instant — Sanity Cost: 0

Performed On: Others

Successfully casting this Spell causes all within range of the Caster (friend and foe alike) to suffer from gloomy thoughts, and they will become depressed. The effect of this is that all targets of the Spell must make a Will Test, with Failure causing them to lose Sanity equal to one-half the caster's Will (double for a Dramatic Success), as well as suffering a -1 to all Tests for a number of Rounds equal to the Caster's Will (doubled for Dramatic Success). Failure to cast the Spell means spell effects do not occur, while a Dramatic Failure results in the caster losing Sanity equal to the his Will, and he suffers a -1 to all Tests for a number of Rounds equal to his Will.

## Conjure Element

Range: Touch — Vitality Cost: 2

Duration: Instant — Sanity Cost: 0

Performed On: Special

This simple Spell is one that all mages learn when starting their walk down the path of magic. This Spell, once cast, produces one element. This element can be contained in a vessel or container of some sort, and in some cases, may serve as a light or heat source.

- **Fire:** A burst of magical flame which can be used to ignite a fire, or light a torch or a lamp. Dramatic Success summons the flame, and it continues to burn for a number of Rounds equal to the Caster's Will.
- **Air:** Creates a gentle breeze swirling around the Caster for a number of Rounds equal to his Will. On a Dramatic Success, this breeze lasts for one day. The breeze is strong enough to cool and refresh the Caster, but it is not strong enough to put out open flames.
- **Water:** Summons one gallon of water, which can be stored in a bucket, flask, or other vessel. A Dramatic Success summon two gallons of water.

- **Earth:** Summons a fist-sized rock, and a Dramatic Success summons a man-sized rock.
- **Magic:** Summons a globe of light which sheds light in a 60-foot radius, and lasts for a number of Rounds equal to the Caster's Will. With a Dramatic Success, this light not only lasts for one day, but it will float above the head of the Caster.

Failing to cast the Spell means the Caster has failed to summon the element, while a Dramatic Failure has the Caster suffer Vitality damage equal to his Will, and makes him unable to cast spells for one day.

## Cure Disease

Range: Touch
Vitality Cost: 5
Duration: Instant
Sanity Cost: 0
Performed On: Self, Others

This Spell is one that many of those who consider themselves to be healers seek to learn. The reason for this is that mastery of this spell aids in the healing of those suffering from the effects of disease. When this Spell is successfully cast, and a person who suffers from a disease is touched, the disease is automatically cured. Even though the disease is cured, any damage or Ability levels the character has lost due to the disease is not healed, and these injuries must heal naturally. In addition, this Spell only works on one disease, and if the target suffers from multiple diseases, the Spell must be cast once for each type of disease. A Dramatic Success on casting this Spell not only cures the target of the disease, but also does not cost the Caster any Vitality to cast.

Failing to cast the Spell means the disease is not cured, while a Dramatic Failure not only results in the disease not being cured, but causes the Caster to contract the disease himself.

## Familiar

Range: Touch

Duration: Instant

Performed On: One Animal

Vitality Cost: 15

Sanity Cost: Special

Those skilled in the magical Arts soon learn that they might need a little aid in their daily lives. Familiars are normal animals that serve not only as protector and companion, but act as a storehouse of Sanity which a sorcerer **can** use. In order to bond with a familiar, the Caster must first have an animal, which can range in type and size from rat or a cat, to a dog to even a lion. Once the respective animal is found or purchased, this Spell can be cast. Successfully casting the Spell results in the animal and the Caster being bonded, and half of the Caster's current Sanity is transferred to the familiar. This bonding has the following benefits:

- Familiar's Sanity is increased by half of the Caster's Sanity (Dramatic Success causes this to be doubled).
- The Caster is able to intuitively know where his familiar is at all times, as well as summon them to his side.
- The Caster is able to use the senses of his familiar, such as sight and hearing. To do so requires the Caster to spend one Round doing nothing but concentrating on their familiar. As long as the Caster takes no Action, he can see or hear through his familiar.
- As long as the Caster is touching his familiar, which requires an Action, he can take back a number of Sanity equal to his Will. The familiar recovers Sanity as per the rate found in **SHADOW, SWORD & SPELL: BASIC.**

Failing to cast this Spell means the animal is not bonded to the Caster, while a Dramatic Failure causes the animal to immediately attack the Caster. In addition, the Caster loses half his Sanity.

There is a limit to the number of Familiars a Caster can bind himself to, and this is based on the Caster's Will. Thus, a sorcerer with Will 9 is able to bond with a total of 9 familiars.

If a familiar dies, the Caster loses access to the Sanity that was retained by the familiar, and suffers a Sanity loss equal to the number of Sanity the familiar had. Sanity that was channeled to the familiar is permanently lost.

## Magic's Luminance

Range: Within 5 feet of the Caster | Vitality Cost: 1
Duration: Hours equal Caster's Will | Sanity Cost: 0
Performed On: nil

This simple Spell creates a small 1-foot diameter globe of light which floats in the air around the Caster. This globe of light sheds radiance in a 60-foot radius. Successfully casting this Spell causes the globe to appear, while a Dramatic Success makes the globe able to move up to 50 feet from the Caster. The globe responds to the Caster's mental commands as it relates to movement. Failing to cast the Spell cause the globe of light not to be conjured, while Dramatic Failure results in the Caster being struck blind for a number of hours equal to their Will.

## Open

Range: Touch | Vitality Cost: 1
Duration: Instant | Sanity Cost: 0
Performed On: Locks

This simple Spell, if successfully cast, opens any lock. A Dramatic Success causes any lock within 20 feet of the Caster to unlock. Failing to cast the Spell means that the lock does not open, while a Dramatic Failure results in the Caster suffering a number of points of Vitality damage equal to their Will.

## Resist Elements

Range: Touch | Vitality Cost: 6
Duration: Hours equal Caster's Will | Sanity Cost: 0
Performed On: Self, Others

Successfully casting this Spell causes the target of the Spell to become repellent to the specific effects of one element. For example, you can cast this Spell to repel mud (Element of Earth) and doing so makes the mud unable to touch the target, as well as to allow them to walk across mud as if it were solid ground. Casting the Spell to protect the target from hail (Element of Water) results in hail not touching the target, but the target can still get wet due to the effects of rain and water. While this Spell is in effect, the specific element in question simply does not affect the target. The duration of this Spell's effect is for a number of hours equal to the caster's Will. Failing to cast the Spell results in the element in question not being repelled, while a Dramatic Failure causes the Caster to suffer Vitality damage equal to his Will.

## Shadow of the Moon

| | |
|---|---|
| Range: Touch | Vitality: 2 |
| Duration: Rounds equal to Will of the Caster plus Degrees of Success | Sanity Cost: 0 |
| Performed On: Self, Others, Object | |

When this Spell is successfully cast, the mage summons a sphere of darkness that is 10 feet in radius that shrouds the mage, and makes him difficult to see. While inside the shroud, anyone trying to attack the mage suffers a -2 to all Tests (-4 with a Dramatic Success). The mage, while inside the shroud, can see normally and is not affected by the darkness. Failing the Test means the Spell is not cast, while a Dramatic Failure blinds the mage, causing him to suffer a -2 penalty to all Tests for a number of Rounds equal to the Caster's Will.

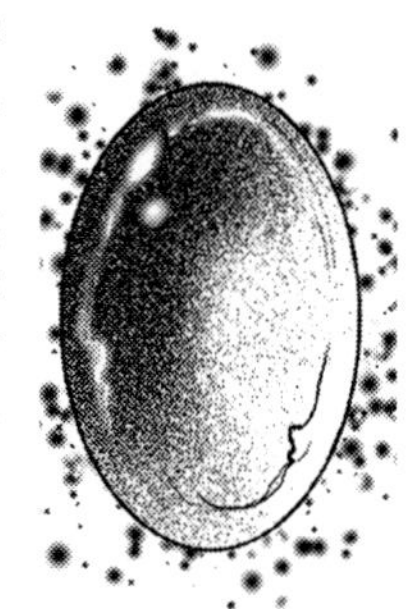

## Silence

| | |
|---|---|
| Range: Feet equal to the Caster's Will | Vitality Cost: 3 |
| Duration: Rounds equal to Caster's Will | Sanity Cost: 0 |
| Performed On: Self, Others, Object | |

This is a simple Spell, but one with many uses for the more subtle acts of thievery. Successfully casting this Spell creates a zone where no sound can be heard or made. The radius is centered on the target, and is equal to the Caster's Will in feet. In addition, if this Spell is cast on a person, the zone of silence moves with the target. The silence lasts for a number of Rounds equal to the Caster's Will (doubled for Dramatic Success). Anyone trapped within the zone suffers a -2 to all Tests due to being unable to hear anything. Bear in mind that even though the zone is silent, those within the zone can still be seen, smelled, and/or touched – they simply make no noise. Failure to cast the Spell causes no zone of silence to be created, while a Dramatic Failure causes the Caster to be struck deaf for a number of days equal to his Will. While deaf, the Caster suffers a -2 to all Tests due to the lack of hearing.

## Span the Distance

Range: Miles equal to Caster's Will
Vitality Cost: 3

Duration: Minutes equal to Caster's Will
Sanity Cost: 0

Performed On: Self, Others

This Spell allows the Caster, or the person on which it is cast, the ability to see great distances. Successfully casting the Spell allows the target to see a number of miles equal to the Caster's Will. The duration of this far-seeing vision is equal to the Caster's Will (doubled for a Dramatic Success). Failing to cast the Spell means that the Spell is not cast, while a Dramatic Failure results in the Caster losing a number of Sanity points equal to his Will, as a result of his visual senses being overwhelmed.

## Sword of the Ghost

Range: Feet equal to Caster's Will
Vitality Cost: 5

Duration: Rounds equal to Caster's Will
Sanity Cost: 0

Performed on: Hand Weapon

This Spell is cast on any hand weapon, and allows the weapon to float in the air. The Caster is able to direct the weapon mentally, and have it attack anyone within a number of feet equal to the Caster's Will. Successfully casting this Spell gives a duration of a number of Rounds equal to the Caster's Will (double for a Dramatic Success). The weapon, while the Spell is in effect, has a Brawl [+10], which is used in conjunction with the Caster's Will to determine the Target Number (TN). Failing to cast the Spell means the weapon is not enchanted, while a Dramatic Failure causes the weapon to attack the Caster. The Spell is only able to be cast on a hand weapon usable one-hand, as two-handed weapons are too heavy for the Spell.

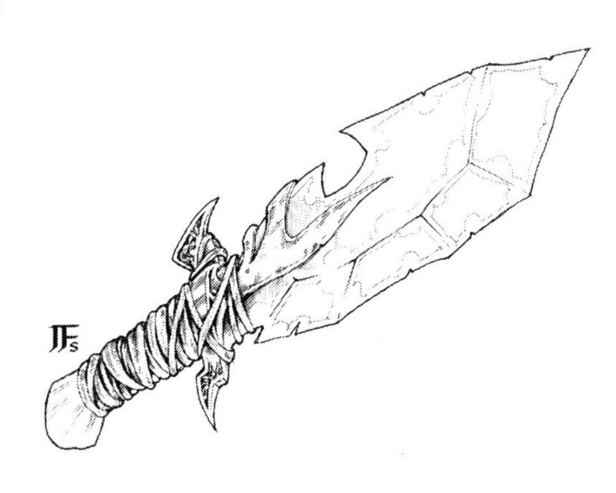

# Traverse

Range: 10 Feet x Will | Vitality Cost: 7

Duration: Rounds equal to Will | Sanity Cost: 0

Performed On: Area

Successfully casting this Spell creates a magical, shimmering bridge capable of supporting 1,000 pounds. The length of this bridge is equal to ten times the Caster's Will, and the Spell lasts for a number of Rounds equal to the Caster's Will (a Dramatic Success has the bridge last for one full day). Failing to cast the Spell results in no magical bridge appearing, while a Dramatic Failure causes the Caster to suffer Vitality damage equal to their Will, as well as Sanity loss equal to half their Will. The bridge is wide enough for one person to cross, and can take any form the Caster desires. It can look like sand, shimmering flames, or even a rainbow. The width of the bridge is a number of feet equal to 10 times the Degrees of Success. Thus if there are 4 Degrees of Success in casting the Spell, the bridge would be 40 feet wide.

# Warning

Range: 1 Mile | Vitality Cost: 2

Duration: Hours equal to Caster's Will | Sanity Cost: 0

Performed On: Object

A simple Spell, which many think is a pointless one to learn, but when used for the first time, the value of the Spell quickly becomes appreciated. Successfully casting this Spell on a object, anything passing with 5 feet of said object (20 feet with a Dramatic Success) has the Caster feel a tingling sensation that alerts them of this fact. Failing to cast the Spell does not cause the warning to take effect, while a Dramatic Failure results in the Caster suffering 6 Vitality damage every time something passes within 5 feet of the spot or object on which the Warning Spell was attempted. This Spell is often used by wizards to alert them when trespassers enter into their strongholds.

# Arcane Spells

Unlike Common Spells (see **Shadow, Sword & Spell: Basic**), Arcane Spells are rare and powerful. Truth be told, all magic is powerful, but what separates Arcane Magic from Common Magic is that these spells date back to a time far in the past.

Those skilled in the Arts of the Arcane Spells are able to perform feats only the Gods can match. Though the power that a sorcerer is able to call upon is great, the price he must pay is even greater. Unlike Common Spells, which can cause a Caster harm if they are miscast, Arcane Spells cost you more than your Sanity – they have the potential to cost you your life.

Just like purchasing Common Spells and Arcane Arts (see **Shadow, Sword & Spell: Basic, Chapter 6**) Arcane Spells are purchased the same way, although they are more expensive. Arcane Spells, just like Common Spells, are always bought at Power Rank 1, and the cost is always equal to twice the Character's Will. To increase a Spell by one Power Rank (see **Shadow, Sword & Spell: Basic, Chapter 6**) the cost is equal to the Character's Will. Refer to **Table 4:1** for quick reference.

**Table 4:1 Magical Arts Cost**

| Rank | 1 | 2 | 3 | 4 | 5 | 6 | 7 | 8 | 9 | 10 | 11 | 12 |
|---|---|---|---|---|---|---|---|---|---|---|---|---|
| New Common Spell | 1 | 2 | 3 | 4 | 5 | 6 | 7 | 8 | 9 | 10 | 11 | 12 |
| New Alchemical Art | 1 | 2 | 3 | 4 | 5 | 6 | 7 | 8 | 9 | 10 | 11 | 12 |
| New Arcane Spell | 2 | 4 | 6 | 8 | 10 | 12 | 14 | 16 | 18 | 20 | 22 | 24 |
| Raise Common Spell Rank | 1 | 1 | 2 | 2 | 3 | 3 | 4 | 4 | 5 | 5 | 6 | 6 |
| Raise Alchemical Art Rank | 1 | 1 | 2 | 2 | 3 | 3 | 4 | 4 | 5 | 5 | 6 | 6 |
| Raise Arcane Spell Rank | 1 | 2 | 3 | 4 | 5 | 6 | 7 | 8 | 9 | 10 | 11 | 12 |

# Banish

Range: 10-foot radius around the Caster

Vitality Cost: 10

Duration: Instant

Sanity Cost: 25

Performed On: Creature

This Spell banishes a summoned creature, be it Otherworldly, Undead or Infernal (see **Chapter 10**). Successfully casting this Spell forces the summoned creature in question to make an opposed Will Test against the Caster's Will. If the creature fails the Opposed Test, it is dispelled and banished. A Dramatic Success, on the casting of the spell roll automatically banishes the summoned creature. If the Spell is failed, the creature is not banished, while a Dramatic Failure in casting this Spell means that the creature is empowered, and gains a number of Plasm or Taint (see **Chapter 10**) equal to twice the Caster's Will.

# Bring Forth Elemental

Range: Within circle

Vitality Cost: 10

Duration: Rounds equal to Caster's Will

Sanity Cost: 15

Performed On: Elemental Object

This is a powerful Spell, and is rarely found in books or scrolls; those who know the Spell jealously guard its secrets. This is is due to the fact that this Spell summons an elemental which does the bidding of the Caster. To successfully cast this Spell and summon an elemental, the Caster must inscribe a circle on the ground and within it place a sacrifice. The sacrifice must be:

- **Earth:** A fist-sized piece of marble
- **Air:** An eagle feather
- **Water:** A pint of water
- **Fire:** A burning fire
- **Magic:** The mage sits in the circle

Once the sacrifice is placed in the circle, the Caster must not engage in movement or be disturbed while casting the Spell. Successfully casting this Spell allows the Caster to summon an elemental that will do the Caster's bidding for a number of Rounds

equal to the Caster's Will (double for a Dramatic Success). Depending on the sacrifice, only one type of elemental is summoned.

- **Earth:** Gnome
- **Air:** Sylph
- **Water:** Undine
- **Fire:** Salamander
- **Magic:** Will-o'-wisp

## Contact

Range: Within circle

Vitality Cost: 12

Duration: Rounds equal to half the Caster's Will

Sanity Cost: 24

Performed On: Others

This is a powerful Spell in that it contacts an Elder God, and allows the Caster to commune with and seek advice from this Elder God. This Spell can be taken multiple times, allowing the Caster to contact other Elder Gods. Thus the Caster must have the spell separately for each Elder God.

**Table 4:2 The Elder Gods**

| Elder God | Summoning Circle Component |
|---|---|
| Azathoth | Blood of a lizard |
| Cthulhu | Ink from a squid |
| Shub-Niggurath | Bile of a goat |
| Hastur | Blood of a rooster |
| Nodens | Blood of a raven |
| Nyarlathotep | Bile of an owl, blood of a hawk, and the eye of a cat |
| Nyogtha | Blood of a ram |
| Tsathoggua | The Caster's blood |
| Yig | Blood of a snake |
| Yog-Sothoth | Blood of a squid and a rabbit |

To cast this Spell requires much from the Caster. First, he must fast for a period of 24 hours, and during that time meditate and prepare himself

mentally and physically for the casting. During this time, the Caster must inscribe the appropriate circle for the God he wishes to contact, and this circle must be made from the appropriate components, or the Spell will not work. In addition, the Caster must know the summoning circle for the God he wishes to contact; if he does not, he cannot contact the God. Once the circle is inscribed, the Caster must chant for 10 Rounds, and in that time do nothing but chant. If the chanting is stopped for any reason, either by the Caster or someone else, the spell automatically fails. Once the chanting is over, and the Spell Test is successfully made, the image of the God appears in front of the Caster. The Caster is then able to ask the God for advice, seek their aid, or ask for some boon. The God remains for a number of Rounds equal to half the Caster's Will (Dramatic Success has the duration last for a number of Rounds equal to the Caster's Will). Failing to cast the Spell results in the God not appearing, and a Dramatic Failure has dire consequences. First, the Caster has their Sanity permanently reduced by a number of points equal to their Will. In addition, the God, as per the Curse Spell, curses the Caster, the effects of which last until the God deems the Caster has learned their lesson.

## Curse

| | |
|---|---|
| Range: Eyesight | Vitality Cost: 6 |
| Duration: Days equal to the Caster's Will | Sanity Cost: 10 |
| Performed On: Others | |

Curses are the practice of using a spell to specifically cause harm to an enemy, object or place in some designated manner. As such, every Curse can only be resisted by a believer's Will. Those skilled in the use of this Spell are also able to break Curses. A Caster coming across a Cursed person, place or object can remove a Curse by successfully reversing the Curse and breaking it. There are three different types of Curses that mages are able to cast.

**People:** Examples of Curses against people are typically related to physical injury: breaking a leg, losing one's hearing, contracting a disease, growing warts, etc.. Most often, when a person is Cursed, the transmission of the attack is related to something personal to ensure success. Ingredients for these Curses must include an item from a holy sanctuary that has been desecrated (cursed), something forcibly stolen from the victim, and something that can transmit the curse to the victim by using air, water, earth, metal, or fire. Internal diseases require a draught of the victim's blood.

**Places:** By desecrating a place, mages leech the life out of a pasture, set a magical booby trap for other mages or spirits, or use it as a tool to make people lose hope. Cursing places is the most difficult type of spell, because the

components and the time it takes to prepare are a huge price to pay for, what some believe, is so little benefit. In order to Curse a place, the practitioner needs to take the life of an innocent, drain their blood into a silver container, and desecrate it through a dedicated ritual chant to a dark God, Goddess, or demon. If the Curse's patron deity accepts the offering, the blood turns black. You'll then have to smear it over the entry points (North, South, East, West) for the Curse to take effect. By murdering an innocent in order to enact the Curse, you create an angry, vengeful spirit that might one day come back to haunt you.

**Objects:** The only type of objects that can be affected by Curses are conductive objects that effectively "transmit" a curse to someone else. Metal is the best conductor, while wood is the poorest. Knives, shovels, picks, necklaces, and sometimes even weapons are perfect for cursing. To Curse an object, you spend 1d12 Vitality and offer it your own blood to power the curse.

Cursing Holy objects requires more spell components, but these can be taken from a temple or other sanctuary. Typically, the ingredients for desecrating Holy objects include blending various body parts into a stew related to the curse you want to store. For example, if you want to Curse someone with smallpox by stealing their necklace, you'll have to use the skin of a smallpox victim in your potion to curse the necklace. Holy objects cannot be used to transmit Curses, but they are an integral part of this Spell as well as many others. Once you successfully use a Cursed holy object in a spell, the object retains its desecration, and you don't have to curse it again.

Successfully casting a Curse, the targeted person or place feels the brunt of what you intended and will suffer 2d12 Vitality damage as well as suffer a -2 to all Tests for the duration of the Curse. An object that is Cursed is always

Cursed, but forces the target to roll their Will to resist the Curse. Failing to Resist causes the person to suffer from the Curse. A Dramatic Success results in the effects of the Curse being doubled. Failure to cast Curse results in the Caster losing 2d12 Vitality, as well as the person being targeted becoming instantly aware of the Caster's efforts. In addition, the Caster is not able to attempt their efforts to curse the object, a place, or a victim again for 1d12 days. A Dramatic Failure means that the Spell was botched so badly that the Caster suffers the effect of the Curse.

## Destroy the Dead

Range: 50 feet | Vitality Cost: 10

Duration: Instant | Sanity Cost: 10

Performed On: Undead

This powerful Spell instantly destroy a number of skeletons or zombies equal to the Caster's Will within a range of 50 feet if successfully cast (Dramatic success doubles the number destroyed). This Spell can be cast against other type of Undead, but it does not destroy them, instead causing them harm. When the Spell is cast, the Undead can Resist, and if they fail, they take damage equal to the Caster's Will (on a Dramatic Success, the Undead takes damage equal to double the Caster's Will). Failing to cast the Spells results in no Undead being destroyed, while a Dramatic Failure causes the Caster to suffer Vitality damage equal to their Will as well as being struck blind for one day.

## Dispel

Range: 10-foot radius around the of Caster | Vitality Cost: 10

Duration: Instant | Sanity Cost: 10

Performed On: Others

This powerful Spell is usually the first Arcane Spell sorcerers seek to learn, due to the fact that learning it allows the Caster to dispel any magic or magical effect within his range. Successfully casting this Spell, one magical effect within range of the Caster is canceled out (on a Dramatic Success, it cancels out all magic). Failure to cast the Spell means the magic is not canceled out, while a Dramatic Failure causes the Caster to nullify their own ability to work magic for a number of days equal to their Will.

# Elemental Harmony

| | |
|---|---|
| Range: Touch | Vitality Cost: 4 |
| Duration: Rounds equal Caster's Will | Sanity Cost: 8 |
| Performed On: Self, Others | |

This Spell is one that recently appeared in a number of esoteric works, and despite the best efforts of scholars, no one knows how the knowledge was discovered. Though there are a few other spells similar to this one, this Spell is the most powerful and useful for certain mages. Many practitioners devote their entire lives to mastering the power of the five known elements. The components for summoning and harnessing elemental spirits are: an object that signifies the human attribute, an object made from the element you're focusing on, and the elemental spirit's secret name. Examples of spell components are as follows:

- **Earth (Brawn):** Stone, crystal, plants, clay, sand, buffalo, bear
- **Fire (Toughness):** Volcanic glass, fire, soot, ash, salamanders or other reptiles
- **Water (Will):** Spring water, holy water, lotus, water lilies, fish, and turtles
- **Air (Quickness):** Butterflies and other flying insects, incense, eagles and other birds
- **Spirit (Wits):** Iron, copper, gold, silver, tin

When this Spell is successfully cast, the target of the Spell takes on the traits of the intended element, and gains a +4 bonus to the associated Ability for a number of Rounds equal to the Caster's Will. A Dramatic Success allows the Caster to radiate the element from his body, which causes damage equal to the caster's Will to anyone who touches them. Failure to cast the Spell indicates the target is not aligned with the element, while a Dramatic Failure causes the target to suffer damage equal to the Caster's Will.

## Enchant

Range: Touch

Duration: Permanent

Performed On: Object

Vitality Cost: See below

Sanity Cost: See below

This Spell allows a sorcerer to enchant an item, thus making it magical. This Spell requires much, not only from the Caster, but from the item that is to be enchanted. Successfully casting this Spell grants a permanent bonus to the item enchanted that can be applied either to Combat, to Damage or to Skill use. For example, a dagger +1 would be a dagger that gives a +1 bonus to the Melee Skill when the dagger is used, a +1 to the DV or a +90 to the maximum damage. Enchanting a pair of boots that help the wearer move silently would provide a +1 bonus to Stealth. A Dramatic Success in casting the Spell shifts the bonus to the next highest value, for example, a +2 to a +3. Failure to cast the Spell means that the item is not enchanted. A Dramatic Failure causes the item to be Cursed, and instead of gaining a bonus, it incurs a penalty. In the example above, the dagger would have a -1 penalty to the Melee Skill. In order to enchant an item, the Caster must have an appropriate item. For example, if you want to make an item that gives a bonus to Hide tests, it must be either a pair of boots or a cloak or some such. Vitality and Sanity Costs depend on the bonus the item will have.

**Table 4:3 Enchant Cost**

| Bonus | Vitality Cost | Sanity Cost |
|---|---|---|
| +1 | 8 | 10 |
| +2 | 10 | 14 |
| +3 | 12 | 18 |
| +4 | 14 | 22 |

Each additional +1 adds 2 extra Vitality and 4 extra Sanity to the cost, cumulative.

## Exorcise

Range: Touch

Duration: Instant

Practiced On: Others, Place

Vitality Cost: 8

Sanity Cost: 12

Excise is, simply put, the laying of one's hands on a victim while chanting fervently to drive out a spirit. This Spell works on houses, taverns, towers, and other buildings that spirits have decided to haunt. While there are no ingredients used to cast this Spell, there are several secret incantations that a

Caster must learn and memorize in order to excise spirits. Successfully casting this Spell drives one ghost or spirit out of a specific person or place. A Dramatic Success not only drives the ghost or spirit from their victim, but the ghost or spirit in question cannot repossess them ever again. In the case of a ghost or spirit choosing a particular location to haunt, that ghost or spirit is repelled from the location and cannot return. Failing to cast the Spell indicates the ghost or spirit still possesses the person or place, and the Caster is unable to attempt to excise the ghost ever again. A Dramatic Failure has dire consequences for the Caster: instead of repelling ghosts and spirits, the person or place acts as a beacon, causing the spirit or ghost in question to automatically possess the Caster.

## Geas

Range: 10 feet plus the Caster's Will | Vitality Cost: 10

Duration: See below | Sanity Cost: 10

Practiced On: Others

Geas is a very powerful Spell that allows a mage to compel others to perform a specific task or undertake a Quest. Such tasks might involve hunting down a specific creature, staying by the Caster's side and acting as a bodyguard until a destination is reached, or some other such task. In the case of a Quest, as long as the Quest does not entail the target of the geas to take undue risks, the target is compelled to undertake the task until it is completed or the terms of the Quest are met. If this Spell is successfully cast, the target is able to resist the Spell, requiring an Opposed Test between the Power Rank of the Caster and the target's Will. A Dramatic Success in casting the Spell means there is no Opposed Test, the spell automatically succeeds, and the target is geased. Failing to cast the Spell indicates the target is not affected, while a Dramatic Failure knocks the Caster out for a number of days equal to his Will. The number of people the mage can affect with this Spell is equal to one-half his Will.

## Plague

Range: Touch | Vitality Cost: 10

Duration: Instant | Sanity Cost: 12

Performed On: Others

When this Spell is successfully cast, and the target of the spell is touched, the victim is infected with one of the diseases found in **Shadow, Sword & Spell: Basic** (see **Chapter 5**). The victim can resist this spell with a successful Resist Test but Failure to do so has them contracting the disease. A Dramatic Success makes the disease harder to resist, and the victim suffers a -2 penalty to their Toughness or Resist Test in fighting off the disease. Failing to cast the spell, the mage does not infect a victim, while a Dramatic Failure causes the mage to contract the disease himself.

## Pillar of Light

Range: Caster
Vitality Cost: 10
Duration: Special
Sanity Cost: 5
Performed On: Self

This powerful Spell summons a pillar of light that is centered on the Caster, and any being looking at him will be struck blind for a number of Rounds equal to twice the Caster's Will. Successfully casting this Spell provides a radius of effect for this light equal to 50 feet (100 feet with a Dramatic Success). As long as the Caster does not move, the light continues to shine. The light is as bright as daylight, and illuminates the area around the Caster. In addition, the light causes damage to all Infernal creatures, equal to the Caster's Will (doubled for a Dramatic Success). Failure to cast the Spell results in no light being summoned, while a Dramatic Failure results in the Caster being struck blind for one day and suffering damage equal to his Will.

## Raise Dead

Range: Caster

Vitality Cost: 8/4

Duration: Special

Sanity Cost: 12/6

Performed On: Nil

This necromantic Spell allows the mage to summon Skeletons and Zombies. The mage must perform this Spell in a graveyard, and if successful, the mage summons a number of Skeletons or Zombies equal to their Will (Dramatic Success provides double this number). These Skeletons obey the mage's commands, and the Skeletons remain animated for one full day. Failure to cast this Spell means the Skeletons are not summoned and raised, while a Dramatic Failure summons the Skeletons, but they attack the mage. To maintain the Skeletons, the Caster must expend 4 Vitality and 6 Sanity for each additional day he wishes them to remain animated.

## Summon

Range: Within circle

Vitality Cost: 6

Duration: 1 Day

Sanity Cost: 10

Performed On: Others

This Spell allows the Caster to summon a Mundane or Infernal creature.

As such, there are literally hundreds of summoning Spells that exist for known creatures, and every one provides suggestions for sample ingredients. Thus, if you want to be able to summon rats as well as cats, the spell needs to be purchased twice: once for summoning rats and once for summoning cats. Commonly, creatures seem to require both tribute and sacrifice in order to be summoned. The tribute and sacrifice is represented by the Vitality (sacrifice) and Sanity (tribute) cost.

Successfully casting this Spell summons the animal. A Dramatic Success causes the animal to be compelled to obey the Caster. Once the animal or creature has performed its service, it returns to whence it came.

Failing to the cast the Spell indicates the Caster is unable to summon any creature for a number of days equal to his Will, as well as the possibility of becoming more susceptible to attacks by vengeful creatures similar to the one they tried to summon. A Dramatic Failure results in the Caster being unable to summon creatures for a number of days equal to twice his Will. During this time, their magical trail and aura are so strong that they are more noticeable to all creatures and spirits, and may be attacked. For each additional Power Rank in this Spell, the Caster is able to summon an additional creature.

## Transformation

| | |
|---|---|
| Range: Touch | Vitality Cost: 6 +1 per person transformed |
| Duration: Rounds equal Caster's Will | Sanity Cost: 10 +1 per person transformed |
| Performed On: Self, Others | |

This Spell allows the Caster to transform themselves, or another person, into the form of another living creature. For example, the Caster can change a sailor into a pig, or can transform both himself and his apprentice into birds. Any special abilities or immunities of the creature transformed into are not gained upon transformation, but physical abilities are. For example, a caster transforms his friend into an Earth Demon. The friend looks like an Earth Demon, but is unable to cast Spells, use Taint, or any of the other abilities of Earth Demons, but they do gain their physical strength (Brawn and Toughness). However, if the Caster transforms himself into a trout, he would not only look like a trout, but be able to swim and breathe underwater as well.

Successfully casting this Spell transforms the Caster and/or another person into another living thing for a number of Rounds equal to the Caster's Will. A Dramatic Success doubles this duration. Failure to cast the Spell means that no transformation is achieved. A Dramatic Failure, however, transforms the target into a misshapen creature which causes them to lose not only a number of Vitality equal to the Caster's Will, but to also lose Sanity equal to the Caster's Will as well. The number of people a caster can transform is determined by their Power Rank in the Spell.

## Ward

Range: Touch  
Duration: Until disturbed  
Performed On: Object, Location

Vitality Cost: 8  
Sanity Cost: 5

A Ward is a magical rune or symbol of magical power which is placed on an object or location that acts as a form of protection. There are a number of Wards a caster is able to use, and this Spell can be taken multiple times in order to learn these various Wards. Thus each Ward spell (i.e., Ward (Blind), Ward (Deaf), etc.) is a separate spell.

*Blind*: Successfully placing this Ward causes the person disturbing it to be struck blind for a number of hours equal to the Caster's Will (a Dramatic Success has the blindness last for that number of days). Failing to cast this Ward results in the ward not being placed, while a Dramatic Failure causes the Caster to be struck blind for a number of hours equal to their Will.

*Deaf*: Successfully placing this Ward causes the person disturbing it to be struck deaf for a number of hours equal to the Caster's Will (a Dramatic Success has the deafness last for that number of days). Failing to cast this Ward results in the ward not being placed, while a Dramatic Failure causes the Caster to be struck deaf for a number of hours equal to their Will.

*Explosion*: Successfully placing this Ward results in all within 10 feet of the Ward suffering 20 Damage from an explosion (Dramatic Success increases this range by 20 feet). Anything that the Ward is placed I on is destroyed by the explosion as well. Failing to cast the Spell results in the ward not being placed, while a Dramatic Failure results in the Ward exploding immediately, causing the spellcaster to suffer 20 Vitality damage.

*Fire*: This rune, when placed, sets off a flame burst when the Ward is disturbed. Successfully casting this Ward results in a fire burst that causes 15 damage (double for a Dramatic Success). Placed on an object which is combustible, the intense heat will consume the object. Failing to cast this Spell results in the Ward not being placed, while a Dramatic Failure causes the Caster to suffer 15 damage as well as destroying the object upon which the Ward is placed.

*Mute*: Successfully placing this Ward causes the person disturbing it to be struck mute for a number of hours equal to the Caster's Will (a Dramatic Success has the muteness last for that number of days). Failing to cast this Ward results in the Ward not being placed, while a Dramatic Failure causes the Caster to be struck mute for a number of hours equal to their Will.

*Shock*: This rune, when placed, fills a 5-foot area with electricity. Successful casting this Ward causes anyone within range of the Ward to suffer 15 electrical damage (double this for a Dramatic Success). Failing to cast this Ward results in nothing happening. A Dramatic Failure results in the Caster being shocked for 15 Vitality damage.

*Stun*: Successfully placing this Ward causes a person who disturbs it to be paralyzed for a number of hours equal to the Caster's Will (the same number of days on a Dramatic Success). Failing to cast this Ward means that nothing happens, while a Dramatic Failure results in the Caster being paralyzed for a number of hours equal to their Will.

*Unmoving*: This Ward is usually placed on objects, such as statues and the like. Successfully placing the Ward causes the object to be permanently rooted to the spot in which it stands. This means that no matter how strong a person is or how much effort is expended, the object cannot be moved. A Dramatic Success allows the Caster to place the Ward on an area 5 feet in diameter. Failing to cast the Spell means the Ward does not function, while a Dramatic Failure results in the Caster being unable to move for a number of hours equal to his Will.

## The Water's Fount

Range: Touch

Duration: Rounds equal to twice Caster's Will

Performed On: Location

Vitality Cost: 8

Sanity Cost: 5

This Spell is one that is often seen as both a blessing and a curse. A blessing because it summons water, but a curse because it is very destructive. Successfully casting this Spell and striking the ground, the Caster summons a geyser of water that reaches up to 100 feet in height, and gushes for a number of Rounds equal to the Caster's Will (double for a Dramatic Success). The total amount of water the geyser gushes is equal to a number of gallons equal to 10 x the Caster's Will. Thus, a Caster has a Will of 10, so 100 gallons of water in 10 seconds (remember a Rounds equals 5 seconds). Anyone caught in the geyser suffers 4d12 points of Vitality damage. Failing to cast the Spell results in the geyser not appearing, while a Dramatic Failure causes the Caster's lungs to fill with water and he begins drowning (see **Chapter 5** of **SHADOW, SWORD & SPELL: BASIC**).

# Alchemy

Hidden within the mists of time and in ancient tomes, there are many lost wonders and knowledge. Those skilled in the magical Art of Alchemy (see **Shadow, Sword & Spell: Basic**, **Chapter 6**) zealously guard their secrets. From time to time, word leaks of new Arts, and an effort is made to discover them.

## Create Homunculus

This Art allows the Alchemist to create a Homunculus, which serves as a tool for the Alchemist's work. In order to create a Homunculus, the Alchemist first needs to acquire the corpse of a dead baby which is then added to a cauldron filled with 4 pounds of wax. The mixture must simmer for two days, while the Alchemist stirs the cauldron every hour. During this process the Alchemist can do nothing else, but watch the mixture and stir it every hour. If the Alchemist stops stirring the mixture every hour during the requisite time period, the mixture is ruined, and he must begin again.

Once the two days are over, a live bat is placed within the mixture, and the lid is placed on top of the cauldron. The cauldron must then cool for one week and the lid must not be removed, nor may the cauldron be disturbed. Moving the cauldron or taking the lid off again ruins the Art mixture. Once cooled, the Alchemist must make an Alchemy Test, with Success leading him to having created a Homunculus (on a Dramatic Success, the Alchemist creates two) which is loyal to its creator and will follow his commands. Failing the Test results in having no Homunculus created, while a Dramatic Failure causes the Alchemist to lose all his Sanity due to seeing a disturbing image in the mix. There is no limit to the number of homunculi an Alchemist is able to create; all they need is the time, materials, and the dedication to do so.

## Create Manticore

Due to the danger that a Manticore presents, this is one of the rarest Arts found in the Alchemist's repertoire. Unlike the lesser Art of Create Homunculus, this Art requires a much larger time commitment on the part of the Alchemist, as well as a great many materials. While performing this Art, the Alchemist can perform no other work other than this Art. If he misses one day, or attempt to perform another Art during this time, the process is ruined. The first step is to prepare a cauldron large enough to work the materials needed for the creation of a Manticore. The cauldron should be no smaller than 100 gallons (price for this varies between 200 SC and 750 SC), and it needs to be built over a furnace capable of creating a flame hot enough to heat the cauldron. The cauldron must be filled with purified water (water that has been distilled), and brought to a boil. While boiling a living lion, a man and a scorpion are added, and the three are allowed to simmer for three days. During this time, the Alchemist must do nothing but keep the fire going, and allow the liquid to remain undisturbed. If the fire goes out during this time, or the cauldron is touched (or even stirred), the creation is ruined.

Once the three days are up, three Distilled Essences (see below), one each of *Essence of Lion*, *Essence of Man*, and *Essence of Scorpion*, are added one at a time over a three-day period. During this process the cauldron must still simmer, and the mix remain undisturbed. After the addition of the third Essence, the following day the cauldron must be brought to a boil, and the cauldron be allowed to boil until the liquid has evaporated, which takes a total of three additional days. Once this time has passed, the Alchemist makes an Alchemy Test, with a success resulting in having an egg appear in the cauldron which will hatch in one week's time (one day's time for a Dramatic Success). This egg is roughly the size of a lion, and will be too heavy to move. It is at this time the fire can be put out, and the whole allowed to cool. At the end of the week (or one day), the Alchemist must cut his palm, and place his bleeding palm on the egg. Upon doing so, the egg will hatch and a living Manticore will emerge. The Manticore will follow the commands of the Alchemist (a successful Animal Handling Test is required). Failing the Alchemy Test means that no egg is formed, and the mixture does not congeal. A Dramatic Failure results in an egg forming, but when it hatches, the Manticore will immediately attack the Alchemist.

## Distillation

The most important Art for any Alchemist, and really the major goal of the Art, is the process of Distillation. Distillation is the process Alchemists use to discover the essence and nature of all life. It is with this Art that they break down living matter into a liquid, and through this liquid, can take on the traits of living creatures. In short, it is the breaking down of an animal or living person, and creating an Essence that once drunk, gives the imbued target a specific trait for a period of time.

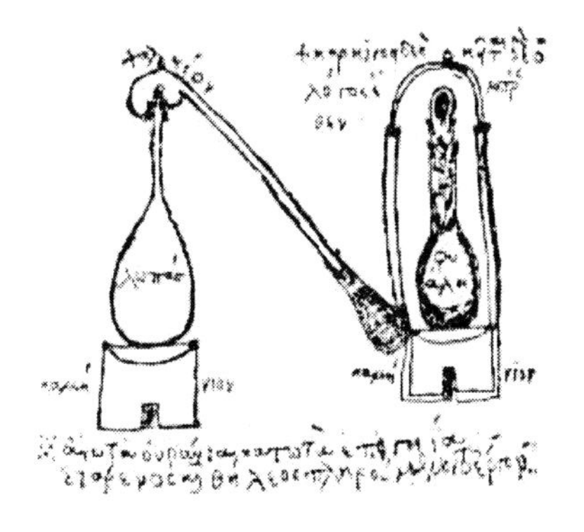

The first step is to create a still large enough to contain the animal or human that is to be distilled. This is filled with water, and allowed to boil; as it boils, the vapor escapes, is trapped in the coil, cools, and collects in the adjacent vessel. During this process, which requires a day, the Alchemist can do nothing but keep the fire hot enough so that the liquid boils. At the end of the day, the Alchemist must make an Alchemy Test, with success indicating he has successfully created an *Essence of...* . The *Essence* is the one trait, or Skill, of the living thing that has been distilled. Note that *Essences* are only made from the listed Traits of a creature. In order to take on this trait, the *Essence* must be drunk. Once drunk, the effect of the distilled trait or Skill lasts for a number of minutes equal to the Alchemist Will (double for a Dramatic Success). Failing the Alchemy Test means the Essence is not created, while a Dramatic Failure causes the still to explode, causing 12 points of Damage, and draining the Alchemist of all his Sanity due to the horror witnessed.

So how does Essence work? Let's say you want to create an *Essence of the Lion* and you want this Essence to give the imbiber claws. You add the body of one lion to the still, and work through the process. At the end of the requisite time, you create an *Essence of the Lion*, and once drunk, the drinker's hands transform into claws, resembling those of a lion. When distilling a human, the Essence created is either one of the Skills the person had, or the Attribute they have (say their Brawn). For example, a warrior who is known for their skill with the sword could be distilled to create an *Essence* which when drunk, would give the drinker the Melee Skill of the warrior.

# The Stone of Life & Death

Known by many names, the most famous of which is *The Philosopher Stone*. This Art is rumored to not actually exist, and is said to be nothing more than a tale told by bards and minstrels. Recently, however, rumors have filtered north from Ku'Kku that the Art was written down, and has been shared among a few Alchemists.

To create a *Philosopher Stone*, a cauldron must be placed over a fire and heated until it glows red. Once heated, water is added to the cauldron and allowed to boil. Once boiled, the heart of new-born baby and the heart of a recently dead person are added to the boiling water. Then a lid is placed over the cauldron, thus allowing the cauldron to become a pressure cooker. This then must boil undisturbed for a period of one week. During this time, the Alchemist can do nothing else but keep the fires burning. If the fire goes out, or the Alchemist performs another Art, *The Stone of Life & Death* is not created. Once the week of boiling is done, the fire must be put out, and the cauldron allowed to cool. It is at this time that the first Alchemy Test is made. Make note of whether this Test is a Success, Dramatic Success, Failure, or Dramatic Failure.

After the week is up, the second Alchemy Test must be made. Again, make note if this Test is a Success, Dramatic Success, Failure, or Dramatic Failure. If both Tests were Successes, a *Stone of Life & Death* is created. If one Success is achieved, a Stone of Death is created. If both Tests failed, the Stone is not created. If both Tests were Dramatic Failures, the Stone explodes and the explosion causes 30 points of damage, as well as draining everyone within 100 feet of all their Sanity. Any Dramatic Successes cause the Stone to be twice as strong. What happens if both rolls are Dramatic Successes? The stone splits in two and both a *Stone of Life* and a *Stone of Death* are created.

## Stone of Death

This stone must be buried in the ground and once buried, each person within range (a 20-foot radius) must make a Toughness Test each day they are exposed for more than an hour; a Failure causes them to contract the disease. A Dramatic Success causes the would-be victim to become immune to the stone's disease, while a Dramatic Failure cuts the incubation time in half. The stone's effect lasts for a number of days equal to the Alchemist's Will. Once these days are up, the stone no longer works. As for the disease the stone causes, the Alchemist determines which disease they infuse into the stone (see **Chapter 5, Shadow, Sword & Spell: Basic** for disease).

## Stone of Life

This stone must be placed in the mouth of a dead body and must lay undisturbed for a number of days equal to the Alchemist's Will. At the end of this time, the body will be brought back to life, though they will only have 1 Vitality. *The Stone of Life* works only once, and can bring back only one person. The person brought back to life retains their personality and all of their memories.

# Manipulation

A rare Art, and one rumored to have been first created in the lost empire now known as the Shimmering Sands. This Art allows the Alchemist to take two creatures and through the process of Distillation, merge the traits of both to create a new creature. It is from the use of this Art that such creatures of myth like Unicorns and Pegasi originate. In order to perform this Art, the Alchemist needs a cauldron large enough to easily fit both creatures. This is placed over a roaring fire, and the cauldron must be heated for a period of 24 hours. Once heated, both creatures are added to it, as well as enough water to cover both. The mix must then boil for one day, and during this time, the Alchemist can do nothing else but ensure the fire is maintained. Once the 24 hours is up, the Alchemist must create two potions using the Distillation Art that contains the Essence of both creatures. Once these Essences are added, a lid must be placed and secured on the cauldron, creating a pressure cooker. The cauldron must then stay over the fire for a period of 2 days. During that time, the Alchemist can do nothing else but maintain the fire, and ensure no harm comes to the cauldron.

After the 2-day period, the fire is put out, and the cauldron is allowed to cool (which takes one week). It is at this time, during the cooling period, that an Alchemist Test must be made. Success indicates the Art has worked, and a creature will emerge from the cauldron that has equal parts of both (a Dramatic Success has two creatures emerge!). For example, if a horse and a lion are used, emerging from it would be a creature with the body of a horse and the head of a lion. Failing the Alchemist Test results in no creature emerging, while a Dramatic Failure results in the cauldron exploding. This explosion causes 40 points of damage.

# Shape the Golem

Once a popular Art in ancient Atlantis, Shape the Golem was created as a means for Atlantean Alchemists to create obedient servants capable of enduring great stress, and serving as their loyal slaves. Though considered lost for many years, the Shape the Golem Art recently emerged in both The League of Cantons as well as Foxpoint in the Merchant League. In order to create a

Golem, the first step is to construct a Golem. This requires the skills of someone who knows how to work with stone. Alchemists may simply hire a sculptor or stone mason to make their Golem, or take the time to learn how to craft one themselves. Once the Golem has been constructed, it must be given a name. The name is then inscribed on a piece of stone. To destroy the Golem, one simply needs to inscribe its name backwards on the same piece of stone or on the Golem itself.

To bring the Golem to life, the Alchemist must procure a human soul that can be infused into the construct. In order to procure the soul, the Alchemist must successfully perform the Distillation Art. The soul is simply an energy source to feed the Golem; it is not in control of the Golem's actions. Once the soul has been distilled, the Golem must be heated in a fire, and when it is burning hot, the distilled soul is then poured on to the Golem. The Alchemist must then make an Alchemy Test, with success causing the Golem to come to life in one hour (instantly with a Dramatic Success). Failing the Alchemy Test results in no golem being created, while a Dramatic Failure causes the Golem to explode for 40 points of damage, and destroys the Alchemist's lab. In order to control the Golem, the Alchemist, or anyone else, must hold the stone with the name inscribed and simply tell the Golem what he wants.

# Researching New Spells and Arts

As Heroes progress, those skilled in the Magical Arts — be it Spells or Alchemy — soon have the desire to create their own Spells and Arts. There really are no hard and fast rules when it comes to this. In the end, it is up to the GM to decide if a new Spell or Art will be permitted. If they say no, so be it. However, what if the GM says yes? Read on.

## The Five Questions and their Answers

There are five steps which a player needs to follow when creating their own Spell or Art. These steps are more along the lines of questions, and answering them is important.

**Table 4:4 Cost of Spell/Art Research**

| | Base | Per/Week |
|---|---|---|
| Common | 500 | 100 |
| Arcane | 1500 | 250 |
| Art | 1000 | 150 |

### What type?

The first question is the most important: What type? Is it an Art or is it a Spell? If it is a Spell, is it an Arcane or Common one? Once answered, this guides the whole creation process.

## What does it do?

More important than type, what does the Spell or Art do? Players and GMs should use the Spells and Arts found in both **Basic** and **Expert** as models and guidelines to follow. The general rule of thumb is that the more powerful it is, the higher the Vitality and Sanity costs will be.

## How much does it cost?

It costs money to create a Spell or Art, and this cost covers the need for research materials, items, and the like. This cost varies depending on what is being researched.

## How long does it take?

The amount of time it takes to research a new Spell or Art depends on two factors: first, the character's Wits, and second, the type of Spell or Art being created.

**Table 4:5 Amount of Time**

| Character's Wits | Length of Time (in weeks) |
|---|---|
| 1 | 24 |
| 2-5 | 20 |
| 6-7 | 16 |
| 8-11 | 12 |
| 12 | 8 |

**Modifiers**

- If it is a Common Spell, the length of time is equal to the time listed in the table.
- If it is an Arcane Spell, the length of time is doubled.
- If it is an Alchemical Art, the length of time is multiplied by 1.5 weeks.

## Success or Failure?

Once all the money has been spent, and the time has been devoted, it is time to learn if the Character's endeavor succeeds or not. Success hinges on a Wits Test, with Success ensuring the Spell or Art is created, and Failure resulting in it not being created. Successfully having created the Spell or Art, the character not only creates a new Spell or Art, but gains 2 XP for their effort (4 XP for Dramatic Success). Failure means the Spell or Art is not created, but the Character is able to devote more time — and money — to try again. The amount of extra time needed is half the Base Time (see above). If this Test fails, the Character can continue to study and conduct research, but the Wits Test suffers a -1 TN, which continues to increase for each additional Test. Succeeding at the second Wits Test (or subsequent ones) allows the Spell (or Art) to be created, but no XP are gained (even if the Test is a Dramatic Success). A Dramatic Failure means that the Spell or Art is beyond the scope of the character to create and the character must stop all work.

## A Few Notes

The above rules assume that the character is doing nothing but working at creating the Art or Spell. Players who want their characters to still adventure, or rule their own Domain, have a much longer task ahead of them. All time requirements are doubled, and in addition, the Wits Test has a -6 TN.

# 5

## Relics

Known by many names, they are collectively referred to as Relics. Relics are ancient, and little is known about them. These are items that exist, and continue to exist. They are objects that defy definition, let alone explanation. Some speculate that they are objects forged via Alchemy, enchanted by Magic, and fueled by otherworldly powers. Others claim Relics are objects from other realms or strange dimensions that touch the world briefly, and when they do, leave the world changed forever. Some whisper in hushed tones that Relics have been placed on this mortal plane by Gods who use them to test the mettle of humankind.

Unlike the items Alchemists and Spellcasters are able to create through Magic, Relics are able to perform many feats. Relics are items so rare that the rumor of one's existence spurs many to action so as to seek ways of obtaining them. Relics are objects that are rare, so rare in fact, that GMs need to consider their use and addition to their games very carefully. Unless there is a good reason to do so, Relics should not enter games that are being run with just **Shadow, Sword & Spell: Basic**. The reason for this is that Relics are very powerful, and have a large impact on the game world as a whole. That is not to say you cannot use Relics with **Shadow, Sword & Spell: Basic**; you can, but be prepared for the change in power levels and the other consequences and ramifications of doing so in the game.

What are these consequences and ramifications? First is power level. It's important to remember Basic's main design goal is all about starting out life as an adventurer. These characters are suppose to be weaker, and giving them access to Relics makes their lives easier. As for the risks, Relics are powerful, but there is a chance that trying to use an item this powerful can lead to harm or even death for your Character. Finally, Relics introduce powers which not only tip the odds in a character's favor, but they have a personal cost which might harm them – or worse, kill them – in their attempt to use the Relic.

Though players are able to create magical items through Alchemy and the Arcane Spell Enchant (see **Chapter 4**), these are lesser creations allowing for simple powers. Relics are objects that the GM creates for specific campaign purposes. Think about the One Ring in Tolkien's *The Lord of the Rings*, or Moorcock's *Stormbringer*. These are items that are as much of a curse as they are a blessing, and the introduction of such an item into a campaign needs to be thought out thoroughly. Care needs to be taken in not allowing too many Relics in the game world, because not only are Relics powerful, but they are also mysterious. Having them become commonplace in the game world takes away from the impact they have. Relics are items that adventures should be built around, and should be used not only to add drama, but to add complications for the players and their characters.

# Creating Relics

GMs are free to create their own Relics to insert and add flavor into their games. Though creating a Relic is relatively easy, a few guidelines need to be followed. First, all Relics need to have a *Name*. Second, all Relics need to have a *History*. Third, you need to decide if the Relic has *Will*. And finally, you need a *Game Effect*. All four of these elements help to not only place a Relic into the SHADOW, SWORD & SPELL setting, but provide both the GM and player characters with enough information to use them in their games.

## Name

All Relics have a Name, and this Name can be simple or descriptive. When coming up with a Name, be as over the top or archaic as you want. Example of Names can be something as simple as Morr's Dagger, or as flowery as The Grand Cloak of the Veiled Stars.

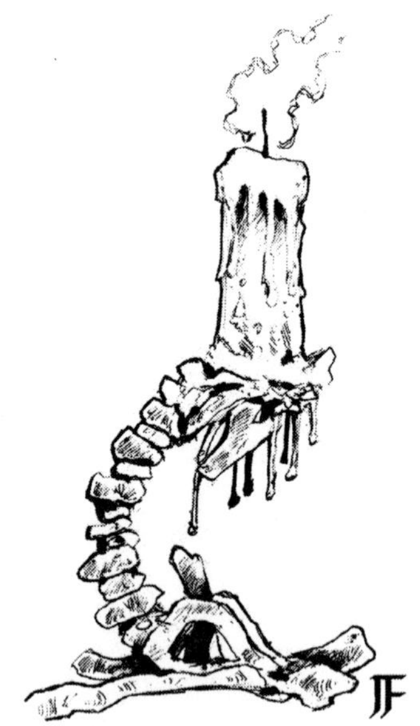

## History

A Relic's History is very important, and this History needs to span the period of time from when the Relic was first created to its first appearance. Some histories are simple, while others are lengthy and detailed. No matter what level of detail you choose, the History should be something that will inspire adventures.

### Will

Will is what differentiates a Relic from the enchanted items player characters create. Not all Relics have Will, but those that do are very powerful. Relics with Will have it listed. In order for a character to use a Relic, she must overcome the Relic's Will to do so. For more on Will, see below.

### Game Effect

The Game Effect is the power the Relic has. All Relics have certain powers and effects usable by one possessing the Relic. GMs creating their own Relics should be careful not to give them too many powers, , or to make them too powerful. If creating more powerful Relics, these Relics should have a high Rank in Will.

## Using a Relic

Most Relics work automatically, meaning that if the Relic is a cloak, ring, or other such item, the user of the Relic is able to call upon the power of the Relic as an Action. Relics with Will are a different matter, however.

### Relics Exerting Will

Some Relics, due to their nature, power or creation, have Will. These Relics are so powerful that they seek to dominate those weaker than themselves. Anytime the user wishes to use the Relic, she must make an Opposed Will Test with the Relic. A successful Test for the user results in her being able to use the Relic, while failure means trouble. What type of trouble? It depends on the Degrees of Failure.

**Table 5:1 Relic Degrees of Failure**

| Degree of Failure | Effect |
|---|---|
| 1-2 | -1 to all Tests for a number of Rounds equal to Relic's Will |
| 3-4 | Relic does not work for a number of Rounds equal to Relic's Will |
| 5-6 | -2 to all Tests for a number of Rounds equal to Relic's Will |
| 7-8 | Relic does not work for 1 Day |
| 9-10 | Relic causes harm to others |
| 11-12 | Relic causes harm to user |

In the case of Relics with Will, it is important to know how badly the user fails the Opposed Test. The higher the Degree of Failure, the more dire the consequences are for the would-be user.

In the case of a Relic causing harm to others, it is up to the GM to decide how this plays out. For weapons, the Relic attacks any of the Hero's companions, no matter how much the Hero does not want this to happen. The way the weapon attacks is left up the Gamemaster. Some suggestions are that the weapon leaps from the Character's hand and attacks a nearby companion. Or, no matter who the Character is attacking, her weapon misses the mark and instead hits a nearby companion. If the Relic is not a weapon, but a object, the harm caused to others is more mercurial. If it is an object aiding a skill, the result might be beneficial. For example, a object that allows you to hide, might make your easier to be seen by those looking for you.

## Option: Appeasement

In order to appease a Relic exerting its Will over the Character, the Character can opt to sacrifice some of herself to the Relic. This is done by allowing the Relic to drain a number of Vitality points equal to the Relic's Will score. Once this is done, the Relic allows the Character to use it for one day.

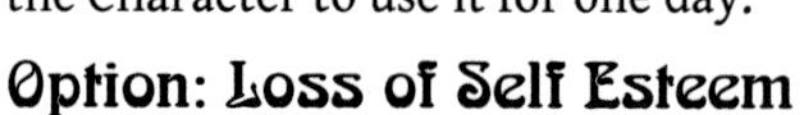

## Option: Loss of Self Esteem

Another option that allows for more drama, and plays up the themes of Curses, is to have the Character's Sanity suffer every time the Relic exerts its Will. Every time the Character fails to dominate the Relic, she loses a bit of her Sanity. The number of Sanity lost is equal to the Degrees of Failure. Thus, if the Degrees of Failure is 6, the Character loses 6 Sanity.

## Option: Some Relics Above the Rest

Another option, and one that runs closer to the ideas found in the works of such writers as Moorcock and Tolkien, is to have only swords and rings possess Will.

# Sample Relics

## The Band of Iron

**History:** A simple band of iron, this Ring's origins and history are a mystery to all. The Ring is smooth to the touch, and is impervious to any tool or flame. Where did it come from? Who created it? These are questions to which no one has the answers.

**Will:** 10

**Effect:** Placing the Ring on the finger causes the wearer to turn invisible. As long as the wearer continues to wear the ring and stands still, she gains a +6 TN Bonus to hiding, +4 if walking, and +2 if running. Though invisible, Undead and Infernal creatures as well as Spirits are able to see the wearer. If the wearer overcomes the ring's Will, she will be able to see anything that is hidden.

## Boots of the Shadow

**History:** The Cult of Caim is said to be masters of silence and the art of death. Their cultists, who are nothing more than assassins, are rumored to possess numerous items that can aid them in the practice of their "religion." The Boots of the Shadow are one example of such an item, and it is said that many of these sets of Boots exist, and can be found throughout The World.

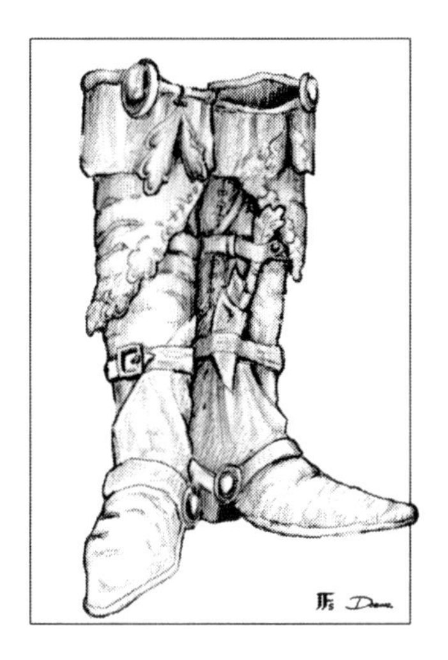

**Will:** 0

**Effect:** While wearing these plain looking Boots, the wearer is very difficult to track. Those trying to track the wearer suffer a -4 to their Tracking Test. If the wearer makes a successful Will Test, the Boots bestow the ability to muffle the noise that a wearer makes for a number of Rounds equal to their Will. This effect of silence means the wearer gains a +2 bonus to their Stealth Tests (+4 if a Dramatic Success). Failing to activate the power of the Relic, the wearer suffers a -2 to their Stealth Tests (-4 if a Dramatic Failure) for a number of Rounds equal to their Will.

## Crowtan's Claw

**History:** The origin of this Relic is shrouded in mystery. There are more stories than facts, but when the Claw has been found, it was said to signify that evil is near. The Claw is a long, black talon, some 3 feet in length, and carved across the Claw are strange runes which glow with a faint yellow light when Infernal and Undead creatures are nearby.

**Will:** 5

**Effect:** This Claw, once held, gives all within 20 feet a +2 bonus to Fear Tests. A Will Test allows the holder of the Relic to cause 12 damage to all Infernal and Undead creatures within 20 feet of the holder, and a Dramatic Success causes 24 damage to all Infernal and Undead creatures within the same radius. This power can only be used once per day. Failing the Will Test means that no damage is caused, while a Dramatic Failure results in the holder of the Claw suffering 12 damage.

## Dagger of the Ray

**History:** No one knows this Dagger's origin. Though it has been seen from time to time over the years, there is no record of one person ever possessing it. The Dagger is a simple one, made of solid gold, and dull to the touch. Despite its dull edge, the Dagger is said to be lethal when used in combat.

**Will:** 8

**Effect:** Though made of gold, the Dagger is as strong as steel, and shows no sign of age or tarnish. Those struck by the Dagger take normal damage, and continue to lose 2 Vitality for a number of Rounds equal to the wielder's Brawn. In addition, any wound caused by the Dagger is hard to heal, and for every 2 points of damage suffered, only 1 point is healed.

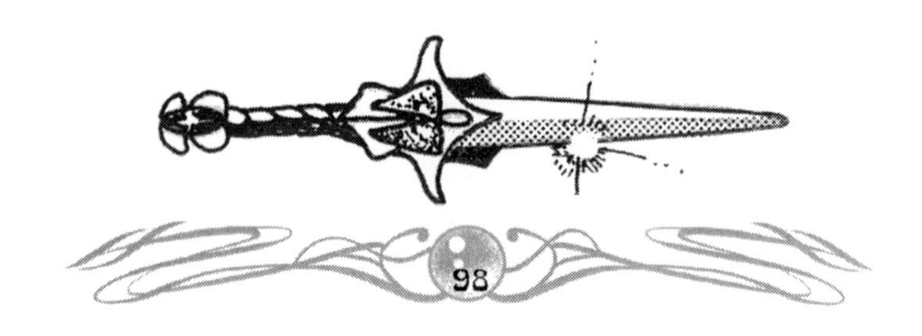

## Eyeglasses of Greycloak

**History:** Large is the shadow looming over the magical community associated with the name Greycloak. This family, rumored by some to originally hail from remote Atlantis, has been known to create magic items and Relics of great power, and have had kings bow down to them in obedience. Whether this is a legend or the truth no one knows, but from time to time, Spells, items, or Relics surface, and the Eyeglasses of Greycloak are just one such example. These Glasses are simple in a appearance, consisting of copper frames and thick glass.

**Will:** 0

**Effect:** Putting these Glasses on allows the wearer to read any one language. She understands the content, and if she chooses, can transcribe what she is reading into a language that she is literate in.

## The Key

**History:** Many of these Keys are said to exist, and they are a boon to those who seek to enter areas that have doors or unlock any lock that impedes them.

**Will:** 0

**Effect:** Placing this Key in any lock automatically unlocks it.

## Quill of the Writer

**History:** No one knows when the Quill was created, it just appeared as several others similar quills have. Numerous Quills of this type are said to exist, and those who make their living as scribes, or enjoy writing, cherish them greatly. No matter where it is or who possesses it, those who make their living through writing seek out these Quills, and guard them closely.

**Will:** 0

**Effect:** Dipping the Quill in ink, and placing it on a sheet of paper, the Quill will automatically write anything one person says. There is no need to dip the Quill in ink again, it simply writes. Once the talker stops speaking, the Quill stops writing.

## Roland's Finger

**History:** Many years ago when the League of Cantons went to war against the City-States of Döârn, there was a renowned priest, known only as Roland the Pious. Roland was rumored to be able to channel the powers of the gods, and with a touch could heal the sick and bring the dead back to life. Roland died during the Battle of the Crying Moon, and he gave his life to ensure that

the orphans of the war would be safe. Many sought to take a piece of the hero, and his grave was robbed, fortune hunters selling him off piece by piece. Though many claim to have a piece of the hero, the Finger is the only piece that has been seen and verified.

**Will:** 6

**Effect:** Roland's Finger is able to heal a person suffering from any disease. Each time the Relic is used, it must "rest" for one hour. Failing to let the Relic rest has the consequence of causing the holder of the Relic to contract the disease that she was trying to cure.

## Sword of Ullrich, the Bringer of Storms

**History:** Ullrich, the Bringer of Storms is a named feared by many who sail The Reach and the Berg Sea. A feared warrior, he led a fleet of raiders and carved a bloody swath through Noricum, Bǣrgøstēn and The League of Cantons. It was flush with victory that Ullrich turned his attention to creating his own throne and ruling his own domain. Seeing the untapped and wild area known as The Wastes of Mictlan, the Bringer of Storms and his raiders came ashore and were never seen again. It was many years later that an iceberg carved a swath on the shores of the League of Cantons. Imbedded in the ice was Ullrich's sword.

**Will:** 14

**Effect:** This plain looking two-handed Sword grants a +2 Bonus to Melee. To use any of the other powers of this Relic weapon, the user must overcome the Sword's Will. Overcoming the Sword's Will, the user can use one of the following powers:

- Cause Fear in all within 20 feet.
- Burn an opponent with a searing cold flame for 6 points of damage.
- Drain Vitality from an opponent equal to the Sword's Will, and heal the Sword's wielder of that quantity of Vitality damage.

# 6

# Libraries, Ancient Tomes & Books

## Libraries and Their Use in Fantasy RPGs

With the amount of books that player characters come into contact with during the course of their adventuring careers, the utility of the library is often overlooked. From serving as a springboard for adventures, to research tools for scholarly player characters, the library offers many options to GMs looking to interject something new into their game. Since most fantasy RPGs are set in a pseudo-medieval world, libraries from our medieval history can be used as templates for libraries within the game. The question remains: what were libraries like during the Middle Ages, and how can they be used in the game?

Historically, libraries as we know them were extremely rare in medieval Europe. When they could be found, they were typically connected with a monastery, cathedral or church. It was not until the High Middle Ages that libraries became more widespread. The early libraries were mendicant libraries. Friars established these libraries, and since their vow of poverty did not allow for owning books, friars relied on donations to build their own libraries. The mendicant library was used for education, and is considered by many scholars to be the model used for university libraries.

During the High Middle Ages, education moved away from the monastery to universities. It was the growth of these universities that led many to seek an education, and often this education was not one based in theology. With the high cost associated with books in the era before printing, most students could not afford their own books. Students studying theology at a monastery might be given their essential books from the monastic order's library. In 1228, the

General Chapter of the Dominicans ruled that all brothers sent to study at a university had to have three books. These books usually consisted of the ***Bible***, the ***Book of Sentences***, and Peter Comestor's ***Historia Scholostica.*** Students not attending monasteries or church-run universities relied on lending libraries for their books.

Lending libraries were private libraries maintained by stationers, who for a fee, copied books and rented text books out in sections. Students would rent a book section by section, and make their own copies. This gave the student access to the needed books, and allowed him to build his own library of books. University authorities supervised this closely, and regulated the fees stationers could charge, and the worthiness of the rented texts.

Before movable type was invented, all books were copied by hand. Monks, or stationers, would copy a book word for word, and the process could take months; in the case of the ***Bible***, this process could take years. Monks would not only copy the text, but illuminate the pages with illustrations and create a work of art. The act of copying was such an expensive endeavor that only the very wealthy could afford to own a book. When movable type was invented this changed, and allowed books to be reproduced cheaply and quickly.

In the early Middle Ages, the rarity of books meant that most of a library's collection consisted of scrolls and loose pages. The contents of these pages were ancient texts dating to the time of the Greeks and Romans, and their organization was often haphazard. Libraries of this time were very small, and most could store all their books in a locked cabinet. By the late Middle Ages, collections became large and libraries were divided into two sections.

The main section of the library was known as the *magna libraria* or public library. This section of the library was a large room where scholars could go to consult a large reference collection of important books. These books could not leave the library, and in the case of Merton College, Oxford, the best copy of each book the library owned was chained to the shelves. The second section was a communal library, or *parva libraria*, and was open at regular hours and loaned out duplicate copies of books and specialized works to members of the institution. Others could consult these books, but they could not remove them from the library.

Libraries spent a great deal of their time safeguarding their collections. From chaining books and locking extra copies in chests, libraries wanted to ensure their books stayed in the library and remained intact. Libraries throughout Europe had many rules dealing with book treatment and storage. In the Sorbonne library, rules prohibited anyone from carrying a light into the library for fear it would cause a fire. Some libraries had rules stating that books had to be arranged in such a way that they were separate from each other. This prevented tightly packed shelves from damaging books as they were used. Swearing of oaths to not damage books was not unheard of either, and the Heidelberg library required anyone wishing to use their library take such an oath.

For people wanting to borrow a book, it was customary to pledge another book or item of equal value as a deposit guaranteeing the return of the borrowed book. For some libraries, this was an acceptable arrangement and allowed access to new titles. Monasteries did not lend out their books, and threatened to excommunicate monks caught lending books. The church frowned on this, and encouraged leniency or annulled penalties so that poor scholars could have access to their books. Some libraries went further, and required all borrowers to return a new copy of each book borrowed along with the original.

Introducing libraries into a fantasy roleplaying game is an easy task, and all it takes is a little work on the GM's part. Libraries can be a source of adventure. New books can be added by the player characters who are hired by a library to find them. This can be accomplished in many ways, but perhaps having the player characters steal books from other libraries offers the most opportunity. Besides being hired to acquire new texts, characters can be hired to track down books thieves, book vandals, and delinquent borrowers. Aside from their use as a source of adventures, libraries can be used by player characters for research. From researching new spells or historical facts dealing with a current campaign, the library can be a viable tool for GMs to dispense information.

Libraries are a great device for Gamemasters, and with a little effort, they can add a new dimension to games.

# Books and their Use

Numerous examples exist in the literature on which **Shadow, Sword & Spell** draws from for the inspiration of books not only serving as a tool but a plot device. Books, especially in the **Shadow, Sword & Spell** setting, assume a very important role. Not only do they provide information, but they provide a means for mystically oriented characters to learn new Spells or Arts. Books, this term being used in a general sense, take many shapes and sizes, ranging in form from a clay tablet, a scroll, stone discs, leather-bound book, to any other form the GM desires.

## Using Books

Heroes owning books may, if time permits, use them to aid in Skill Tests. Now, before you start thinking your players' Heroes will be using books to aid them in combat, there are some rules governing this.

In order to use a book, your Hero needs to have the ability to read the language in which the book is written. If he cannot read the language the book is written in, he cannot use that book.

Assigning a Time to Read to a text is largely arbitrary. If you create your own books for the game, then do what you like. The length of time necessary to read a book may be due to the actual length of the book or the need to go through the book slowly due to its being written in an older version of the language. Here are a few rough guidelines that GMs can use when dealing with the Time to Read.

A short book, or one that has been translated into the current form of the language, takes 6 days or hours.

A book of moderate length or one that is in an older version of the language takes up to 12 days to read.

## Reading vs. Skimming

The first step in actually using a book is to decide whether you wish to read the book to absorb all of its information or skim it to find a pertinent piece of information.

### Skimming

A reader skims books to find information pertaining to a particular topic, question or problem. When skimming a book, the Time to Read is in hours. If a Hero wishes to skim the book more quickly, a Language Test needs to be made, with Success allowing the reader to subtract half of their Wits from the Time to Read. (A Dramatic Success, allows the reader to subtract their full Wits). If the reader is fluent in the language of the text, half the Wits is subtracted from the Time to Read automatically. For a fluent reader to take advantage of the Dramatic Success, roll 2d12 and on a result of 2, the player may subtract his Character's full Wits. The minimum number of hours that the Time to Read may be reduced to is 1 hour.

Successful language Tests provides a +1 bonus to a roll of the appropriate Skill for that particular task. If the Test result is a Dramatic Success, the Character finds detailed information applying to the situation, thus obtaining a +2 bonus.

For example: Greycloak XXX (Wits 10) is skimming ***The Necronomicon*** in an attempt to find information helping him answer a question on magical sympathy. As noted above, it takes 24 hours to skim the book to see if it has information pertaining to his problem. A Successful Language — Elder Tongue Test, reduces his time by 5 (half his Wits) hours, thus lowering the time down to 19 hours, and he gains a +1 to his roll. A Dramatic Success on this roll would reduce the Time to Read by 10 hours, lowering the time down to 14 hours, and provide a +2 to the roll.

When a reader fails the Language Test while skimming a book, he either misinterprets the text or fails to find the information appropriate to the situation. The time spent skimming the text is lost, and no benefit is gained. On a Dramatic Failure, a particularly cruel GM might apply a penalty to the Test as the Character draws the wrong conclusions from what he reads. This may also apply to a fluent Character if the player rolls a 24. Remember: just because you understand a language, doesn't mean you come to the right conclusions.

## Reading

When reading a book, a reader is seeking to add the knowledge contained within that book to his own. Reading a book is the only way to learn any Spells that are in the book. When reading a book, the Time to Read is always listed in days. The same rules apply for reducing the amount of time as noted above, except that the time is subtracted in days. On a successful Test, the reader gains Experience Points towards the particular Skill or Spell that he is interested in, and only that particular Spell or Skill. On a successful roll, the character earns 3 XP toward the Skill or Spell (6 XP for a Dramatic Success). The player may apply this XP to any Skill or Spell that the text covers, including specialties.

So what happens in the event that the book in question has multiple Spells or multiple Skills? The Character is still able to learn the other Spells or Skills, and must repeat the process again.

For example: Edward (Wits 8) reads ***The Book of the Sacred Magic of Abra-Melin the Mage*** (Time to Read: 12 days). His player makes a successful Language - Ancient Tongue Test subtracting 4 (half his Wits) from the 12 days time period, and finishes reading the text in 8 days. Since his Test was successful, he gains 3 XP which may be applied to the Lore Skill or Excise Spell. So learning the Lore Skill, Edward re-reads the book a second time, makes a successful Language – Ancient Tongue Test, and finishes reading the book in 8 days. Since the Test was successful, he gains 3 XP which he applies to acquiring the Excise Spell.

A failed Test while reading the book means the reader spent the maximum amount of time on reading the book, and reduces the XP gained to 1 point. A Dramatic Failure means that not only did the reader waste their time reading the book, but he gains nothing from the text, and may rip the book apart in frustration as he finds parts of the text unreadable or discerns that the book is worthless to him.

## Aiding in Work

Books aid those having Skills in Study, Profession, Trade, and Lore. Using a book that contains information falling under one of these Skills offers a +1 bonus to the Target. This bonus may only be gained if the book is appropriate to the Test.

For example, a Hero is dealing with a law question; using Law books would give the bonus, but books on Animal Husbandry would be useless in this endeavor. Books can only be read during non-pressure situations, that is, when Heroes have peace and quiet to do their work. Heroes attempting to use a book in the middle of a battle, during a time sensitive situation (such as running from a pack of ghouls), or, worse, using a book on the wrong topic, is not permitted.

# Creating Books

In **Shadow, Swords & Spell**, books are more than simple plot hooks; they are objects of history and importance that impact the game. All books need to be created with a mind towards their history and importance. In addition, though printing is now an active business and more works of antiquity are being printed, there are numerous works dating back to a time that predates the invention of the printing press. Still found are manuscripts, journals, hand-copied books, and even scrolls; all of these works offer much to those who not only find them, but also use them.

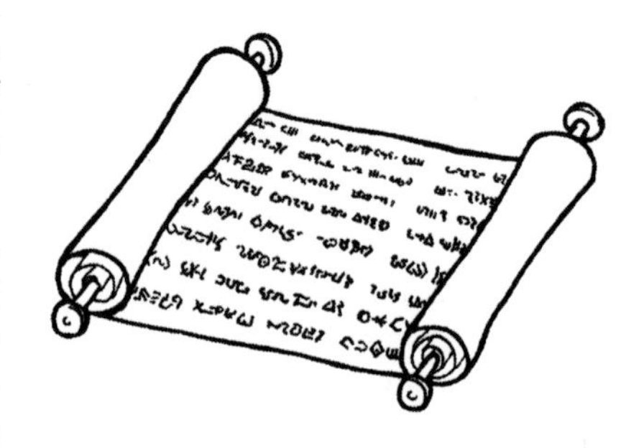

Works can be either magical or non-magical. Magical books are ones used by spellcasters, and through them, they can learn new Spells or Arts. Non-magical works are those that are used to learn information, or are consulted during a task. Regardless of whether these books are magical or non magical, they are treated similarly in how they are described. All books have the following information:

**Title:** This is self-explanatory; this is the title of the work.

**Author:** Who wrote it, if known.

**Language:** The TN needed to beat in order to read the book, as well as the language in which it is written.

**Time to Read (TR):** The length of time it takes to read the book.

**Description:** What the work is, what it contains, and what it looks like.

**Effect:** The game effect of the work.

# Sample Books

***1000 Eyes***, Author Unknown, Language (Ancient) 20, TR 32.

Measuring two feet in diameter, this marble plate is 6 inches thick. Carved on one surface and continuing in a spinning circle ending is the center, the plate is said to contain many mysteries. Those who've said they have read it state the writing is rather crazed and discusses the beliefs of Nodens. The plate also contains the spell Contact – Nodens, as well as the skill Lore (Nodens).

***Bestiary of Greycloak***, Gregor Greycloak XV, Language (Old Tongue) 11, TR 14.

This slim book is a compendium of information about all creatures great and small. From monsters to animals, if Gregor Greycloak XV studied them, they were described and detailed in this book. Measuring no more than 8 inches in height and numbering 300 pages, this book is written in a tight, clear hand. Reading this book, and using this book, the reader gains a +1 bonus to all Lore skills involving animals and monsters.

***The Codex of Ba'am***, Ba'ma, Language (Catharian) 15, TR 15.

Numbering 333 pages and contain 33 chapters, *The Codex* is the life work of General Ba'ma, who fought against the forces of chaos and is said to have helped pave the way to the creation of the Kingdom of Cal'thar and its being dominated by clan rule. *The Codex,* to those who've read it, is a master work on the science of war. Reading and using this book the reader gains a +1 bonus to all Tactics and Bureaucracy Tests.

***Plates of Mortram***, Author Unknown, Language (Runic) 19, TR 18.

Consisting of 20 clay plates covered with a dense runic script, the origins of this work are unknown. The plates first came to prominence in Wall, but soon disappeared. What is known is that the plates were supposedly found in The Wastes, and contain alchemical lore. Those willing to spend the time studying

the plates find knowledge on the following Alchemical Arts: Distillation, Transmutation, and Vitriol.

***The Necronomicon***, Abdul Alhazred, Language (Ancient) 20, TR 24.

This is a vile work of pure evil, and the book's true history is not known. It is said to be ancient, and and that it predates The World in many ways. Numerous attempts have been made to destroy the book, but every time the book returns. Those who have seen it all describe the book in the same way: numbering close to 1,000 pages and bound by a leather-covered wood binding, the pages are yellowed with age, and the words are in a reddish-black ink. The entire book is closed by a metal clasp, and the book feel light despite its size. The work contains numerous amounts of information on demons, devils and other cursed things. Those reading the book are able to learn Lore—Demons, Lore—Devils, and Lore—Elder Gods. In addition, the work contains the Arcane Spells Banish, Contact, Dispel and Summon. As per the Reading rules (see above), a character who is willing to read the book multiple times, eventually gains XP to learn everything this book has to offer. However, reading this book, or reading it multiple times does come with a price, that price is sanity lost. Each time reading the book, the reader must make a Will Test, with Failure having them loose 5 Sanity (10 Sanity for a Dramatic Success).

***The Scroll of Bliss***, Mapaw, Language (Elder) 15, TR 10.

This scroll is said to contain the secrets of life written by a Hegemony shaman known only by the name Mapaw. Written on the cured hide of a white horse, the scroll is written with a deft hand. The scroll fills the hide and Mapaw divided the hide into 50 columns. Those reading the scroll discovers that it contains the spell Sanctify.

***The Scrolls of the Tentacles***, Author Unknown, Language (Ancient) 20, TR 24.

This bundle of fourteen scrolls are always found resting in an ancient, threadbare sack that appears immune to fading and aging. The scrolls are tied in a bundle with a cord made from human hair. The scrolls are written in a strange language, and those who read it have been known to go insane. The scrolls, if read, teach all that is known of the god Cthulhu, and upon reading them, the reader gains the skill Lore—Cthulhu at Base Rank. In addition, the scrolls teach the reader the Arcane Spell Contact, and the caster gains a +2 Bonus to summoning Cthulhu.

# 7

# Mass Combat

As your Hero grows in fame and prestige, she will eventually come into contact with armies. The world of **SHADOW, SWORD & SPELL** is a violent one, and various powers clash in battle. The rules governing Mass Combat are straightforward and allow you to quickly run mass combat on the table top. These rules cover small squads as well as large armies. These simple rules are designed to allow both the Gamemaster and players to fight out battles involving these armies quickly and easily.

The first thing to keep in mind is that this system is narrative in scope, and this has been done intentionally. Mass Combat is very complex, and typically involves miniatures, counters, and terrain, as well as a lot of time. This is not a knock against wargames and miniatures. Hell, growing up, wargames and miniature wargaming consumed a lot of my free time. However, for a roleplaying game, the needs are quite different. Often war, or a clash of armies, is just one small facet of an adventure. There isn't a need to have a detailed, drawn out battle. Instead, Mass Combat for has been reduced down to a few simple dice rolls. This system is designed to allow not only armies but small units to clash. It allows the Gamemaster and players to deal with Mass Combat quickly and efficiently.

## Basics

Before going into detail, it's important to note that all armies have six basic elements. No matter the type of troops, these common elements quickly allow you to assess the strength or weakness of various troops. These elements are: ***Unit Type, Unit Rating, Quality, Size, Engagement Rating,*** and ***Hooks.***

**Unit Type** is simply the type of unit with which one is dealing. The Unit Type can be infantry, cavalry, and the like.

**Unit Rating** is a simple stat which takes into account a unit's training, skills, abilities, and the like. Over time, this stat can and does improve.

**Quality** is not only partially based on the **Unit Rating,** but it takes into account the weapons, armor, mounts, and any other type of special abilities that the unit might have.

**Size** is a simple concept, and is mainly comes down to the number of soldiers found in the unit.

**Engagement Rating** is the number used to see if you win or lose a battle.

**Hooks** are well, hooks. They are similar to the Hooks that individual Heroes have.

Combat involves two armies declaring tactics, taking the calculated ***Engagement Scores***, a few other factors, and then rolling 2d12. This result is added to the Engagement Score, and whichever side has the highest number, wins. Combat continues until one side is destroyed, retreats or surrenders.

With the basics out of the way, let's go into detail about how the system works.

# Armies

Armies are comprised of a number of units, ranging in size and type. Armies are controlled by the player, as well as the Gamemaster. When armies take to the field, the army with the highest Quality chooses their opponent and this is followed by the next highest Quality, and so on. There is no limit to the number of units which can attack an opposing unit.

## Unit Type

The Unit Type is a simple concept that serves as a brief description of what that unit is. **Table 7:1** shows the breakdown of the Unit Types found in the game.

**TABLE 7:1 UNIT TYPE**

| Type | Explanation | Example | Starting Unit Rating |
|---|---|---|---|
| Infantry, Light | Poor offense, poor defense, cheap | Peasant militia | Below Average |
| Infantry, Medium | Good offense, good defense, average cost | Trained soldiers | Fair |
| Infantry, Heavy | Great offense, great defense, expensive | Knights on foot | Average |
| Mounted, Light | Good offense, poor defense, cheap | Barbarian Horsemen | Fair |
| Mounted, Medium | Good offense, good defense, average cost | Mounted soldiers | Fair |
| Mounted, Heavy | Great offense, great defense | Mounted knights | Average |
| Artillery, Light | Good offense, poor defense | Peasant Archers | Average |
| Artillery, Medium | Good offense, good defense | Trained Archers | Average |
| Artillery, Heavy | Great offense, good defense | Siege engines | Fair |
| Skirmishers, Foot | Good offense, poor defense, fast movement | Assassins, Scouts | Fair |
| Skirmishers, Mounted | Good offense, good defense, fast movement | Mounted Scouts | Fair |
| Creature, Large | Good offense, good defense, hard to control | Elephants | Fair |

## Unit Rating

Unit Rating is based on several factors: training, experience, and toughness. This Rating ranges between Untrained and Elite.

So how is the Unit Rating decided? **Table 7:1** gives you the starting Unit Rating for each type of unit. Each year a unit stays active and does not disband, it gains a new level to the Rating, up to the maximum of **Average**. The only way to raise a unit's Rating above an **Average** one is through the actual engaging and winning of combat and battles. Each victory a unit wins causes their Rating to rise to the next level. Any time a unit is routed in battle, their Rating drops by a level.

## Mixing Troops

Sometimes two types of units need to be combined to form a much larger larger army. Sometimes new soldiers need to be added to a unit to replace those lost in battle. This merging of units or adding new soldiers to replace those lost in battle has an effect on the Rating, and actually adjusts it lower. Compare the two ratings of both units, and reduce the Rating by one rank based on the Rating of the unit with the higher value.

**Table 7:2 Unit Rating**

| Rating | Quality |
|---|---|
| Untrained | 30 |
| Poor | 60 |
| Below Average | 90 |
| Fair | 120 |
| Average | 150 |
| Good | 180 |
| Excellent | 210 |
| Elite | 240 |

For example, you have a unit of 50 Heavy Infantry with a Rating of Good. You bolster this number with an additional 50 troops, whose Rating is Fair. Looking at the 2 ratings, you make the new unit's Rating Average.

## Quality

The quality of a Unit is determined by **Table 7:2**. Each Rating has a Quality which is the starting total for a unit.

## Size

How many troops does the unit have? If you have the money to field that many troops, that is the size of the Unit.

# Combat

Combat is fast and simple. Before doing anything, you need to determine if any of the sides in the combat is defending. Basically a side that is defending is waiting for the attackers to arrive. Defending pretty much covers anything from staffing a keep to holding the high ground. If no one side is Defending, than Initiative is determined. Each side rolls a d12, and the highest number wins. The winner decides which units they are attacking.

There are three steps all battles have in common: ***Determine Tactics***, ***Calculate Engagement Score***, and then Battle! (that is, roll the dice and decide the outcome!).

# Step One: Tactics

Each side in a battle decides what their tactics will be for the battle in question. This is a single decision made for the entire army as a whole. This is done not only to make bookkeeping easy, as well as the mass combat easier, but it takes into account the fact that each army's units are working together to achieve a specific goal.

**Table 7:3** lists the Tactics available, as well as the effect each of these Tactics has in combat. To use this table, you need to compare your Tactic(s) to your those of your opponents, and this gives you the effects.

## Option: Army Tactics

This option allows each side of an Engagement to decide on a Unit level what the tactics are. This allows for one Unit to Charge, while another one can Evade, and so forth. This option allows for a little more strategy, although it does make the combat last longer, but it is a good option if you wish to run battles with a modicum more of choices, and with a little more complexity.

**Table 7:3 Tactics**

| Tactic | Attack | Surround | Hold | Charge | Snare | Retreat |
|---|---|---|---|---|---|---|
| Attack | +10 CA | +10 CA | — | -20 ES | +10 CA | +10 ES |
| Surround | -10 ES | — | +30 CA<br>+20 ES | +10 CA | -10 CA | +10 ES |
| Hold | -10 CA | +20 CA | No Combat | +20 CA | +20 CA | No Combat |
| Charge | +20 CA | +10 ES | +10 CA<br>+10 ES | +20 CA | +20 CA | +20 ES |
| Snare | +10 ES | -20 ES | -20 ES | +20 CA | — | -10 CA |
| Retreat | +20 CA | -10 CA | No Combat | +30 CA | -10 CA | No Combat |

CA = Casualty
ES = Engagement Score

## Tactic Descriptions

### Attack

This is pretty straightforward and the most effective, in which both sides attack each other. This is one of the better tactics to use against forces that are Holding or Retreating, but it is more risky against other types of tactics. However, no matter the risk, this is the most effective tactic to employ.

### Surround

The army is attempting to surround the enemy from all sides, and means to pin them in. This is a tactic that is very effective against forces who are Holding.

### Hold

Like Attack, this is a straightforward tactic. The Army is staying put, holding their ground, and waiting for the action to come to them. For armies that are staffing a fortification or manning a fort, this is pretty much the default tactic.

### Charge

One of the most deadly attacks. Charging allows you to attempt to overrun an opponent and get through their first line of defense. Charging is a tactic that has both a high risk and a high reward. The reward is that it can kill many troops. The risk is that it leaves the attacker open to a counter-attack.

### Snare

This tactic is one when you are trying to lure the opponent into making an attack when they are not ready, or do not know the full scope of your forces. A snare is a classic bluff that is often employed against an opponent who might be unwilling to commit to a attack.

**Table 7:4 Engagement Score Modifiers**

| Situation | ES Change |
|---|---|
| Army outnumbers opponent less than 2 to 1 | +10 |
| Army outnumbers opponent 2 to 1 | +20 |
| Army outnumbers opponent 3 to 1 | +30 |
| Army outnumbers opponent 4 to 1 | +40 |
| Army outnumbers opponent 5 to 1 | +50 |
| Army outnumbers opponent 6 to 1 | +60 |
| Army outnumbers opponent 7 to 1 | +70 |
| Army outnumbers opponent 8 to 1 | +80 |
| Army outnumbers opponent 9 to 1 | +90 |
| Army outnumbers opponent 10 to 1 | +100 |
| Army outnumbers opponent 11 to 1 | +110 |
| Army outnumbers opponent 12 to 1 | +120 |
| Army outnumbers opponent 13 to 1 | +130 |
| Army outnumbers opponent 14 to 1 | +140 |
| Army outnumbers opponent 15 to 1 or greater | +150 |

**Table 7:4 (continued)**

| Situation | ES Change |
|---|---|
| Army is in the Domain of the Ruler | +30 |
| Army has beaten the enemy before | +20 |
| Unit Rating is two Ranks higher than opponent | +20 |
| Attacker is springing an Ambush | +15 |
| Allied force has been Routed | -50 |
| Battle is at night | -20 |
| Army has sun at their back | +20 |
| Attacker besieging defender's Stronghold | +10/week |
| Siege Defender has no food | -15/week |
| Surprise attack by defender | +15 |
| Mounted units fighting in woods, mountains, swamps or Stronghold | -25 |
| Infantry fighting in swamp | -25 |
| Archers fighting in woods or swamp | -25 |
| Artillery fighting in swamp or woods | -25 |
| Army outnumbers opponent 15 to 1 or greater | +150 |
| Battle being fought in snow | -10 |
| Army is Retreating | -50 |
| Army is Routed | -100 |
| Army is advancing | +40 |
| Battle being fought in the desert | -10 |

**Table 7:4 (continued)**

| Situation | ES Change |
|---|---|
| Battle being fought in snow | -10 |
| Army is Retreating | -50 |
| Army is Routed | -100 |
| Army is advancing | +40 |
| Battle being fought in the desert | -10 |
| It is raining | -15 |
| It is snowing | -20 |
| Army is defending | +10 |
| Army has the high ground and is defending | +20 |
| Defending a Stronghold | +40 |
| Must cross shallow water | -10 |
| Must cross deep water | -20 |
| Defending a town | +15 |
| Army has Medium Fatigue | -15 |
| Army has Severe Fatigue | -30 |
| Defending a narrow gap or pass | +40 |
| Defending a Bridge | +50 |
| Army has artillery | +30 |
| Army is advancing | +40 |
| Battle being fought in the desert | -10 |

**Table 7:5 Battle Result**

| | Winner | | | Loser | | |
|---|---|---|---|---|---|---|
| ES Difference | Casualties | Action | Fatigue | Casualties | Action | Fatigue |
| 1-12 | 0 | Hold | None | 10 | Hold | None |
| 13-24 | 0 | Hold | None | 20 | Hold | None |
| 25-36 | 10 | Hold | None | 20 | Retreat | Medium |
| 37-48 | 10 | Hold | None | 30 | Retreat | Medium |
| 49-60 | 20 | Retreat | Medium | 40 | Retreat | Medium |
| 61-72* | 0 | Hold | None | 30 | Retreat | Medium |
| 73-84 | 20 | Advance | Medium | 50 | Retreat | Severe |
| 85-96 | 30 | Advance | Medium | 60 | Retreat | Severe |
| 97-108 | 10 | Advance | None | 50 | Retreat | Severe |
| 109-120 | 0 | Advance | None | 30 | Rout | Severe |
| 121-132 | 10 | Advance | None | 70 | Rout | Severe |
| 133-144 | 10 | Advance | None | 70 | Rout | Severe |
| 145+ | 10 | Advance | None | 100 | Rout | Severe |

* Maximum Result is winner's tactic was Hold

**Notes:**
Casualties is the number of troops the army loses.
Action tells you the action that each Army takes as a result of the attack.
Hold: Army is standing their ground.
Retreat: The Army is leaving the field of battle. They are still able to attack.
Rout: Enemy is fleeing they are unable to counter attack.
Advance: Army is pressing the attack, and can continue to attack units who are retreating or that have been routed.

### Retreat

Put simply, you are leaving the field of battle. Instead of fighting, your forces are more concerned with getting out of harm's way then fighting.

For the purposes of these rules, each side would write down their Tactic, and then each side declares their Tactic simultaneously. Once the Tactics are known, **Table 7:3** should be used to see what effect the tactics play on the battle. The effect is one of several things: a modifier to the number of Casualties, a change in the Engagement Score, the fact that combat does not take place, or there is no effect.

**Table 7:6 Tactics ES Adjustment**

| Tactics Skill | ES Bonus |
|---|---|
| 1-5 | +20 |
| 6-10 | +40 |
| 11-15 | +60 |
| 16-20 | +80 |
| 21+ | +100 |

## Step Two: Engagement Score

All armies have an Engagement Score, which is always equal to the Army's Quality (see above). This score rises and falls, depending upon the various conditions that occur as detailed in **Table 7:4.**

## Step Three: Battle!

Once each side in a battle has calculated their final Engagement Score, each side rolls 2d12 and adds the result to the Engagement Score. Whoever has the highest total wins.

To determine the results of the battle, subtract the losing side's total from the winning side's total, and look at the result on **Table 7:5**. This table gives you the battle's effect on each side.

## Step Four: Aftermath

Once each side has attacked, both sides note their casualties. The winner of the attack can decide if they want to continue fighting, and if so, the process begins again until one Army is completely destroyed or surrenders. If one side retreats from combat, then the battle is over. Fatigue plays a role as well, and depending on what level of Fatigue a Army has, their ES is adjusted:

Medium Fatigue -25 ES

Heavy Fatigue -50 ES

Strongholds and Sieges

Attacking or defending a Stronghold is handled in the same way as normal Mass Combat, with a few slight changes:

When figuring out the troop ratios in determining the Engagement Score, the defender has three times as many troops. This takes into account being within a Stronghold.

The defender takes only one-half the casualty total.

The defender ignores Retreat and Rout results.

Attackers wishing to lay siege can do so, and each week their Engagement Score is adjusted by +10. Defenders, when they run out of food, suffer not only a -15 adjustment to their Engagement Score each week, but also suffer double the number of casualties in combat.

Defenders are able to attack at anytime as long as their Tactic is not Hold. If the Defender does so, this gives them a one-time +15 Engagement Score bonus due to their launching the surprise attack.

## Heroes and Units

Your Hero's Skills have a direct effect on a unit or the units they command. When a Hero commands a unit, her Tactics Skill raises the unit's ES by a number of points, as determined on **Table 7:6.**

In addition to the bonus to the Engagement Score, a Unit being led by a Hero can never be Routed.

# Hooks

Every unit has a Hook. Hooks are similar to the Hooks Heroes have, but for Units, they have the following effect.

## +50 ES Bonus

By playing the Unit's Hook, the Unit can give themselves a +50 ES Bonus for the purposes of the combat. This bonus is only in effect for one Engagement; any follow-up combats due to pressing the attack do not receive the bonus.

## Boost Quality by 1 Level

By playing the Hook, the Unit is able to raise their Quality for that combat by 1 Rank.

# Building Armies

So how do you build an army? With money.

To derive the cost of the Army, you simply find the cost of the soldier or mercenary type on the Hireling, Services & Specialist Tables in **Chapter 4.** In addition, you need to figure out the cost to arm the troops and provide them with armor and/or shields, and multiply that by the number of troops you want to purchase.

For example, you want to field a unit of 50 archers armed with longbows and short swords, and all wear chainmail.

Archer costs 5 SC

Chainmail is 40 SC

Longbow is 50 SC

20 Arrows is 8 CC

Shortsword is 7 SC

The total of this is 97 SC 8 CC.

Multiplying 97 SC 8 CC by 50 troops, it costs you 4,858 SC (400 CC is converted to 8 SC) to buy and field this unit. Remember, you must pay the monthly rates to keep the archers in your employ.

# Combat Example

So, how does all of this work? Combat between Armies is easy, and once you go through the process and run your first combat, the system will click, and you'll quickly be able to lead armies and take to the battlefield easily.

Hearing that a barbarian horde is approaching his Domain, Tobara Darkenhand has slowly built up an army in order to defend her holdings, as well as push back the threat of the impending fight. Having heard the reports for the past few months, Tobara has assembled her forces, and they are as follows:

Archers – Artillery, Medium (100), Quality Average, Unit Rating 150

Infantry – Medium (50 foot soldiers), Quality Fair, Unit Rating 120

Mounted – Medium (50), Quality Fair, Unit Rating 120

Her scouts report that the barbarians forces are the following:

| Tobara's Forces Engagement Score | 2d12 Roll | Total | Difference | Total | 2d12 Roll | Barbarian Forces Engagement Score |
|---|---|---|---|---|---|---|
| Archers Engagement Score 270 | 15 | 285 | 114 Tobara Winner | 171 | 11 | Mounted – Light Engagement Score 160 |
| Infantry – Medium Engagement Score 240 | 3 | 243 | 27 Barbarian Winner | 270 | 20 | Mounted Skirmishers Engagement Score 250 |
| Mounted – Medium Engagement Score 240 | 20 | 260 | 85 Tobara Winner | 175 | 5 | Mounted – Light Engagement Score 170 |

Mounted – Light (100), Quality Fair, Unit Rating 120

Mounted – Skirmishes (50), Quality Good, Unit Rating 180

Mounted – Light (100), Quality Fair, Unit Rating 120

How do you determine how many men of a given type there are in a Unit? By buying them. Tobara has spent a great deal of coin to outfit and assemble her forces. As for the Unit Rating, remember, this is set by **Table 7:1.**

Tobara's player assesses her situation and looks to see what modifiers she has for her Unit Ratings. Since her forces are in their Domain, they each gain a +30. In addition, they are Defending, which gives them a +10 bonus. Finally, Tobara has Tactics (+20), which confers a +80 to each unit's Unit Rating. The total bonuses thus equal +120. Thus, Tobara's units now have the following final Unit Ratings:

- Archers – Artillery, Medium (100), Quality Average, Unit Rating 270
- Infantry – Medium (50 foot soldiers), Quality Fair, Unit Rating 240
- Mounted – Medium (50), Quality Fair, Unit Rating 240

The Gamemaster assesses the situation to see what modifiers exist for her Unit Ratings. Since the barbarians' leader has Tactics (+40), the units now have the following Unit Ratings:

- Mounted – Light (100), Quality Fair, Unit Rating 160
- Mounted – Skirmishes (50), Quality Good, Unit Rating 220
- Mounted – Light (100), Quality Fair, Unit Rating 160

Both sides declare their Tactics. Tobara declares that her forces are attacking, while the Barbarians declare that they are Attacking. Since Tobara is Defending, the Barbarians declare which units they are attacking. The breakdown is as follows, as well as any additional modifiers that these attacks have:

- Mounted Skirmishers (+20 for being Skirmishers, +10 for outnumbering opponent 2 to 1), attack Infantry
- Mounted – Light attacks Archers
- Mounted – Light (+10 outnumbers opponent 2 to 1) attacks Mounted – Medium

Both sides, calculate their Engagement Score, which is determined by taking the Unit Ratings and adding any Modifiers. The Engagement Scores are:

Both sides now roll 2d12 for each Unit, and add that number to the Engagement Score. The results are compared and this is used to see which Unit wins. Here is the breakdown:

With the differences known and the winners and loses known, both sides refer to **Table 7:5** to see what the results are.

Archers win; they suffer no casualties, and their next Action is to Advance. Conversely the Barbarians Mounted – Light lose 30 horsemen and are Routed.

Tobara's Infantry – Medium loses; they suffer 20 casualties, and their next Action is to Retreat. Conversely, the Barbarian's Mounted Skirmishers suffer 10 casualties and their next Action is to Hold.

Tobara's Mounted Medium win, and they suffer 30 casualties and their next Action is to Advance. Conversely, the Barbarians suffer 60 casualties, and their next action is to Retreat.

| Tobara's Forces Engagement Score | Barbarian Forces Engagement Score |
| --- | --- |
| Archers Engagement Score 270 | Mounted – Light Engagement Score 160 |
| Infantry – Medium Engagement Score 240 | Mounted Skirmishers Engagement Score 250 |
| Mounted – Medium Engagement Score 240 | Mounted – Light Engagement Score 170 |

Both sides reassess their forces, and then decide what to do the next Round. Combat proceeds for two more Rounds, and during those Rounds, Tobara and her forces suffer heavy casualties, but succeed in repelling the barbarian horde.

# 8

## Politics & High Stakes

In **SHADOW, SWORD & SPELL: BASIC**, the primary assumption about adventures is that they are centered around survival. Your Hero is worried about his next meal, or if he has enough money to repair his armor, or hell, whether he can replace it. Adventure is all about survival, not only dealing with the physical dangers, but the dangers more mundane. As your Hero grows, his outlook grows and changes as well. Gone are the days when he is selling his sword to the highest bidder. He now leads his own band of cutthroat mercenaries. Or, his own gang of thieves. Or, he is working behind the scenes in the just as lethal political theater of "the game of thrones". Adventures for these heroes take on a special challenge for the Gamemaster. What challenge? How do you make it interesting?

It is not that adventures for more powerful heroes are difficult to create, it's just that they are different. Look at the *Kull* short stories of Robert E. Howard. Here is a hero who has gained the throne, and he must not only deal with byzantine plots, but antagonists who want him dead. More and more, his adventures center around the various factions involved. For a more recent example, look to David Sim's **High Society**, in which the main character, Cerebus, not only has to deal with a political election, but also the fallout from the election's results. This, in turn, leads him to dealing with the various religious factions (see **Church & State I** and **Church & State II**), and his eventual appointment as Pope. Though at first blush these seem like dull adventure prospects lacking risk of harm, this is far from the truth, as often, the higher the stakes, the greater the risk you run of being killed.

Keep in mind that your Hero has henchmen, hirelings, and hangers-on who need not only action, but more importantly, money. Often it is this need to keep the troops happy that spurs action. Heroes who have been given lands and titles have obligations which might mean mustering armies, staffing outposts, or serving as diplomats to far distant locations. Remember with the Scheming rules (see **Chapter 1**) and the Domain rules (see **Chapter 3**) that these are perfect for adventures as well.

# Political Campaigns

Leading armies, slaying powerful beasts or even partaking in a gang war is rife with adventuring possibilities. However, sometimes shifting the focus to political adventures offers just as many adventuring opportunities, as well as the impetus for creating some memorable game moments. How do you create political campaigns, let alone adventures? You talk with your players.

The first question that needs to be asked is a simple one. What type of game do you want? The answer to this helps guide the campaign's direction, as well as gives you the overall goal. There are many ways to answer this question. Here are a few examples:

- *The Heroes have made a name for themselves, and are now assigned to the king, emperor, or top of the leadership ladder, and now protect the ruler in question.*
- *The Heroes have been appointed to a remote outpost, and must work to bring rival factions to the bargaining table and negotiate a peace treaty.*
- *The Heroes have been given a Domain, and must work to tame it and lead it in a civilizing direction.*
- *Due to their deeds, the Heroes are elected to the senate, ruling council, or other type of government body, and now need to survive the back-room politics.*
- *The Heroes are of a pious nature, and have worked their way up the rungs of their religious organization's ladder, and must deal with various factions.*
- *The Heroes decide to become merchants, and must not only deal with the rise and fall of trade prices, but the effects of organized crime.*

Political campaigns can take place at any time. These campaigns are not limited to Heroes leading armies; in fact, sometimes, political campaigns are just as effective with weaker Heroes. As a general rule of thumb, the following table is a good reference tool in figuring out the starting level for a political campaign. This table includes Power Levels, as discussed in **Chapter 3**.

**TABLE 8:1 POWER AND POLITICS**

| Power Level | Political Campaign |
|---|---|
| Average/Above Average | Ordinary adventurers, newly joined soldiers in a mercenary band, young nobles |
| Experienced | Village leaders, law enforcers, sergeants in a mercenary band |
| Seasoned | Experienced politicians, skilled law enforcers, minor nobles |
| Veteran | Senators, senior political figures, command officers, powerful nobles |
| Legendary | Top government officials, generals, warlords, powerful nobles |
| Mythic | Kings, emperors, heads of church |

Though not necessary, it does not hurt for the Gamemaster to have a theme or a goal, as this will give the players and the campaign a sense of direction. This goal can range from the clichéd concept of taking over the world to something as simple as bringing peace to a war-torn kingdom. These type of campaigns are far more effective if there is a goal in mind. Why? Because it offers the Gamemaster an easy reference point in creating adventures.

Party unity is not a requirement for a political campaign. It is very easy to have each player be part of a different faction, or to be on opposite ends of the political spectrum. This type of campaign requires more work by everyone involved, as well as flexibility, but campaigns based on rivalry are fun not only to run, but to take part in. If you choose to do a rivalry campaign, the players need to be able to work against each other, while not having their characters become inactive. In addition, the players must be willing to be patient when the GM is dealing with each rival or faction. The only real guideline for a rival type campaign is that players should have a little game experience when working against each other, as beginning players have too much to deal with in this type of campaign.

# Villains and Adversaries

The key component to any political campaign is an effective villain or an advisor. They are essential not only for good political campaigns, but all campaigns. Keep in mind they do not have to be uber-powerful demi-gods capable of destroying cities with a flex of their arms. Villains and adversaries can be the apparently weak clerk, who through family connections and blackmail, is able to get a lot done behind the scenes. All villains and adversaries, regardless of type have a few things in common: **Power Base**, **Goals**, **Motivations**, and ***Je Ne Sais Quoi.***

# Power Base

A Power Base is a source of influence, personal resources, and skills that Villains use to accomplish their goals. A Power Base could also be a secret, be it one in which a certain bastard son lives, to one in which the Count's wife is having an adulterous affair with her brother-in-law. It is with this Power Base that the villains are able to gain influence as well as nudge events so as to harm or hinder the player characters. Networking is another important power base, and it is through their personal connections and networks of owed favors that the Villain is able to assert his will. Position is an even more important power base, because it is through a given position that resources are able to be used to thwart the actions of the player characters. Finally, the most important power base is Wealth. It is money which allows votes to be bought, judges to be paid, as well as nefarious individuals to be hired.

# Goals

Just as the Heroes have their own Goals, Villains have Goals as well. Goals are important to the Villain because they aid Gamemasters in creating adventures. Goals take many shapes and forms, from acquiring vast sums of wealth to taking the crown for themselves. Some examples of villains' Goals include:

- Restoring family honor
- Reclaiming a birthright
- Protecting trade interests
- Destroying a specific group of people or a tribe
- Breaking the control a religious sect has on a government
- Bankrupting a rival business owner, trader or merchant
- Taking control of a religious sect, temple or monastery
- Discovering the key to Godhood
- Enslaving a group of people to feed the constant need to build an empire
- Uncover a lost relic which would enable the summoning of a demon

While Goals might be melodramatic or over the top, however, they are extremely important to the Villain. It does not matter how strange a goal seems as, for the Villain, the Goal is their driving force. No action is too debased, no deed unjust, if it means that the Villain's Goal will be met.

## Motivation

Though a Goal is a villain's driving force, it is their Motivation that drives the Villain to accomplish their Goal(s). Motivation ranges from such simple concepts as love to more complex emotions such as envy. Emotions are important, and it is these emotions which a GM should use and mull over when giving his Villains their motivations.

## Je Ne Sais Quoi

*Je Ne Sais Quoi* (from the French, literally meaning, "I do not know what") is that special something that makes a Villain, well... a Villain. This is the edge that villains have. To think of it another way, if the player characters have Hooks, then the villains have *Je Ne Sais Quoi*. It is this which makes the Villain a match for the player characters, and should come into play often. *Je Ne Sais Quoi* can range from anything from allies (a Villain's close confidant or ally who works to prevent the characters from disrupting the Villain's plan) to something like popularity (the Villain is popular among the denizens of the city, and no one will think the Villain is actually a Villain).

## Wrap Up

By thinking about a Villain's Power Base, Goal, Motivation and *Je Ne Sais Quoi*, you should have a Villain that is able to seriously challenge the players and their characters. A Villain does not end there. More important than these traits, the Gamemaster needs to ensure that his Villain is as well-rounded as the players' characters. Why is the Villain the way he is? What is his personality like? What does he look like? What makes him tick? All of these should be kept in mind, and are just as important as the Villain's stats.

**TABLE 8:2 TRADE GOODS AVAILABLE**

| 2D12 Roll | Trade Goods | Base Unit Cost | Units Available (Tons) | Trade Code |
|---|---|---|---|---|
| 2 | Weapons | 40,000 SC | 3d12 | A |
| 3 | Grain | 500 SC | 1d12 x 10 | F |
| 4 | Lumber | 800 SC | 1d12 x 10 | I |
| 5 | Fruit | 1000 SC | 6d12 | F |
| 6 | Precious Metals[1] | 100,000 SC | 1d12 ÷ 2 | LG |
| 7 | Stone[2] | 15,000 SC | 1d12 ÷ 2 | M |
| 8 | Vegetables | 1000 SC | 6d12 | F |
| 9 | Livestock | 9000 SC | 5d12 | F, L |
| 10 | Historical Artifacts | 30,000 SC | 1d12 ÷ 2 | LG |
| 11 | Spices | 10,000 SC | 3d12 | LG |
| 12 | Textiles | 3500 SC | 6d12 | LG |
| 13 | Fish | 8,000 SC | 1d12 x 5 | F |
| 14 | Ores[3] | 50,000 SC | 1d12 | I |
| 15 | Crystals | 20,000 SC | 1d12 ÷ 2 | LG |
| 16 | Wine | 8500 SC | 5d12 | LG |
| 17 | Gems | 50,000 SC | 1d12 ÷ 2 | LG |
| 18 | Handicrafts | 10,000 SC | 1d12 x 10 | LG |
| 19 | Silk | 40,000 SC | 1d12 | LG |
| 20 | Oil[4] | 15,000 SC | 1d12 x2 | I |
| 21 | Salt | 40,000 SC | 2d12 | I, F |
| 22 | Armor | 60,000 SC | 3d12 | A |
| 23 | Oil (edible)[5] | 30,000 SC | 3d12 | F |
| 24 | Cotton | 18,000 SC | 3d12 ÷ 2 | LG |

Notes:
1. Includes gold, copper, silver and platinum
2. Includes marble
3. Includes iron, pigments, and coal
4. Includes whale oil and lubricants
5. Includes palm oil, olive oil and any type of oil consumed

# Trade

Contrary to what some might think, trade is the life blood of The World. It is trade which makes life possible, brings wealth to certain regions, and often provides a chance for the lucky to make their wealth. With the size of The World, and the diversity of available goods, some heroes might decide that a life of adventure is too risky, and that it is far safer to buy and sell goods.

Trade goods run the gamut from such luxury items as spices, and gems, to more mundane items such as grain.Through careful buying and judicious selling the potential for those to make money are great. It is through trade that the profit potential on such items have led to the formation of Merchant House in The League of Merchants, to the funding of individual known as Merchant Princes. This section provides some simple rules to adjudicate such trade.

**Table 8:3 Price Multiplier**

| Degrees (+/-) | Purchase Price Multiplier | Sale Price Multiplier |
|---|---|---|
| 12+ | 0.8 | 2.0 |
| 9-11 | 0.85 | 1.75 |
| 6-8 | 0.9 | 1.5 |
| 3-5 | 0.95 | 1.25 |
| 0-2 | 1.0 | 1.0 |
| -1 to -2 | 1.25 | 0.95 |
| -3 to -5 | 1.5 | 0.9 |
| -6 to -8 | 1.75 | 0.85 |
| -9 to -11 | 2 | 0.8 |

## Trade Procedure

Characters wanting to buy goods in order to sell them for a profit, may attempt to engage in speculation. To do that, the characters must first determine what goods (and how much) are available for purchase. This is done by rolling on the **Trade Goods Available** table below. The units available (in tons) is then determined. These units are the total number available for purchase. Characters may purchase as few or as many as they wish. Units may also be split, but doing so incurs a penalty of 1-6% (1D12 ÷ 2).

Once the characters have determined what goods are available for purchase and in what quantities, they can then determine the purchase price by making a Merchant test. The degrees of success (or failure) determine the purchase price multiplier, as shown on the Trade Value table below. For example, suppose a character is trying to buy several units of grain and achieves 6 degrees of success. On the table, there is a 0.9 purchase price multiplier for 6 degrees of success. Multiplying 0.9 and the base unit cost of grains (500 SC) yields 450 SC, which is the price per unit at which the character is able to purchase this trade good.

When it comes time to sell an item, the character once again makes a Merchant test, with the degrees of success (or failure) determining the sale price multiplier (see **Table 8:2**). It is important to remember that the sale price multiplier, like the purchase price multiplier is applied to the base unit cost, even if the character had purchased a trade good at a price higher or lower than the base unit cost.

**Table 8:4 Supply**

| Population | Trade Code | | | | | |
|---|---|---|---|---|---|---|
| | **A** | **F** | **I** | **L** | **LG** | **M** |
| 1-249 | +25% | -50% | +25% | -45% | +40% | 0% |
| 250-499 | +15% | -35% | +20% | -30% | +40% | 0% |
| 500-999 | 5% | -15% | +10% | -15% | +20% | +5% |
| 1,000 - 2,499 | 0% | 0% | +10% | 0% | +20% | +5% |
| 2,500 - 4,999 | -5% | +15% | +5% | +15% | +10% | +5% |
| 5,000 - 6,999 | -15% | +35% | +5% | +30% | +10% | +10% |
| 7,000 - 9,999 | -25% | +50% | +2.5% | +45% | 0% | +10% |
| 10,000+ | -35% | +65% | +0% | +50% | -10% | +15% |

**Codes:**
A – Arms
F – Foodstuff
I – Industrial
L – Livestock
LG – Luxury Goods
M – Metals

# Additional Rules

The system presented above is intended to be very simple and straightforward, but some players and Game Masters may desire further complexity. For them, the following additional rules may be employed.

**TABLE 8:5 DEMAND**

| Population | Trade Code | | | | | |
|---|---|---|---|---|---|---|
| | A | F | I | L | LG | M |
| 1-249 | +20% | 0% | +35% | 0% | +50% | 0% |
| 250-499 | +25% | +10% | +30% | +10% | +40% | +10% |
| 500-999 | +30% | +15% | +25% | +15% | +30% | +15% |
| 1,000 - 2,499 | +35% | +20% | +20% | +20% | +20% | +20% |
| 2,500 - 4,999 | +40% | +25% | +15% | +25% | +15% | +15% |
| 5,000 - 6,999 | +45% | +30% | +10% | +30% | +10% | +10% |
| 7,000 - 9,999 | +50% | +35% | +5% | +35% | +5% | +5% |
| 10,000+ | +50% | +40% | +0% | +40% | +0% | +0% |

**Codes:**
A – Arms
F – Foodstuff
I – Industrial
L – Livestock
LG – Luxury Goods
M – Metals

## Brokers

If the characters wish, they may employ a local broker to aid in the sale (but not purchase) of goods. A broker grants a +1 to the TN of the Trade test, up to a maximum of +5. Brokers work on commission, earning 5% of the final sale price per +1 TN. No more than a single broker can be employed per sale.

## Supply and Demand

Each type of trade goods has a code listed on the Trade Goods Available table. These codes are used in conjunction with the **Supply and Demand** table below.

Depending on a market's population, there are varying degrees of supply and demand for each type of trade goods. The first number is the supply multiplier and the second is demand modifier. These multipliers are applied to the base unit cost before any other modifiers. If the supply multiplier is listed as "-," that means that type of trade good is unavailable in the market in question.

For example, grain is a foodstuff that sells for 500 SC per unit. In a location with a population between 1 and 249 people foodstuffs is plentiful, so they cost less per unit (500 SC × (-50%) = 250 SC). Demand, however, in an area with a population between 7,000 and 9,999 people is much greater, so selling grain the sell price is increased by +35%,of the standard price per unit.

The tables above are easily altered. Indeed, Gamemasters are encouraged to create custom tables that reflect the peculiarities of individual locations in their campaigns. Likewise, additional modifiers can be employed to affect the supply and demand multipliers, such as location, local economic factors, as well as armed conflicts. Of course, there is no need to introduce such complexities into the system unless the players enjoy the added detail.

# Experience Points

In **SHADOW, SWORD & SPELL: BASIC**, guidelines are given for awarding Experience Points. In Expert, Heroes still gain Experience Points, but due to the nature of the threats faced, Heroes gain Experience Points in different ways. Heroes still gain them from adventuring and the like. However, in **Expert**, other means of gaining experience exist.

In **Chapter 3**, we talked about gaining XP from the Domain a Hero has. In **Chapter 5**, we talked about gaining XP from successfully reading books. Finally, we talk about gaining XP from successfully creating a new Spell or Alchemical Art in **Chapter 4.** There are other ways to gain XP, and the following table gives you some idea of the other types of XP characters can earn.

**Table 8:6 Experience Awards**

| | |
|---|---|
| Buying new goods for sale | 1 XP/1000 crowns |
| Traveling to a new region | 1 XP/500 miles |
| Finding new goods to sell | 1 XP/1500 crowns |
| Starting a new business | 4 XP |
| Founding a Domain | 1 XP |
| Having retainers equal to half your Resolve | 1 XP |
| Having retainers equal to your Resolve | 2 XP |
| Raising an army | 1 XP |
| Leading an army into battle | 1XP |
| Winning a Battle | 1 XP |
| Starting a Scheme | 1 XP |
| Successfully Pulling off a Scheme | 2 XP |
| Expanding a Domain | 2 XP |
| Traveling | .5 XP for each 200 miles traveled |

# 9

# Setting & The World

## What is a Setting?

In **Shadow, Sword & Spell: Basic**, we introduced The League of Merchants. This "setting", if you will, was designed to serve as the proving ground for Heroes. The region is ideal for young adventurers, and offers many opportunities for Gamemasters to set their own adventures there, as well as to expand on the material to their hearts content. However, over time, Heroes grow powerful, and they begin to wonder what lies beyond a small region. Their desire is to explore.

Pulp fantasy novels and magazines, from which much of **Shadow, Sword & Spell's** inspiration is derived, is rich in the tradition of exploring the world. Think of Howard's Conan, or Kull and the stories where his heroes explore the larger world and discover adventure. Even in more "modern" works such as Moorcock's works, *Elric* wanders the Young Kingdoms in search of his lost love (Cymoril), his peace (Tanelorn), or for other opportunities. World spanning is important, especially if the hero is searching for land to claim as their own, a throne to take, or new markets where they can buy and sell goods.

Unlike **SS&S: Basic**, **Expert** has a setting. Unlike **Basic**, **Expert's** setting is larger and offers many opportunities for GMs to put to use. Like **Basic**, this setting is only barely detailed. A lot is left blank so you can take it and create what you want. Where we describe aspects of the setting, this is done in very broad strokes. We do this for a few reasons.

First, a fantasy game without a setting is not useful. A setting helps give context to the rules, but also serves as an example for Gamemasters when creating their own game world environments. In addition, a setting helps set a tone for the game. Think of **Game Workshop's** *Warhammer Fantasy Role Play*, **TSR's** *Greyhawk*, Dave Arneson's *Blackmoor*, or even **Judge's Guild** *City State of the Overlord* (as I type this I realize I have just dated myself). These settings stand the test of time not only because of the tone, but also due to the hook. The hook for a setting is important, and should be summed up in one succinct sentence. For example, let's use *Warhammer Fantasy Role Play as an example.* What is the hook? A grim world of perilous adventure. That hook is a perfect descriptive element, and when kept in mind, helps you create adventures and other aspects of the world for your players.

Another reason a setting is useful is because it sets a baseline that players and Gamemasters alike can use in their games. This baseline provides not only inspiration for players in creating their characters, but also for GMs in creating their own adventures.

Finally, the other reason to provide a setting is that it is fun to create a world, no matter how large or small it is.

# Setting Design

Before diving into the setting for **Shadow, Sword & Spell: Expert,** let's talk about the nuts and bolts of setting design. Setting design is relatively easy, as well as offering numerous rewards. However, when faced with a blank piece of paper, many world builders fall into two groups:

1. World builders with stage fright
2. World builders with too many ideas

There might be other groups, but over the years, these are the two groups of setting designers commonly found. What follows are the guidelines and lessons we've learned over the years. There might be other ways to approach setting design, and our methods are not the only ones to follow, but through the years this method has worked for us. Before writing any history, drawing any map, or naming any feature, you need to ask yourself one simple question: *What type of campaign do I want?*

The answer to this question is important, and answering it helps guide you in the building of your world. Is your campaign going to be centered on exploration? If so, will it consist of trekking across massive landmasses like some fantastical Marco Polo or Lewis & Clark? Or is your campaign going to center on oceanic exploration, where new lands are discovered? Is war going to be the focus? Are two kingdoms at war? Cities? Tribes? The answers to these questions help guide you in the creation of your setting. How? For two kingdoms, you need to come up with the bare bones of who rules, why they are fighting, and what the two kingdoms look like geographically. For two cities, these same questions are useful as well, but you are more confined to a smaller area. For tribes, this region is an even smaller.

With the answer to what type of campaign you want, the process of creation begins. Often this is seen as a daunting task. It really isn't. World building is just as enjoyable as creating adventurers, running a weekly game, and devising clever encounters to pit against the player characters. Where the struggle comes in, is the type of campaign you create. When you boil all the advice down, all the options and the possibilities, you are left with two types of settings: Encyclopedia or Sandbox. Each has its own pluses and minuses, and both are very rewarding.

Encyclopedic Settings are those where you strive to detail everything. Encyclopedic settings are ones that show off the creativity of a Gamemaster, and the thought that goes into one of these settings often serves as a springboard for other ideas. Another advantage is that the Gamemaster is ready for any question a player asks, and creates a richness of detail that makes the world seem truly alive. The downside of this is that often the bulk of this material never comes into play. Though nothing goes to waste, per sé, the details do go to waste if they never leave the confines of your note-filled workbooks. Players might not even care to ask what the lineage of a certain ruler is. Their concerns are more primal, like who is paying them, how do they afford a new sword, or how they can learn a new spell. Examples of Encyclopedic Settings are found in sprawling multi-volume fantasy epics such as Robert Jordan's *Wheel of Time*, J.R.R. Tolkien's *Lord of the Rings*, Raymond E. Feist's work, M.A.R. Barker's *Tékumel*, N. Robin Crosby's *Hârn*, and **TSR/Wizard of the Coast**'s *Forgotten Realms* (originally created by Ed Greenwood).

These settings are rich and brimming with detail; however, most of this detail is not needed. So, should you not create a setting like this? No. Go for it! Keep in mind that often the bulk of your creation is for your own enjoyment.

So if an Encyclopedic Setting is one end of the spectrum, a Sandbox is the other. What is a Sandbox Setting? It is a setting where you purposely leave areas *empty*. Instead, you think about the area where you plan to have your adventures take place, and you flesh it out in broad strokes. One example of this is The Merchant League region found in **SHADOW, SWORD & SPELL: BASIC**. That is a sandbox to play in. Only the bare minimum is written up, and as your adventurers explore, details are figured out. Growth is more spontaneous and details are created as players ask questions, or as you need them. Sandbox campaigns are rewarding in that everyone has a hand in shaping the growth. However, some GMs find them daunting because they often have to "wing it." This is a good thing, because some of the best creations are the ones you make up as you go along. The key to a Sandbox is that all you need are a few notes, as well as a notebook in which you can jot down what you create.

The game world of **Shadow, Sword & Spell** is a Sandbox. It is designed this way to serve not only as an example, but because we want you to make the game world your own.

Ok, with the basics out the way, what follows is the setting we have created for **Shadow, Sword & Spell.** Those who have read **Basic** have seen just a small portion of this world. Though the world is large, much of it is left blank, and we invite you to add your own ideas and creations to it. Hell, even areas we have developed and mentioned are open to you. We have provided you with the building blocks and a slight blueprint. Take it, and let your imagination run wild!

# The World

## Atlantis

Very few know of Atlantis, and what is known is only rumor. An ancient kingdom, the sorceresses and mages living here are said to be immortal. Is this true? No one knows, as those who have sailed to Atlantis have not lived to tell the tale. And if they have lived, they never return to share the tale. From time to time, ships hailing from Atlantean ports appear seeking to trade with the powers of the North. A few ports are rumored to be open to trade, but no one has been able to confirm this. There is presently a rumor that the land is home to immortal wizards who have been turned into undead as a result of the working of powerful magic. As for the truth of this rumor, no one has lived to confirm or deny it.

## Bærgøstēn

Hugging the Berg Sea's western shores is the realm of Bærgøstēn. The fjords and sheltered coves of this landscape hold what many jokingly refer to as *civilization.* The tribes that live here are some of the best sailors found in The World, and their dragon-headed boats have been seen sailing not only the Southern Sea, but the Azure Sea as well. The numerous rivers which flow south to the Cantons and the City States of Döârn have borne witness to these ships as well. A hearty people, these tribal folk are the only ones brave – or foolish – enough to venture into the Wastes seeking glory.

## Beidha

The great seafaring nation of Beidha is ruled by the Dynasty of Jade, who have led the people for close to 1,200 years. Beidha's navigators are a constant sight on both the Azure Sea and The World's oceans. For the past twenty years, Beidha has been in a constant state of war with Nipur. It is a testament to the Navy and soldiers of Beidha that the Dynasty of Jade has not been overrun. Despite their fearless nature, the Beidhans are known for their skills in science, mathematics, and Alchemy. It is their Alchemy which the Kingdom is best known for, and the current Maharajah, Deviprasad Sukhjinder XXVIII, is perhaps the greatest living Alchemist walking the land.

## Cal'athar

Stretching along the eastern coast is the small kingdom of Cal'athar. Though The Shimmering Sands border this land to the west, Cal'athar is a rich, teeming land. Her people are expert sailors, shipbuilders, and explorers. Cal'athar has no central government or rulers. Instead, the land is tribal, and the ancient tribes who once lived here have grown and developed into clans that dwell on their ancestral lands and carry out the work of their forefathers. The exact number of clans is unknown, but some speculate that there are close to 200 of them. Some clans are rich and powerful, and their homes resemble large cities, others are poor and downtrodden. The head of each clan can be either male or female, and are known as either Dasho (male) or Ashi (female). The only requirement to be head of the clan is that one must be the eldest. As the saying goes: "*The clans are like flowers: many, unique, and blooming.*"

# Cathar

This large northern kingdom is thought by many to be one of the oldest in existence. Ruled by an Empress, Cathar's origins date back some 3,000 years. Known as the Earthly Celestial Bureaucracy, Cathar's Empress leads this bureaucracy and seeks to bring order to the world's chaos. A kingdom of artists, poets, and sculptors, the refined scholarly air in Cathar hides an efficient and highly trained militaristic way of life. Soldiers are considered to be the highest level of society, and all nobles live to fight. Military matters and warfare are the domains of the nobility, and other aspects of life are left up to the workers and non-nobles. Merchants seek the numerous goods produced here, and other kingdoms import the military techniques and weapons to use as their own.

# Catha

If there is one place you can call the center of all evil, Catha is it. It is within this city that Nergal takes human form and leads His people. It is here where foul magics are created and practiced and diseases are crafted. All of this is done to feed the great machine of war. Those who have survived their visit to this city state the same thing: it is built in a fetid swamp whose air is filled with living clouds of flies, the stench of death, and the wretched living. At the center of the city can be found the tower known as Nergal's Finger. This black edifice reaches into the sky, and at its top sits the earthly form of Nergal, surveying all of His domain.

# City-States of Döarn

An ancient empire that once stretched all the way to the west, this Empire was ravaged by internal strife, and had the bad luck of suffering from weak emperors as well. It was this weakness which led to the collapse of the Empire, and the establishment of the various City-States that now dot the land. Döârn is a collection of city-states, each of which is led by a general who commands her own private armies. These generals war against each other, as well as try to conquer new lands so they can expand their private empires. If someone could unite all the city-states as a whole, many feel the Empire of Döârn could well live again. The citizens of the City-States share a kindred past, but their present is marked by the ebb and flow of peace and war. Though the time of endless conflict is over, war and skirmishes take place between the various generals and their armies. Though many feel the only trade that

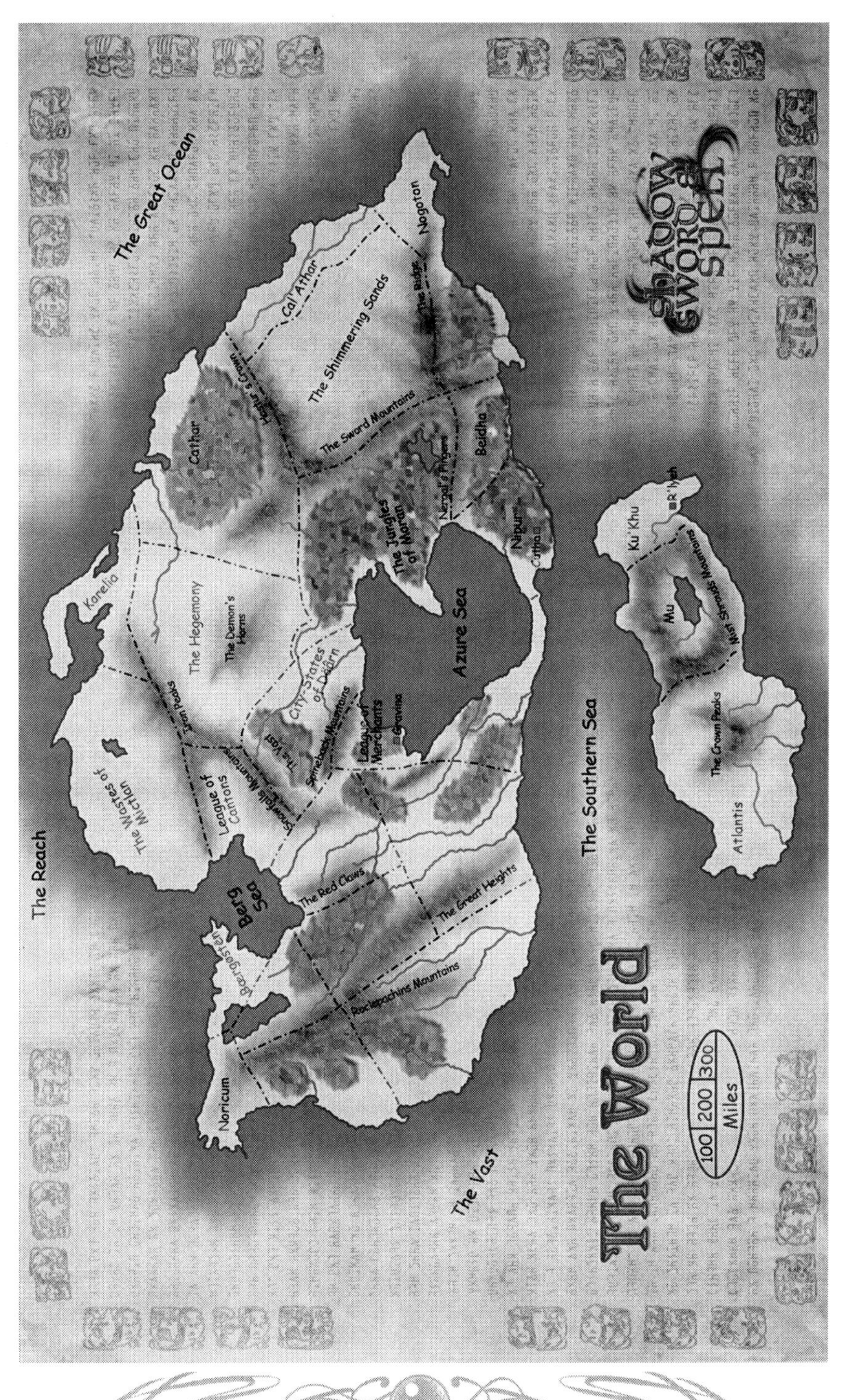
The World
100
200
300
Miles
Shadow Sword & Spell
The Great Ocean
The Reach
The Vast
The Southern Sea
Azure Sea
Berg Sea
Cathar
Cal Athar
Nogoton
The Shimmering Sands
The Ridge
The Sword Mountains
Beidha
Nergal's Fingers
The Jungles of Moran
Nippur
Karelia
The Hegemony
The Demon's Horns
City States of Da'arn
Iron Peaks
The Wastes of The Mictlan
League of Cantons
Spineback Mountains
League of Merchants
Gravina
The Red Claws
The Great Heights
Noricum
Ku'Khu
R'lyeh
Mu
The Crown Peaks
Atlantis

the City-States have is war, nothing is further from the truth. A diverse culture with a focus on agriculture can be found here, as well as a growing class of writers, dramatists and poets.

## The Hegemony

This vast steppe is home to various tribes of nomads known only as the People of the Plains. The various groups roam the steppes surviving, raiding, and warring amongst themselves. Little is known of these tribes, but from time to time the various clans unite under the banner of a Kahn and descend upon more civilized lands and plunder them. Despite many attempts, the Hegemony has been proven time and time again to be untamable, as well as unconquerable. The diverse number of tribes, the lack of any sustained industry or agriculture, The Heg, as many call it, is a wild grasslands region of the Hegemony whose inhabitants are just as wild. When not warring amongst themselves, the tribes are frequently found raiding along the borders. Some tribes do trade with various kingdoms, usually furs as well as horses in exchange for iron and implements forged by them.

## Jungles of Moarn

Nestled along the eastern shores of the Azure Sea lie the dense, mist-shrouded jungles known as Moarn. The jungles' green, living wall of trees hides numerous secrets, and no known kingdom or power has been able to claim them for themselves. All attempts to claim these secrets have failed, and even Nipur avoids conflict with Moarn at all costs. Small tribes of men and women are found throughout the jungles, who war amongst themselves as well as trade with the various merchant houses (see below) that have set up trading posts along the coast. These trading posts are considered to be the only form of *civilization* found in the region.

Visitors to the coasts of Moarn report that merchant houses from The League of Merchants, the City-States of Döârn, as well as Cal'athar, can be found here. Along the western borders with Cathar, trading posts are found as well, and it is rumored that even mountain passes linking Beidha to the jungles exist. Explorers who have survived the jungles' depths tell of ruined cities hidden deep in the jungles, as well as numerous statues and monuments dedicated to the god, Seth. Also rumored to lurk in the deepest reaches of the jungle are Snake Men, who according to the Moarn tribes, still teem within the shadows, working for their priest kings.

## Karelia

Located to the north is a rocky, icy region known as Karelia. A hard land that only the strongest can survive, the various barbarian tribes living here know one thing: struggle. When not fighting each other, the tribes of Karelia war with the Hegemony to the south, Cathar to the southeast, and the creatures from The Wastes of Mictlan. Hidden in the valleys and glaciers of Karelia are the ruins of an ancient race that once called this place home. The tribes now living here are unique, and have their own beliefs and way of life. The only thing they have in common with one another is their god, Chairoum. Chairoum is a cruel God, and wants His children to be strong. That is why they constantly war, so that they can grow strong.

## Ku'Kku

No one goes here unless they have the desire to die. A strange race calls this land home, and in R'lyeh, a temple dedicated to Cthulhu stands.

## The League of Cantons

Nestled in the midst of the high alpine lands of this region are small domains known as Cantons. These Cantons once consisted of the various tribes that embraced civilization in this region. The Cantons are independent, and though they govern themselves, they have formed a League in order to protect their mutual self-interests. There are fifteen Cantons found in this region, each of which has its own industry and way of life. The League is also known for its scholars and sages, and many feel The World's knowledge is to be found here, contained in the numerous libraries dotting the land.

## The Merchant League

The heart of commerce for the Azure Sea, and her cities are quickly gaining in power, wealth, and prestige. The League, though small, will be a force to be reckoned with in the years to come. For details on The Merchant League please refer to **SHADOW, SWORD & SPELL: BASIC**.

## Mu

Ringed by mountains, some whisper dragons live here. There are a few trading posts nestled along Mū's north and south coasts which trade with the various tribes that live in Mū's interior. Some has penetrated the mountains ringing the land, and tales of walking monsters and tribes of aboriginal warriors hunting these creature with weapons of gold are plentiful. These tribes place a value on ivory, and see gold as nothing but a worthless metal. Gold, silver, and platinum are found in the mountains. and the tribesmen use it to create weapons and other goods. In the center of the land is a giant lake, and it is said that the waters cover an ancient city of the gods.

## Nipur

This small tropical kingdom is ruled by a feudal lord, who is seen as the earthly form of the god Nergal (see page 152). Nipur is an evil place, and rumors persist that hidden deep in its jungles are a set of ruins in which a rift is located through which the evil inhabiting The World passes. Though some feel this is nothing more than a rumor or myth, Nipur's military is known to have a heavy presence within the jungles. Currently, the southeastern portion is rocked by war between Nipur and Beidha. The origin of this war is a simple one – Nipur wants to expand their borders, and Beidha is in their way. The war has raged for close to twenty years, and is a constant presence in the two regions. The conflict ebbs and flows like the tides, and the last major clash was two years ago. Nipur is currently marshaling its forces, and will soon spill across the Beidhan border. What this means is anyone's guess.

### Catha

If there is one place you can call the center of all evil, Catha is it. It is within this city that Nergal takes human form and leads His people. It is here where foul magics are created and practiced and diseases are crafted. All of this is done to feed the great machine of war. Those who have survived their visit to this city state the same thing: it is built in a fetid swamp whose air is filled with living clouds of flies, the stench of death, and the wretched living. At the center of the city can be found the tower known as Nergal's Finger. This black edifice reaches into the sky, and at its top sits the earthly form of Nergal, surveying all of His domain.

## Nogoton

The Empire of the Golden Sun. The earthy realm of the Eternal Celestial Dragon who sits upon the Sun Throne and rules all that He gazes upon. Nogoton is a mysterious place who existence is unknown to most, where only a few in the west have been lucky enough to visit. It is a major oceanic power in the southeast, and the kingdom is known for numerous products, specifically silk, jade, and amber. Perhaps the greatest export is the mystics, who wander the land seeking knowledge and dispensing guidance to those who are willing to listen.

## Noricum

Though one of the smallest kingdoms, the people of Noricum are known for their skills in battle, their abilities in magic, and the bloody civil war that is spilling into other regions. At one time, the warrior-mystics of Noricum could be found leading and training other armies, and Noricum mercenary companies found work fighting throughout The World. Then came the Time of Blood. Mog Ruith, once the God of the people, was slain by Buddakapula, a rival God who coveted Mog Ruith's power. The people of Noricum are broken into two sects devoted to the two Gods, and have fought a never-ending war for 50 years, and the once proud land is awash with blood, pain, tears, and death. No longer contained within their own borders, the sect of Buddakapula still fights with Mog Ruith's survivors. This fighting has even claimed innocent lives in far away Gravina.

## The Shimmering Sands

Hemmed in by the mountains to the north, west, and south is a vast desert known simply as The Shimmering Sands. Legend holds that the desert covers an ancient civilization destroyed when its peoples tried to capture the god Hastur in order to attempt to tap His power. The entire empire was destroyed, and the kingdom is now a desert dotted with ruins and some oases. Due to the shifting sands, ruins often appear and beckon any who are foolhardy or daring enough to enter and explore. Despite appearances, a variety of life can be found here, usually located in the numerous oases which dot the land. Numerous tribes live at these oases, trading with the various nomads who roams the sands. These nomads, according to some, are the descendants of the civilization that once existed here. They now wander the sands atoning for their sins, and pray to Hastur for His forgiveness.

# The Waste of Mictlan

Imagine a place dotted with ice, snow, steam, geysers, volcanoes, and bubbling mud pits. Imagine a land that is filled with poisonous gases, rivers of lava, and ponds of boiling tar. This gives you some idea of Mictlan. If there is a place where old gods walk, strange creatures roam, and death lives in the air, Mictlan is that place. All who have seen this place have been forever changed by it. The secrets which lie here are many, and evil festers that will one day break free and devour The World. Mictlan is a place of wild magic, and creatures who are spawned in these areas. Rumors abound that there are tribes of humans living in the wastelands. These tribes appear from time to time, raiding along the border of the Hegemony and the League of Cantons. Due to the nature of the Waste and the dangerous creatures that inhabitant it, the League of Cantons insures that the border is well protected. A series of keeps dot the entire border with the Waste of Mictlan, and the garrisons stand a constant vigil.

# Geographic Features

## Bodies of Water

There is a great variety of geographic features found in The World. Due to the vast size and scope of The World, this variety is too great to fully detail here. This is especially true with regards to the various bodies of water. There are five oceans and one sea around which all life revolves.

### Azure Sea

Occupying the center of The World is a vast, inland body of water known as the Azure Sea. The countries that ring it are the powers who vie for dominance, and their ships can be found sailing from port to port, buying and selling goods. Numerous islands dot these waters and hide a multitude of wonders, riches, and threats. One of the threats in the Azure Sea are the pirates who plague the shipping lanes. Another threat is the vast monstrosities lurking in the depths, that occasionally surface to wreak havoc. A canal some 2 miles wide and 500 feet deep connects the Azure Sea to the Southern Sea. The canal has always been here; who made it is is a mystery still to this day.

### Berg Sea

Named for the number of icebergs which float within its confines, this Sea is a challenge to sailors, and only the most daring do so. In addition, due to The Waste of Mictlan being located on its eastern shore, this is doubly a challenge. Finally, another threat sailors must face when sailing the Berg Sea are pirates, who have created hidden bases within and atop some of the largest icebergs.

## The Great Ocean

Bordering the eastern realms and reaching toward the rising sun is a body of water simply known as the Great Ocean. Though islands are scattered along the coastal waters, like The Vast, eventually these small landfalls give out and all that can be seen is the open water. What lies to the horizon? No one knows.

## The Reach

Stretching along the top of The World is the icy region known simply as The Reach. This ocean typically has a thick sheet of ice covering it, and only the coastal waters are readily navigable. However, during winter, the sea ice often reaches south and blocks the waters off. The ice is so thick that barbarians and other creatures have been seen walking, hunting, and warring across it. In addition, some tribes sail the vast ice in boats designed to skate across the frozen surface, as if they were on water.

## The Southern Sea

The waters that bridge the mainlands from the southern continent is known simply as the Southern Sea. This Sea is traveled heavily by the kingdoms of Nipur, Beidha, and Nogoton, and these powers tend to fight more than they trade. Other countries can be found here trading, and also seek new markets to exploit. Due to the location of the southern continent, and the fact that it contains a vast array of strange peoples, creatures, and things, the Southern Sea is a challenging environment as well. If there is one place which sailors consider to be the most dangerous to sail in the world, it is the Southern Sea.

### The Vast

The western ocean has been called The Vast for centuries. The origins of this name are many, but if pressed, scholars state the name is based on the simple fact that no one has explored it fully. All attempts to discover if any landmasses lie to the west have failed due to the explorers sent there vanishing without a trace. Though small islands can be seen dotted along the coast, these landmasses give way, and those who have sailed the Vast for months turn back due to no major land being found.

# Gods

Though the League of Merchants have their own deities, they are not the only ones found in The World. Numerous Gods can be found in the various nations and regions, as it seems that each culture and kingdom has their own religions as well as deities. What follows is by no means an exhaustive list. There are far too many religions, cults, sects, and gods to adequately chronicle here. These are the most well-known, as well as being tied to the lands that have been previously noted above.

## Ardud Lili

When the world was dark and new, there was a God known only as Moma, who carved His kingdom out of the very marrow of Chaos. Naming His realm Mictlan, the domain became the final resting place for all souls. It was also where evil was born and from which monsters emerged, and it was from here that Ardud Lili, the Temptress and Mother of All Demons, arose. She and Her children overthrew Moma, and and took control of Mictlan. Sitting atop Her throne carved from the skull of the dead God, She seeks power and Queenship over all. Ardud Lili is worshipped by those who seek power, crave authority or seek to enslave all. Her worship is hidden in small shrines and Her children seek to bring Her more worshippers. She is depicted as a beautiful woman, draped in shadows, whose unearthly beauty brings pain to all who gaze upon Her.

## Azathoth

One of the many Gods worshipped in mysterious Atlantis, Azathoth is seen as the Light Bringer and Source of All Life. Often depicted as a fiery sun, the priests preach that Azathoth lies at the center of the universe giving and taking life. Though heavily worshipped in Atlantis, the worship of Azathoth has spread north with sailors, travelers, and merchants. The most important sect devoted to the God is found in Davenport, located in The Merchant League. As to the beliefs and tenets of the faith, no one knows. Worship of

Azathoth is kept a secret, and those who are devoted never talk to non-believers. Rumors hold that worship centers around sacrifice and fire.

## Buddhakupula

Noricum worships one God, and this God is the one who created the world. Always depicted as bluish-black in color, Buddhakupula has one face, four arms, and His body is festooned with the bones of His enemies. He carries a knife and cudgel, and in one hand carries the head of Mog Ruith, the God who once held sway in Noricum. Buddhakupula is a Blood God and His worshippers feel that it is the blood of His enemies which feed him as well as protect his people. The devoted, notably the priests, tattoo their bodies blue and carry both a knife and cudgel. This is a cult which is quickly gaining a foothold in the south, and rumors persist that the sect can be found not only in Gravina and Wall in The Merchant League, but in Bæ̀rgøstēn and the Cantons.

## Caim

God of Night, Death, Murder, and Strife. Caim is a deity whose worship has spread throughout The World. Worshippers of Caim tend to be those who are the lost or who lurk in the shadows. The central tenet of the worship of Caim is the eating of the dead. By eating the dead, one shows one's determination as well as gaining the power of the dead. Ghouls are said to be the Children of Caim, and rumors abound that Ghouls are the high priests in the religion of this God. There is no central site of worship. Sects and cults are found in numerous locations, where the faithful gather and consume the flesh of the dead.

## Chairoum

God of the North Wind, Memory, Knowledge, and War. Chairoum is the primary deity worshipped by the barbarians of Karelia. Chairoum is seen as a fickle, angry God, whose mood changes on a whim. He is said to have three eyes, with the third resting in the middle of His forehead. It is this eye which is said to see All, and allows Chairoum to chronicle all that He sees. Chairoum is an uncaring God, and He wants nothing from His worshippers; thus, His faithful should expect nothing as well.

## Cthulhu

Ancient are the ways of Cthulhu. This is a God who has touched the world for eons. According to legend and lore, as well as his worshippers, Cthulhu came to the world in a flash of light, and when the world ends, He will be there collecting the souls of all, including the Gods. Though rumors abound that His main temple is located in R'lyeh, sects devoted to Cthulhu are found in many

BKM·2010

places. It seems as if every major city has at least one temple dedicated to Him. Though the thoughts of Gods are beyond the ken of men, scholars, and theologians, Cthulhu is associated with Death, Dreams, Destruction, and Knowledge. It is the aspect of Knowledge which attracts the worship of scholars, sorcerers, and sages to this deity.

## Hastur

At the dawn of time, there was Hastur. He emerged from the Void, and His coming heralded all life. It was He who battled Cthulhu, and the sparks of their battle created the stars that fill the sky. The unblinking eye, Hastur sees and knows All. According to legend, Hastur was driven mad after piercing the Veil of Time and witnessed the end of all life. It was seeing the paradox of a world with no time that caused Him to go insane. Some also whisper that it was the civilization once living in the region known as The Shimmering Sands that not only destroyed their civilization, but drove the God mad. The fact that numerous ruined statues, as well as relics, bearing his likeness dot the landscape of the Shimmering Sands lends credence to this. There are many small cults and churches scattered throughout The World which are dedicated to Him.

## Haziel

Though no one would “love” the Goddess Ardud Lili, there is one who does, and it is Her mate and general, Haziel. The God of War is Haziel, who marshals Mictlan’s hordes of demons and leads them into war. A strong God, He is depicted as a large muscular man, red in color, with the head of a bull. He is always naked, and carries a massive sword that only He can hold. Haziel is widely worshipped among warriors, pit fighters, and soldiers. He is also a favorite of the barbarian tribes found throughout the north.

## Mog Ruith

A dead God, once the only deity of Noricum. The God died at the hands of Buddhakupula, which signified the start of the conflict between the two sects in that nation. Though many feel that Mog Ruith is dead, His worshippers are still active and it should be noted that miracles are still performed. Mog Ruith is seen as the world’s creator, as well as being the Life Bringer. He is depicted as a single flame, with a human head. Since His murder, images of Mog Ruith can be found everywhere.

## Mulciber

When a fire destroys, it is Mulciber. When a storm rages and claims the livestock of a farmer, it is Mulciber. The God of Punishment and Destruction,

Mulciber is viewed as an angry storm cloud. His worship is widespread, and temples can be found dedicated to Him throughout the world. His devotees tend to be those who seek to punish wrong-doers or those who have survived some form of destruction. Prayers are always said to Mulciber before crops are planted or buildings are constructed.

## Nergal

The main god of Nipur; while other deities are known in that land, Nergal is the one and only true God. He is the God of War and the Plague, and this God is often depicted as a skeleton dressed in armor, wielding a sword covered with maggots. Nergal's worshippers tend to be those who've suffered from illness, and the most important are considered to be lepers. The city of Cutha itself is considered to be the most important temple to Nergal, and it is from here that the plague priests lead their followers in spreading sickness. Though Nipur is the major region of worship for Nergal, small sects to the deity can be found in all major regions of The World.

## Nodens

A mysterious Goddess whom many feel is more myth than reality. Although there are no known temples to Her, the mark of Nodens – which is a white hand holding an orange sun – can be found scrawled on walls, streets, and even doors throughout The World. Rumors abound that Nodens is worshipped heavily by those living in the Region of the Amber Petals in The Merchant League, as well as throughout the League of Cantons. Who worships Nodens? Those who come to the cult do so because they search for something – power, vengeance, knowledge, peace, punishment – and hope to gain it.

## Nyarlathotep

The Trickster, the Tempter, the Seducer, and the Liar. When malice lies in the heart of a person, you will find Nyarlathotep. When someone's jealousy leads to murder, Nyarlathotep is there. A dark God who offers no promises, nor keeps His word, Nyarlathotep and His worshippers are seen as liars. Gamblers appeal to Him for luck. Those wishing to swindle others appeal to Him. It is said no one willingly worships this God, that instead misfortune compels them to do so. Worship of Nyarlathotep is found throughout The World, but His most important temple is found in Nogoton, at the top of a mountain perpetually shrouded in clouds. Other temples and shrines can be found in all major cities, frequently in gambling halls, near merchant areas, trading halls, and markets.

## Nyogtha

Sitting at the bottom of The Vast is a realm of swirling seas and terrible creatures. It is here that Nyogtha rules, and it is His constant anger which causes all storms. His domain is the water, and though known by many names, all kingdoms worship Nyogtha, the Lord of Water and Master of Storms. Worshipped by sailors, merchants, and farmers, anyone who depends on water for a living pray to Him. Fickle and short of temper, sailors have learned to always make a sacrifice to Him before setting sail, whereas farmers make a sacrifice to Him before the first planting and after the last harvest. His temples and shrines are always located near a body of water, and His priests always wear the color blue. His symbol is a crashing wave, pierced by a lightning bolt.

## Qu'Tangles

He who comes with the dawn and devours the night. He whose blood fills all, and through him life flourishes. The beginning and the end. A dead god. Once the sole god of the various tribes of the Jungles of Moarn, Qu'Tangles was killed by Seth, who nows where his skin as a cloak. Strangely, hidden among the jungle's depth are shrines to this god, and his priests still carry out their worship. Many of these priests whisper to have been granted visions by him, and some feel it is only a matter of time, before Seth is made to pay.

## Seth

Lying in the center of the earth gnawing at the roots is Seth, the Great Snake and Devourer of All Life. Seth was once a might mortal sorcerer who discovered immortality and craved godhood. He challenged Qu'Tangles and slew Him. Assuming His shape, Seth rose above Qu'Tangles's people and became the deity of the Serpent People of the Jungles of Moarn. Seth is an angry, power hungry God who even now still craves power. All are put upon the earth to fuel Seth's anger. Though His worship is based mainly within the jungles, small cults devoted to Him can be found throughout the world. Those seeking power, or eternal life, typically come to His worship.

## Shub-Niggurath

A decadent God, Shub-Niggurath is always depicted as an androgynous God, possessed of both male and female genitalia, and whose slightest gaze causes lust in all. Seen as the ruler of fertility, some view Him/Her as the igniter of passion, desire, and love. Worship of this God centers around sex, in all of its forms. A favorite of the wealthy and powerful, devotion to Shub-Niggurath is found in all regions of The World. Though temples dedicated to Him/Her tend to be small and secret, some take the form of brothels, sex clubs or feasting halls.

# Titles of Nobility and Governing

Due to the sheer variety of governments found in The World, there are many types of Titles and Ranks to be found. What follows are merely some of them.

## General Ranks

There are eleven common Titles found in The World. Though the names might vary depending on the region, the hierarchal rank is important. The following table lists the common Ranks of nobility.

| Table 9:1 Titles |
|---|
| Emperor, Empress |
| King, Queen |
| Prince, Princess Royal (First Born) |
| Prince, Princess |
| Duke, Duchess |
| Marquessa, Marchioness |
| Earl, Countess |
| Viscount, Viscountess |
| Baron, Baroness |
| Baronet |
| Knight |

## Bærgøstēn

All of Bærgøstēn is led by the Konge (male) or Kaven (female). To aid in this method of rule, as well as to insure that no one has full authority, Bærgøstēn's various villages are led by a Jarl, who swears fealty to the Konge.

## Beidha

At the highest rung of Beidha is the high king known as the Maharajah (male) or Maharani (female). All report to him or her, and their word is law. Underneath the Maharajah or Maharani are the Rajah (male) or Rani (female), who rule over the various provinces, and these are combined into a state. The provinces, or Sabah, are how Beidha is broken up into easy to rule sections, and ruling these provinces are Nawab. Kshatriyas are the warrior nobles of Beidha, and they make up the bulk of the Noble class.

## Cal'athar

The head of each clan is known as the Dasho (male) or Ashi (female).

## The Hegemony

The leader of each tribe is known simply as Kahn. When all the various tribes unite and follow the banner of one, this leader is known as the Kha-Khan.

## League of Cantons

There are no central rulers; instead the leader of each Canton is known as The Elder. Each Canton is an oligarchy, and the Elders of each Canton meet in what is known as a Landsgemeid, which is an assembly of between 5, 7 or 9 members. If a Canton is unable to meet the numerical requirement, the number is reduced until it is. To insure that there is never a deadlock, the Landsgemeid must always have a odd number of members.

## League of Merchants

There are no central rulers, as each city is run by a collection of Guilds or Councils.

## Nipur

There is but one ruler of Nipur, and he is the Emperor.

## Nogoton

At the highest rung of Nogoton rests the Emperor or Empress. Though there is an Empress (or Emperor) and her (or his) word is law, the entire country is a giant bureaucracy. Underneath the Emperor or Empress is the Wang, of which there are two. One Wang rules the Eastern part of Nogoton, and the other the West. Each Wang oversees two provinces which are led by the Gung. Each province is broken up into four regions, and each is in turn ruled by a Hou. The regions are further divided into six areas, which are rules by a Bi. To further add to the layer of government and confusion, each area is divided into eight districts, which are each led by a Dse. Finally each district is broken into ten lands, which are each ruled by a Nans.

## Noricum

No one knows who, or how, the tribes are led.

## The Shimmering Sands

The leader of each tribe is known as the Malik, and this person must always be the eldest male. There are no other divisions, regardless of whether the tribe is nomadic or if it is settled at an oasis.

# Backgrounds

As you recall, in **SHADOW, SWORD & SPELL: BASIC** we introduced the concept of Backgrounds.

Because of the wide range of possible options, Backgrounds consist of two parts: a Culture and a Modifier. Cultures include Primitive, Barbarian, Civilized, and Advanced. Modifiers, as their name implies, modify the Culture by adding a quality to it, such as "Decadent," "Nomadic," or "Southern." By combining the two in various pairings, you can create many different Backgrounds, each of which has its own unique characteristics. Thus, you can create a Nomadic Barbarian character who will have different bonuses and penalties from a Southern Barbarian Character.

Included here are the ones found in **Basic** as well as new ones inspired by The World. Each of these Backgrounds include Native Language. The Native Languages are found in **Chapter 2**, pages 5-7. When picking a Native Language for your character, these are the ones you choose from.

# Cultures

As noted above, there are four Cultures you can choose for your character. They are:

## Primitive

A Primitive character belongs to a pre-literate culture, lacking metal-working, large permanent settlements, and having no social structure larger than the family or clan. Generally, Primitive characters come from a hunter-gatherer background. Historical examples of Primitive cultures include Australian aborigines, African bushmen, and many Pacific islanders. Literary examples include Robert E. Howard's Picts and Michael Moorcock's Yurits.

**Background Bonuses:** Athletics at Base Rank, Survival at Base Rank, Fluency in Native Language, +1 Action Point

**Background Penalty:** The ability to read and write is purchased as a separate skill from Language.Barbarian

A Barbarian character belongs to a culture that lacks the large permanent settlements and organization of Civilized societies, but possesses many other advances, such as agriculture, metal-working, and, in some cases, literacy. Historical examples of Barbarian cultures include Celts, Huns, and Vikings. Literary examples include Robert E. Howard's Cimmerians and Tolkien's Rohirrim.

**Background Bonuses:** Athletics at Base Rank, Melee at Base Rank, Fluency in Native Language

**Background Penalty:** The ability to read and write is purchased as a separate skill from Language.

## Civilized

A Civilized character belongs to a culture that possesses large permanent settlements, powerful central governments, and engages in large-scale civic engineering projects. Historical examples of Civilized cultures include imperial China, ancient Egypt, and the Romans. Literary examples include Robert E. Howard's Aquilonians and Fritz Leiber's Lankhmarites.

**Background Bonuses:** Bureaucracy at Base Rank, Diplomacy at Base Rank, Fluency in Native Language

## Advanced

An Advanced character belongs to a culture whose achievements far outstrip those of their contemporaries, both in scope and in magnificence. Advanced cultures may even possess magic and/or sciences otherwise unknown in the world. There are no historical examples of such cultures, but literary ones abound, such as Michael Moorcock's Melnibonéans or the Red Martians of Edgar Rice Burroughs.

**Background Bonuses:** Lore at Base Rank, Study at Base Rank, Fluency in Native Language, +1 Action Point

**Background Penalty:** -1 TN when attempting socially-oriented Tests with members of "inferior" cultures.

# Modifiers

The following is a small selection of Modifiers that can be applied to the four Cultures. All Modifiers grant small bonuses and penalties to Skill Tests. Generally, this consists of either a single +2 bonus or two +1 bonuses. A greater number of bonuses are possible, but any bonuses above +2 (in aggregate) must be counter-balanced by a -1 penalty for each additional +1. Thus, a Modifier that granted a +1 bonus to three different Skill Tests would also include a -1 penalty to a single Skill Test.

With this in mind, each Gamemaster can create as many Modifiers as desired for her campaign. Here are a few examples to illustrate how it is done:

## Atlantean

You hail from the mysterious southern kingdom known as Atlantis. What secrets you know would make others quake in fear.

**Bonuses:** +1 Lore, +1 Sense, +1 Study (Emphasis of choice)

**Penalty:** -1 Empathy, -2 Diplomacy

## Beidhan Jade Warrior

The warriors of Beidha are known for their skills, and one area that stands out the most is their versatility.

**Bonuses:** +1 Defend, +1 Profession (Sailor), +1 Tactics

**Penalty:** -2 Diplomacy, -1 Streetwise

## Catharian Bureaucrat

It takes many individuals to insure that the great bureaucracy of Cathar runs smoothly.

**Bonuses:** +3 Bureaucracy, +1 Diplomacy

**Penalty:** -2 Brawl, -2 Melee

## Catharian Legionnaire

The highest rung of Cathar society is the warrior. Dedicated to pursuits not only martial but artistic, Legionnaires are a dichotomy of violence and creators of great beauty.

**Bonuses:** +1 Art (Emphasis of Choice), +1 Melee, +1 Performance (Emphasis of Choice), +1 Tactics

**Penalty:** -2 Empathy, -2 Diplomacy

## Decadent

Your character's culture is in a state of decline.

**Bonuses:** +1 Bureaucracy, +1 Streetwise

**Penalty:** -2 Empathy

## Eastern

Your character's culture is located in the "mysterious East."

**Bonuses:** +1 Bureaucracy, +1 Lore

**Penalty:** -1 Socialize

## Haughty

Your character's culture considers itself superior to others.

**Bonuses:** +2 Intimidate

**Penalty:** -1 Bargain, -1 Empathy

## Magi

Magi are considered by many within Beidha to be the most educated and skilled in the sciences.

**Bonuses:** +1 Lore, +1 Study (Mathematics), +1 Study (Religions)

**Penalty:** -1 Brawl, -1 Defend, -1 Melee

## Mercantile

Your character's culture is renowned for its traders.

**Bonuses:** +1 Bargain, +1 Diplomacy

## Maritime

Your character's culture is a sea-going one.

**Bonuses:** +1 Athletics, +1 Profession (Sailor)

## Martial

Your character's culture holds warfare in high esteem.

**Bonuses:** +1 Defend, +1 Melee, +1 Tactics

**Penalties:** -1 Diplomacy

## Mountaineer

The high alpine pastures, and the plentiful mountains of the League of Cantons has made many into sought after guides.

**Bonuses:** +1 Athletics (Climbing), +1 Observe, +1 Survival (Mountains)

**Penalty:** -1 Empathy, -1 Streetwise

## Mystic

There are some in Nogoton who are in tune with the unseen and mystical. They are a people who are said to be able to read the future in the drifting clouds, and can tell when trouble is too come.

**Bonuses:** +1 Divination, +1 Empathy, +1 Lore, +1 Sense

**Penalty:** -2 Brawl, -2 Melee

## Nogoton Navigator

Nogoton is known for their sailors, and for many their navigator's are the most sought after.

**Bonuses:** +1 Profession (Sailor), +2 Study (Navigation)

**Penalty:** -1 Diplomacy, -1 Streetwise

## Nomadic

Your character's culture has no permanent settlements.

**Bonuses:** +1 Animal Handling, +1 Ride

## Northern

Your character's culture hails from the frozen North.

**Bonuses:** +1 Survival, +1 Track

## Pious

Your character's culture is very devoted to the gods.

**Bonuses:** +2 Study

## Scholarly

Your Character's culture holds knowledge and scholarly pursuits in high esteem.

**Bonuses:** +1 Diplomacy, +2 Study

**Penalties:** -1 Melee, -1 Brawl

## Sorcerous

Your character's culture make regular use of magic.

**Bonuses:** +1 Resist, +1 Study

**Penalty:** -1 Diplomacy, -1 Socialize

## Southern

Your character's culture is found in the burning South.

**Bonuses:** +2 Survival

## Tolerant

Your character's culture is welcoming to outsiders.

**Bonuses:** +1 Diplomacy, +1 Empathy

## Warrior of the North

Your character' hails from Bærgøstēn, and they are known for their ferocity in battle.

**Bonuses:** +1 Brawl, +1 Melee, +1 Survival (Tundra)

**Penalty:** -2 Diplomacy, -1 Empathy

# 10

## Creature Design

The world of **Shadow, Sword & Spell** teems with life. This chapter is designed to help you design creatures to challenge, aid, and harm your player characters. Like everything else in **Shadow, Sword & Spell**, creature design is simple and straightforward, geared toward ease of use and designed to foster fun roleplaying rather than realism.

Creatures are dangers that Heroes face from time to time, and they offer challenges on which Gamemasters can base adventures. Most creatures want nothing more than to be left alone, so they only attack when threatened. Some creatures have evil lurking within their hearts, and will attack no matter the situation. These evil creatures offer GMs many opportunities to pose a threat and challenge to all, not just the player characters.

Four types of creatures – Natural, Otherworldly, Undead and Infernal – exist in the world of **Shadow, Sword & Spell**. These creatures encompass the monstrous threats that characters will face during their adventuring lives.

Natural creatures are native to the natural physical world, and run the gamut from common animals to werewolves and even giants. Natural creatures also include zombies, skeletons and the like. These creatures are native to the physical world. Otherworldly creatures are creatures native to other planes of existence, which makes it difficult for them to remain in the natural world. In order to manifest in the physical world, Otherworldly creatures expend Plasm, which is the force that fuels everything these creatures do. Otherworldly creatures, since they do not have physical bodies, do not have the Vitality Ability; instead, their Plasm acts and substitutes as this Ability. Undead are creatures who have died, and their bodies or spirits live on. The final type of creatures are Infernal, and, like Otherworldly, they are not native to the physical world, dwelling in realms outside the scope of man.

At first blush, both Otherworldly and Infernal creatures come from other planes of existence, why aren't they both classified under the Otherworldly heading? The simple answer is that Infernal creatures have Taint, which is the power that fuels them and the abilities they call upon. The more complicated answer is that Infernal creatures are what are classically known as devils and demons.

# Creature Design Steps

Regardless of whether a creature is Natural, Otherworldly, Undead or Infernal, all creatures are created the same way — with Creature Points. As is the case with character creation, creature creation has six easy steps. These steps are:

**Step 1:** Determine Power Level

**Step 2:** Purchase Abilities with Creature Points

**Step 3:** Purchase Traits with Trait Points

**Step 4:** Purchase Skills with Skill Points

**Step 5:** Calculate Plasm, Taint or Vitality, and Initiative Rating

**Step 6:** Assign one hook

**Step 7:** Pit creature against player characters

So how does this process work? Simple. For example, let's say you want to create a dog. In order to create a dog, you have to take into account that a dog, by its nature, is not tough, and because of this, you decide the Power Level is Feeble, which means that the dog has 20 Creature Points to use in building it. The maximum for any Ability is 6. You have 15 Trait Points which you can use to purchase Traits, and 30 Skill Points to purchase Skills.

## Step 1: Determine Power Level

Determining the Power Level sets up all the steps for creating a creature. The stronger the creature, the more points you have to build it with. **Table 10:1** gives the available Power Levels and the points available to build your creatures.

**TABLE 10:1 CREATURE POWER**

| Power Level | Creature Points | Trait Points | Skill Points | Max Ability Score |
|---|---|---|---|---|
| Infirm | 15 | 15 | 25 | 5 |
| Feeble | 20 | 15 | 30 | 6 |
| Weak | 25 | 20 | 35 | 7 |
| Below Average | 30 | 20 | 40 | 8 |
| Average | 35 | 25 | 45 | 10 |
| Above Average | 45 | 25 | 50 | 12 |
| Experience | 55 | 30 | 55 | 14 |
| Seasoned | 65 | 30 | 65 | 16 |
| Veteran | 75 | 35 | 75 | 20 |
| Legendary | 85 | 35 | 85 | 22 |
| Mythic | 95 | 40 | 95 | 24 |

## Step 2: Purchase Abilities with Creature Points

All creatures have the same Abilities that character have. You purchase these Abilities the same way as you do when creating a character.

## Step 3: Purchase Traits with Traits Points

All creatures have Traits. Traits are the facets of a creature that makes them a creature, and unique in some fashion. What follows is a list of unusual Traits that can be chosen to give creatures unique abilities or "powers". Not all creatures need to have special Traits. However, most creatures do have Traits from the list that follows, even if it is something like Size, a Bite or Claw attack, or something else that is inherent to its nature. However, this section is provided to aid the GM in creating creatures that have special talents and traits that differ from Heroes, Villains, and NPCs. Please note that each Trait has a "cost". In addition, there are a number of Traits listed as "Drawbacks". These Traits are negative ones in that they do not provide the creature with any benefits, but instead limit it in some fashion. Drawbacks grant the creature a number of additional bonus Creature Points that may be added to their total.

## Acidic

The creature's saliva is acidic, and can burn others, increasing the Damage Value of the creature's bite by 1. The creature must have a natural bite, stinger, touch or other form of physical attack to take this Trait.

**Cost:** 1

## Attack Bonus

The creature is particularly talented or skilled at combat, and gains a bonus to all Attack Tests. A conditional Attack Bonus only applies to attacks against a certain type of target (such as members of certain species or factions), or attacks under certain conditions (such as in extreme heat or cold or underwater); this reduces the build point cost of the Attack Bonus to one-half its normal cost, rounded up.

**Cost:** 5 (+1); 10 (+2); 15 (+3)

## Attack Penalty (Drawback)

The creature is less talented or skilled at combat. A creature with this drawback suffers a penalty to Attack Tests, either all the time or under certain conditions. A conditional attack penalty only applies against a certain type of target (such as specific creatures), or attacks under certain conditions (such as in extreme heat or cold ); this reduces the build points provided by the penalty to one-half its normal bonus, rounded up.

**Bonus Points Provided:** 5 (-1); 10 (-2); 15 (-3)

## Bite

Bite is what it implies; it causes damage. In addition, the Bite can be linked to other Traits, such as Acidic saliva (see above). The damage a Bite causes is d12+Brawn.

**Cost:** 1

## Bony Spurs

Bony spikes protrude from the creature's joints, giving it a jagged profile, and making it dangerous to touch. Anyone touching the creature, either due to combat, or some other means, takes a 1 DV attack.

**Cost:** 2

## Breath

The creature is able to breathe flames, cold, poison, darkness, acid, or other harmful substances. This Trait is useful against opponents not only in hand-to-hand combat, but also when the creature is not that close to its target. To use this ability, the creature must make a successful Quickness Test to hit its target. Creatures with the Breath Trait always have a Range and Damage listed.

**Cost:** 6

## Brittle Bones (Drawback)

The creature's bones are so weak that they cannot withstand hard or sudden impacts (falling, being struck by blunt weapons and the like). The creature also takes an additional 1D12 points of damage from any fall greater than 10 feet in height (see **Basic** page 57). The creature cannot possess this drawback if it already has the Skeletal Reinforcement trait.

**Bonus Points Provided:** 2

## Claws

Claws are what they imply; they cause damage. The damage Claws cause is d12+Quickness.

**Cost:** 1

## Combat Fear (Drawback)

The creature is gripped by an inexplicable fear whenever facing a dangerous or frightening situation. After Initiative is rolled, but before the creature takes its first action in combat, it must make a Will Test. If the creature fails the Test, it is shaken for the rest of the encounter, suffering a –2 penalty on Attack and Skill Tests. If the Test succeeds, the creature overcomes its momentary fear and negates the ill effects.

**Bonus Points Provided:** 2

## Control

The creature is able to control something, be it animals, elements or the like. To use this ability the creature must make a Will Test, with success indicating that the creature successfully controls the target of the control attempt. The number of targets/objects the creature can control is equal to its Will stat. The duration is equal to one-half the creature's Will, and the range is equal to the creature's Will x 5 feet.

**Cost:** 8

## Curious

The creature is intensely interested in new knowledge and experiences, and gains a +1 TN to any Test it attempts either for the first time, or while in pursuit of some knowledge or experience it has never had or seen before.

**Cost:** 1

## Damage Reduction

The creature takes less damage from whatever the source of the damage is, depending on the object or the circumstance. Examples of this might be damage reduction against flames, poison, steam, cold, heat, physical attacks, iron, etc. As for the reduction in damage, the reduction is half.

**Cost:** 3 per type of reduction

## Disease

The creature carries a Disease that can be passed on to an opponent via bite, claw, horn, gouge, breath or physical contact. The target is able to resist the disease as per the rules in **SHADOW, SWORD & SPELL: BASIC.**

**Cost:** 5 per each Disease

## Drain

Creatures that have the Drain Trait can drain Abilities, Vitality, Sanity or Resolve. Drain can be linked to a bite, claws or any other physical attack. In addition, the Trait can be take multiple times if a creature can drain more than two different things, such as Brawn and Will. A creature can drain 5, 10 or 15 points and the cost is based around this.

**Cost:** 4 (Drain 5 Points), 8 (Drain 10 Points), 12 (Drain 15 Points)

## Elasticity

The creature is able to bend and twist its body in unnatural ways, allowing it to squeeze into and through very tight spaces. Consequently, the creature can squeeze through an opening or passage one-fifth as wide and tall as its height, in inches, although it does so very slowly compared to its normal movement rate (movement is reduced by half).

**Cost:** 2

## Extra Arms

The creature possesses an additional pair of arms, which look and behave exactly like its other arms. As a species with more than two arms, the creature gains a +2 bonus on Athletics (Climb) and Brawl Tests. For the purposes of combat, both extra arms are treated as "off hands" (that is, you still have only one primary hand).

**Cost:** 3 (per set of extra arms)

## Fear

The creature is able to cause Fear in its targets, and those able to do so have a Rank in this ability that must be purchased, and is applied to a target's Will Test when they make a Fear Test. For example, a creature has Fear -2; when faced by this creature, a Hero's Will is reduced by 2 points for the purpose of the Fear Test. The Fear value can range from -1 to -6.

**Cost:** 4 per point of Fear

## Fierce

The creature is naturally aggressive, or becomes angry when threatened. Creatures with this ability must make a Will Test once they takes damage. If the Test is failed, the creature becomes enraged. As a result, its Brawn and Toughness are temporarily increased by 2 points each, and its Vitality is temporarily increased by 15 Points. In addition, both its Will and Wits are temporarily lowered by 2 points each. Fierce lasts for 1d12 Rounds, and while in this state, the creature is immune to all Fear Tests and ignores any modifiers associated with lost Vitality. As soon as the Fierce state passes, the creature's Abilities return to normal, and the boosted Vitality disappears.

**Cost:** 3

## Flight

The creature is able to fly, whether due to having wings or some ability to make its body lighter than air.

**Cost:** 2 (Wings), 4 (Body Change), 6 (Magical)

## Frailty (Drawback)

The creature's body is particularly vulnerable to the ravages of poison, disease, heat, and other ailments. It also has trouble stabilizing when it is severely wounded. The creature takes a –2 penalty on all Toughness Tests, including Tests made to heal or stabilize after unconsciousness.

**Bonus Points Provided:** 2

## Gaze

The creature is able to cause damage with just a look. This ability has a range, and in order to use it, the creature must make a Successful Quickness Test. Damage and the gaze's effects vary from creature to creature, and are detailed in the description for each creature with this ability.

**Cost:** 2

## Gills

The creature possesses a set of gills allowing it to draw oxygen out of water. The gills appear on its neck, chest or back (near the windpipe or lungs). Consequently, the creature can breathe both in and out of water, and never has to worry about the possibility of drowning.

**Cost:** 1

## Glider

The creature has fleshy flaps that allow it to glide on wind currents. The creature may glide through the air as though flying, but only while descending in altitude. For every 20 feet in altitude that it descends, the creature may move 80 feet horizontally. Thus, if it leaps off a 40-foot tall structure, it may glide horizontally for 240 feet. If a updraft is caught, the creature is able to continue gliding.

**Cost:** 2

## Gore

The creature is able to use tusks or horns to attack an opponent, and does Quickness+1 in damage.

**Cost:** 1

## Head Butt

The creature's skull is thick, allowing it to use its head as an effective weapon. The damage a Head Butt causes is equal to Toughness.

**Cost:** 1

## Heat/Cold Susceptibility (Drawback)

The creature's body does not react well to particularly hot or cold temperatures. The creature takes double damage from prolonged exposure to extreme heat or cold, as well as weapons, spells and the like.

**Bonus Points Provided:** 1

## Horrific Visage

The creature has a terrifying appearance, and those looking upon it are struck with fear that shakes their resolve. This ability is always "on", meaning that whenever the Heroes comes into contact with the creature, they are affected by the creature's appearance. The effect of this Horrific Visage is such that the opponent must make a Will Test, with Failure causing them to lose 1 Sanity (4 Sanity on a Dramatic Failure).

**Cost:** 5

## Horns

The creature has either a single horn or a set of horns that it is able to use as a weapon. The damage caused by Horns is Brawn+1.

**Cost:** 1

## Hug/Squeeze

This ability allows a creature to damage an opponent by squeezing or hugging them (either by enfolding the Hero in its arms, coiling around them with its body, or any other physical means it can use to squeeze them). In order to use this ability, the creature must make a successful Brawl Test to grab its opponent. Those trapped can try to break out by making a successful Brawn Test. For every round trapped in the hug or grip of the creature, the opponent suffers a cumulative -1 to the Test. For example, if the opponent has been in the hug for 3 Rounds he would suffer a -3 to the Test. The damage from this ability is equal to the creature's Brawn + Toughness.

**Cost:** 2

## Hypersensitivity

The creature is particularly sensitive to its surroundings, and gains a +2 bonus on Investigation and Observe Tests.

**Cost:** 2

## Infernal

This ability is usually found in creatures that originate from Otherworldly realms, called the Infernal Realms, and confers to the creature an aura of evil that requires all within 10 feet of it to make a Fear Test. Upon failing this Test, the person feels uncomfortable, as well as having a desire to flee as quickly as possible. Infernal creatures are immune to normal weapons, but weapons that have been blessed by a religious figure cause them double damage.

**Cost:** 6

## Immunity

Creatures with Immunity suffer no damage when they come into contact with whatever it is to which they are immune. For example, if the creature is immune to Fire, it suffers no damage from fires, no matter how hot they are, or if attacked by a fire-based weapon or from spells of fire.

**Cost:** 4 per Immunity

## Invisibility

The creature has the ability to become Invisible, and an invisible creature gains a +2 to its Initiative and is at a -4 TN to be Hit. Creatures with this Trait can remain Invisible for a number of Rounds equal their Will.

**Cost:** 3

## Insubstantial

Insubstantial is the ability that allows the creature to shift its body from a solid state to a gaseous or ghostly state. In this state, all physical attacks pass through the creature harmlessly, causing no damage. In addition, while in this state, the creature is unable to make any physical attacks.

**Cost:** 4

## Kick

The creature causes damage by kicking. The damage is equal to Brawn +2.

**Cost:** 1

## Leaper

The creature gains the ability to leap incredible distances. The creature gains a +5 bonus on all Athletics (Jump) Tests or any other Tests where the GM rules that this Trait has bearing. The distance a creature is able to jump is equal to its Brawn x 2 feet.

**Cost:** 1

## Lethargy (Drawback)

The creature has trouble reacting quickly to danger. Consequently, it suffers a –2 TN to all Quickness or Quickness-based Tests.

**Bonus Points Provided:** 3

## Light Sensitivity (Drawback)

The creature's eyes are unable to adjust to bright light. Abrupt exposure to bright light (such as sunlight) blinds the creature for 10 Rounds, and it suffers

a –1 TN on attacks, Investigation Tests, and Observe Tests as long as it remains in the brightly lit area.

**Bonus Points Provided:** 1

## Manifest

The creature is able to enter into the physical world and allows insubstantial creatures to make physical attacks.

**Cost:** 3

## Mindslave (Drawback)

The creature has certain mental deficiencies that make it harder to resist mind-influencing effects. It suffers a –2 TN on all Will or Resist Tests.

**Bonus Points Provided:** 1

## Moan

The creature has a voice, roar or growl that it uses against an opponent, causing damage. In order to use its moan, the creature needs to make a successful Quickness Test.

**Cost:** 3 (10' Range), 4 (20' Range), 5 (30' Range), 6 (40' Range)

## Natural Armor

The creature possesses some type of natural armor that makes it harder to injure. The creature gains the number of points of AV that function exactly like other types of artificial armor.

**Cost:** 1 per point of AV

## Natural Armor Penalty (Drawback)

The creature is particularly susceptible to attacks. A creature or species with this drawback suffers more damage from attacks directed against it than usual. Creatures with this trait generally cannot possess the Natural Armor trait (see above).

**Bonus Points Provided:** 1 per additional point of damage per successful attack (maximum 10). Cost is halved if it works against a single type of attack.

## Night Vision

The creature is able to see in the dark as easily as it sees in full daylight, and ignores all penalties while fighting in the dark.

**Cost:** 1

## Poison

The creature is poisonous – be if it produces venom, poisonous saliva or secretes poison – and causes damage to an opponent because of this poisonous nature. Unless noted otherwise, this type of poison is natural in nature. Anyone successfully hit by a poisonous creature must make a successful opposed Toughness Test or will be poisoned, and will take damage equal to the Degree of Success. Poison can be secreted, spit or administered via bite. They could be be poisoned by a stinger, touching the skin, or some other such means.

**Cost:** 2

## Plasm

The creature is able to tap into a source of power outside the scope of men, that fuels its abilities. This power, once drained, ends the creature's hold and ties to the physical world, and it must rest to regain more Plasm. When creatures with Plasm manifest in the physical world, they expend Plasm. Every Round the creature is in the physical realm, it costs them 1 Plasm. Once the creature's Plasm is reduced to 0, they leave the physical realm and return to their home realm, and must rest while they regain their Plasm. Depending on how many Creature Points are spent, this resting period can be in Rounds, Hours or Days, and Plasm is regained at a rate equal to the creature's Will.

Calculating a creature's Plasm is determined in Step 5, below.

**Cost:** 8 (Plasm regained in Days), 10 (Plasm regained in Hours), 12 (Plasm regained in Rounds)

## Prehensile Tail

The creature possesses a tail that can grasp and hold objects. A Prehensile Tail grants a +2 TN to Acrobatics Tests. It also allows the creature to grasp and manipulate a small, simple object, such as a dagger. A Prehensile Tail cannot be used to operate a piece of equipment that requires opposable digits or fine motor control. A creature can "hang" from its Prehensile Tail indefinitely by wrapping it around a larger object, thereby freeing up its other limbs. The Prehensile Tail is not dexterous or strong enough to fire ranged weapons or to make melee attacks. However, it can be used to make Hug/Squeeze attacks.

Creatures cannot possess both a Prehensile Tail and the Tail Trait (see below).

**Cost:** 2

## Rejuvenation

The creature is able to heal damage suffered, and regrow lost limbs. Creatures with this Trait can regain 1d12 Vitality as an action. To regrow a missing limb takes 1d12 days to regrow.

**Cost:** 6

## Second Wind

The creature can shrug off minor wounds with ease. Once per day, the creature can heal itself of a number of points of Vitality damage equal to its Toughness score.

**Cost:** 1

## Scent

The creature possesses an acute sense of smell, allowing it to track prey with ease. Creatures with this ability are able to smell an opponent within a 40-foot range. If upwind, the distance is doubled, and if downwind, the distance is halved. The range can be increased for each additional point spent.

**Cost:** 2 +1 Point for each 10-foot increment (maximum of 100 feet)

## Shift

Through magical means or by creating a rift or portal, the creature is able to shift its position by 5 feet as an Action. Shifting requires a Will Test, with success allowing the creature to shift. A Dramatic Success allows the creature to shift 10 feet. Failing the Test means the creature does not shift, and a Dramatic Failure causes the creature to lose 5 Vitality or Taint.

**Cost:** 4

## Size

The creature is larger than most. Size has a scale starting at 1, and progressing up to 12. As a creature gets larger, there is an effect on the creature such that they become stronger and heartier, but slower. In addition, if a creature reaches extremely large sizes, it becomes slower in thought as well, thus suffering Wits reductions. The following table shows the effect of Size.

**Cost:** 5 for each Size.

**Table 10:2 Sizes**

| Size | Height | Effect |
|---|---|---|
| -6 | 2" | -6 Brawn, +6 Quickness |
| -5 | 4" | -5 Brawn, +5 Quickness |
| -4 | 6" | -4 Brawn, +4 Quickness |
| -3 | 1' | -3 Brawn, +3 Quickness |
| -2 | 2' | -2 Brawn, +2 Quickness |
| -1 | 4' | -1 Brawn, +1 Quickness |
| 0 | Normal Height 6' | nil |
| 1 | +8' | +1 Brawn |
| 2 | +10' | +2 Brawn, +1 Toughness, -1 Quickness |
| 3 | +12' | +2 Brawn, +2 Toughness, -2 Quickness, -1 Wits |
| 4 | +16' | +3 Brawn, +2 Toughness, -2 Quickness, -1 Wits |
| 5 | +20' | +3 Brawn, +3 Toughness, -3 Quickness, -2 Wits |
| 6 | +24' | +4 Brawn, +3 Toughness, -3 Quickness, -2 Wits |
| 7 | +28' | +4 Brawn, +4 Toughness, -4 Quickness, -3 Wits |
| 8 | +32' | +5 Brawn, +4 Toughness, -4 Quickness, -3 Wits |
| 9 | +36' | +5 Brawn, +5 Toughness, -5 Quickness, -4 Wits |
| 10 | +40' | +6 Brawn, +5 Toughness, -5 Quickness, -4 Wits |
| 11 | +44' | +6 Brawn, +6 Toughness, -6 Quickness, -5 Wits |
| 12 | +48' | +7 Brawn, +6 Toughness, -6 Quickness, -5 Wits |

## Spawn

The creature is able to create creatures of the same type, thus if a vampire choose, they can create a new vampire through draining a human of all their blood. This can be done via a bite, some set of circumstances, or other means detailed in the creature's description.

**Cost:** 10

## Speed

The creature is extremely fast, giving it the ability to chase down an opponent, or allowing it to have quicker reaction times. Creatures with this Trait gain a +1 to their Initiative Tests, as well as double their movement.

**Cost:** 4

## Spellcaster

The creature is able to work magic, and has at least one Spell it is able to perform. Creatures that have Taint or Plasm fuel their spells with either Taint or Plasm, and not Vitality. In the case of Arcane Spells, creatures fuel the Sanity cost with Resolve.

**Cost:** 8 (Per Common Spell), 10 (Per Arcane Spell)

## Spirit Animal

Creatures with this Trait gain a +1 bonus to all Abilities (Brawn, Quickness, etc.). In addition, they are immune to Fear, and will aid all creatures within 10 feet of them by granting a +1 Bonus to all Fear Tests.

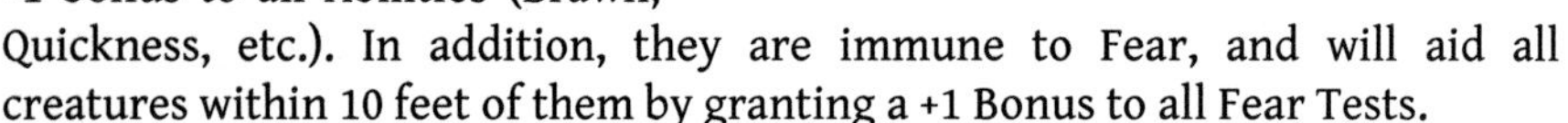

**Cost:** 8

## Stench

The creature has a terrible odor. This smell is so powerful that it makes contact with the creature troublesome, and any within hand-to-hand range of the creature suffer a -1 to all Tests.

**Cost:** 3 (-1 to all Tests), 5 (-2 to all Tests), 7 (-3 to all Tests), 9 (-4 to all Tests), 11 (-5 to all Tests), 13 (-6 to all Tests)

## Stomp

Creatures with this ability are able to stomp creatures smaller then themselves, and cause damage equal to their Toughness x 5 due to their immense size. For example, a creature Size 5 and with 10 Toughness is able to do 50 points of damage to any creature smaller than Size 5. In order to have this Trait, the creature must also have the Size Trait (see above). In addition, Stomp can only be used against creatures that are at least 2 Ranks smaller than the creature in question.

**Cost:** 6

## Swarm

Creatures that Swarm are different from individual creatures. The Wits of the creatures that are in a Swarm gives weaker creatures a chance to stand up to tougher creatures. Creatures that Swarm have Vitality, and in addition, creatures that Swarm cause damage based on their numbers; this damage takes into account their normal means of attack and the like.

**Cost:** 4 for every 25 creatures; thus, for a 100-creature Swarm, the cost is 16 Points

**Table 10:3 Swarming Creatures**

| Number of Creatures | Damage | Vitality |
|---|---|---|
| 1-25 | 1d12 Damage | 25 |
| 26-50 | 2d12 Damage | 50 |
| 51-75 | 3d12 Damage | 75 |
| 76-100 | 4d12 Damage | 100 |

## Tail

The creature possesses a thick Tail. This Tail may be fur-covered, slender, and whip-like or scaly like that of a lizard. Although the Tail improves the creature's balance and can serve as a weapon, it cannot be used for gripping objects. The Tail provides a +2 TN to all Acrobatics Tests. A creature that already has the Prehensile Tail feature cannot gain this Trait.

**Cost:** 1

## Taint

Infernal creatures have Taint, which is the evil of the creature that seeps into the natural world. Taint fuels the Infernal creatures when they manifest in the physical world, and also serves as their Vitality. Once the creature runs out of Taint, it is forced to leave the physical world and return to its native plane where it must "rest" for a number of days equal to its Will. In addition, it costs Taint to stay in the physical world, and every minute an Infernal creature must expend 1 Taint to stay fixed in the physical world.

Calculating a creature's Taint is determined in **Step 5**, below.

**Cost:** 8

## Telekinesis

The creature is able to move objects without touching them, using the power of its mind or personality. The creature is able to move a number of objects equal to its Will, and furthermore, the creature can move up to (Will times 10) lbs. in weight. This weight can either be one object or a number of objects that equal this total weight. Objects can also be moved a number of feet equal to Toughness+ d12; if used as a weapon, an object does damage equal to the creature's Will.

**Cost:** 9

## Thermal Vision

The creature is able to see in the dark due to being able to see various heat sources and the like. This trait cannot be taken with Night Vision.

**Cost:** 1

## Thick Fur Coat

The creature possesses a thick, protective layer of fur over its body. The creature gains a +4 TN on Tests against extreme cold temperatures. In addition, the creature has AV 5 because of the fur, and they cannot take Natural Armor due to the Thick Fur Coat.

**Cost:** 1

## Undead

The creature is Undead, and because of this, it is immune to smoke, heat and cold, and cannot die from suffocation. Furthermore, creatures that are Undead are immune to diseases, poison and Fear. Since they are already dead, these creatures do not breathe, and are thus immune to drowning. That does not mean they are immune to physical attacks, however, and they suffer damage normally.

**Cost:** 8

## Unfathomable

This ability is a special one, and is not easily defined by any of the other traits. Creatures with this ability have it noted in their written description, where it is explained and the game mechanics are detailed. **Cost:** Between 1 and 10

## Wall Crawler

The creature is able to walk on walls and cling to ceilings like a spider. It has tiny barbs on its hands and feet to facilitate climbing, and its fingers and toes secrete a transparent adhesive that allows the creature to cling to smooth surfaces. As long as the creature's hands and feet are uncovered, it can climb perfectly smooth, flat, vertical surfaces. In addition, the creature gains a +3 TN on all Athletics (Climb) Tests.

**Cost:** 1

## Weakness

The creature has a weakness, be it fire, holy water or even direct sunlight. When in contact with or exposed to its weakness, the creature suffers double damage when being attacked by it.

**Bonus Points Provided:** 1 per weakness

## Weak Immune System (Drawback)

The creature's body is weaker than usual, and it has difficulty preventing infections from entering its system; thus, it is prone to sickness and disease. The creature suffers -2 TN to all Toughness Tests to resist the effects of poison, disease, and sickness.

**Bonus Points Provided:** 1

## Webbed Digits

The creature possesses webbing between its fingers and/or toes, and can move more easily through liquids. The creature gains +3 TN on all Athletics (Swim)

Tests. Having webbed digits does not interfere with the creature's ability to grasp or manipulate objects.

**Bonus Point Cost:** 1

## Step 4: Purchase Skills with Skill Points

As is the case with characters, creatures have Sills. Skills tend to be along the lines Brawl, Defend, Dodge and the like, but it is not uncommon for creatures to have Stealth, Survival, and others at the Gamemaster's discretion.

## Step 5: Calculate Plasm, Taint or Vitality, and Initiative Rating

All creatures have Vitality, Plasm or Taint (see above), as well as Initiative Rating. These are calculated in a manner similar to that used to determine these Derived Abilities for player characters. Refer to **Table 10:4** for how to calculate them.

**TABLE 10:4 CALCULATING PLASM, TAINT, VITALITY, AND INITIATIVE RATING**

Plasm = Will × 5
Taint = Will × 5
Vitality = [(Brawl + Toughness) ÷2] × 5
D12 + [(Quickness + Wits) ÷ 2] +/- modifiers = Initiative Rating

## Step 6: Assign Hook

Just like with Characters, Creatures have Hooks. Hooks for creatures work pretty much the same way as it does for the characters (see **Shadow, Sword & Spell: Basic** for the rules on Hooks). The only difference is that they can play the Hook once during the combat.

## Step 7: Pit Creature Against Player Characters

Now's the fun part, of course, using the creature against the players and their characters. Go to it, and enjoy!

# 11

## Creatures Great & Small

The following creatures are ready to use. All you need to add is one Hook.

### Basilisk

| Brawn 8 | Quickness 10 | Toughness 8 | Wits 7 | Will 11 |
| --- | --- | --- | --- | --- |
| Resolve 55 | Vitality 57 | | | |

**Skills:** Brawl [+10], Dodge [+10]

**Traits:**

- *Breath*: Fire [DV 2(30), R 5/15/30, ROF 1/1]
- *Claws:* Claws do d12+Quickness damage.
- *Fierce*: The Basilisk is naturally aggressive, and tends to becomes angry when threatened. The Basilisk must make a Will Test once it takes damage. If the Test is failed, the Basilisk becomes enraged. As a result, its Brawn and Toughness are temporarily raised by 2 points each, and its Vitality is temporarily increased by 15 Points. In addition, both its Will and Wits are temporarily reduced by 2 points each. Fierce lasts for 1d12 Rounds, and while in this state, the Basilisk is immune to all Fear Tests, and ignores any modifiers associated with lost Vitality. As soon as the Fierce state passes, the Basilisk's Abilities return to normal, and the boosted Vitality disappears.
- *Fear -4*: The Basilisk is able to cause Fear in its targets. The Fear modifier is applied to a target's Will Test when they make a Fear Test.

- *Gaze*: R 50', ROF 1/1, successful hit, target must make a Toughness Test, with Failure resulting in their being paralyzed for 1 day, Dramatic Failure target dies.
- *Moan — Hiss*: Effective only against animals, any animal within a 50-foot radius of the Basilisk must make a Toughness Test, with Failure causing them to lose half their Vitality, and a Dramatic Failure causes them to instantly die.
- *Weakness — Weasels*: A weasel's attacks cause double damage.

The Basilisk looks like a rooster, with the tail of a snake. A fierce creature, it is a danger to all life, and has been known to attack with no regard for itself or its surroundings. Like the scorpion, it prefers dry places, and thus they are native to The Shimmering Sands. Though some think this creature is able to turn a person to stone, that is just a myth. A Basilisk is hatched from a cock's egg — a rare occurrence — and they are susceptible to the attacks of weasels.

# Chimaera

Brawn 11 Quickness 10 Toughness 12 Wits 7 Will 11
Resolve 55 Vitality 57

**Skills:** Brawl [+14]

**Traits:**

- *Bite*: Bite does d12+Brawn damage.
- *Breath — Fire:* [DV 6(90), R 10/15/20, ROF 1/1]
- *Claws:* Claws do d12+Quickness damage.
- *Fear -3*: The Chimaera is able to cause Fear in its targets. The Fear modifier is applied to a target's Will Test when they make a Fear Test.
- *Fierce*: The Chimaera is naturally aggressive and angry when threatened. The Chimaera must make a Will Test once it takes damage. If the Test is failed, the Chimaera becomes enraged. As a result, its Brawn and Toughness are temporarily raised by 2 points each, and its Vitality is temporarily increased by 15 Points. In addition, both its Will and Wits are temporarily reduced by 2 points each. Fierce lasts for 1d12 Rounds, and while in this state, the Chimaera is immune to all Fear Tests and ignores any modifiers associated with lost Vitality. As soon as the Fierce state passes, the Chimaera's Abilities return to normal, and the boosted Vitality disappears.

With the head of a lion, a goat's body and a serpent's tail, the Chimaera is a female monster which Alchemists have been known to create. These monsters are thankfully rare, nor do they occur naturally. However, rumors persist that these creatures abound in Nipur and roam freely.

# Deep One

Brawn 9 Quickness 10 Toughness 7 Wits 7 Will 6

Resolve 30 Vitality 40

**Skills:** Athletics — Swim [+13/+14], Brawl [+10], Defend [+11], Melee [+13]

**Traits:**

- *Bite*: Bite does d12+Brawn damage.
- *Claws:* Claws do d12+Quickness damage.
- *Fear -1*: Deep Ones are able to cause Fear in their targets. The Fear modifier is applied to a target's Will Test when they make a Fear Test.
- *Fierce*: Deep Ones are naturally aggressive and becomes angry when threatened. Deep Ones must make a Will Test once they takes damage. If the Test is failed, the Deep One becomes enraged. As a result, its Brawn and Toughness are temporarily raised by 2 points each, and its Vitality is temporarily increased by 15 Points. In addition, both its Will and Wits are temporarily reduced by 2 points each. Fierce lasts for 1d12 Rounds, and while in this state, Deep Ones are immune to all Fear Tests and ignores any modifiers associated with lost Vitality. As soon as the Fierce state passes, the Deep One's Abilities return to normal, and the boosted Vitality disappears.
- *Gills:* The Deep Ones possess a set of gills allowing them to draw oxygen out of water. The gills appear on their necks, chests, or backs (near the windpipe or lungs). Consequently, the Deep Ones can breathe both in and out of water, and never have to worry about the possibility of drowning.
- *Horrific Visage: Deep Ones* have a terrifying appearance, and those looking upon them are struck with fear that shakes their resolve. This Trait is always "on", meaning that whenever your Hero comes into contact with a Deep One, she is affected by the creature's appearance. The effect of this Horrific Visage is such that the opponent must make a Will Test, with Failure causing her to lose 1 Sanity (4 Sanity on a Dramatic Failure).

Grayish-green in color, Deep Ones dwell in the seas, where they worship their dark God, and terrorize those living along the shoreline. Human in size, their heads resemble that of a fish, and their bulging eyes protrude from the sides of their heads.

# Demons

Demons are one of the most powerful and vile creatures in existence today. They are the embodiment of evil, and exist outside the Natural World, and call a different dimensional plane home. Demons manifest in the Natural World in one of two ways, either through a rift or dimensional portal, or by the means of being summoned. Demons are forces of nature that are tied to one of the elements.

## Demon, Air

Brawn 6 Quickness 13 Toughness 9 Wits 10 Will 9

Resolve 45 Taint 45

**Skills:** Brawl [+7], Lore [+10], Resist [+11], Spell — Quicken [+12], Sense [+11], Spell — Refresh [+10], Spell – Air Bolt [+13], Stealth [+15]

**Traits:**

- *Fear -4*: Able to cause Fear in its targets. The Fear modifier is applied to a target's Will Test when they make a Fear Test.
- I*nfernal*: Demons originate from a set of otherworldly realms, called Infernal Realms, and this confers to the Demon an aura of evil that requires all within 10 feet of it to make a Fear Test. Upon failing this Test, the person feels uncomfortable, as well as having a desire to get away as quickly as possible. Air Demons are immune to normal weapons, but weapons that have been blessed by a religious figure cause them double damage.

- *Insubstantial*: This Trait allows the Demon to shift its body from a solid state to a gaseous one. In this state, all physical attacks pass through the Demon harmlessly, causing no damage. In addition, while in this state, the Demon is unable to make any physical attacks.
- *Manifest*: The Demon is able to enter into the physical world, and this allows it to make physical attacks.

- *Spellcaster*: The Demon is able to work magic, and has at least one Spell it is able to perform. The Demon fuels its spells with Taint, and not Vitality. In the case of Arcane Spells, the Demon fuels the Sanity costs with Resolve.
- *Taint:* The Demon has Taint, which is the evil of the creature that seeps into the natural world. Taint fuels the Demon when it manifests in the physical world, and also serves to act as its Vitality. Once the Demon runs out of Taint, it is forced to leave the physical world and return to its native plane, where it must "rest" for a number of days equal to its Will. In addition, it costs Taint to stay in the physical world, and every minute the Demon must expend 1 Taint to stay fixed in the physical world.

Air Demons are known for their ability to hide, and are often employed by more powerful Demons as assassins and spies. Air Demons are human-like, ranging in height between six and seven feet. Slight in build, many feel they are weaker than they appear at first glance. Air Demons have an easier time passing as humans, except for the fact that their skin is white. Air Demons are schemers who work to upset the balance as much as they can.

## Demon, Earth

Brawn 10 Quickness 5 Toughness 11 Wits 11 Will 7

Resolve 35 Taint 55

**Skills:** Brawl [+12], Intimidate [+13], Lore [+7], Sense [+7], Spell – Produce Element [+8], Spell – Earth Bolt [+10], Stealth [+5]

**Traits:**

- *Fear -4*: Able to cause Fear in its targets. The Fear modifier is applied to a target's Will Test when they make a Fear Test.
- *Head Butt*: The Demon's skull is thick, allowing it to use its head as an effective weapon. The damage the Head Butt causes is equal to Toughness.
- Hug: This Trait allows the Earth Demon to damage an opponent by squeezing or hugging them (either by enfolding the Hero in its arms, coiling around them with its body, or any other physical means it can use to Squeeze them). In order to use this ability, the Earth Demon must make a successful Brawl Test to grab its opponent. Those trapped can attempt to break out by making a successful Brawn Test. For every Round trapped in the grasp of the Earth Demon, the target suffers a cumulative -1 to the Test. For example, if the target has been

in the hug for 3 Rounds, she would suffer a -3 to the Test. The damage from this Trait is equal to the creature's Brawn + Toughness.

- I*nfernal*: This ability is usually found in creatures that originate from otherworldly realms, called Infernal Realms, and confers to the creature an aura of evil that requires all within 10 feet of it to make a Fear Test. Upon failing this Test, the person feels uncomfortable, as well as having a desire to get away as quickly as possible. Infernal creatures are immune to normal weapons, but weapons that have been blessed by a religious figure cause them double damage.
- *Insubstantial*: Insubstantial is the ability that allows the creature to shift its body from a solid state to a gaseous state. In this state, all physical attacks pass through the creature harmlessly, causing no damage. In addition, while in this state, the creature is unable to make any physical attacks.
- *Manifest*: The creature is able to enter into the physical world and allows insubstantial creatures to make physical attacks.
- *Spellcaster*: The creature is able to work magic, and has at least one Spell it is able to perform. Creatures fuel their spells with Taint , and in the case of Arcane Spells, creatures fuel the Sanity cost with Resolve.
- *Taint:* Infernal creatures have Taint, which is the evil of the creature that seeps into the natural world. Taint fuels the Infernal creatures when they manifest in the physical world. Taint fuels Infernal creatures as well as acting as their Vitality. Once the creature runs out of Taint, they are forced to leave the physical world and return to their native plane where they must "rest" for a number of days equal to their Will. In addition, it costs Taint to stay in the physical world, and every minute an Infernal creature must expend 1 Taint to stay fixed in the physical world.

Earth Demons are seen as being slow-witted tools usable by the more intelligent Demons. The truth is, that while Earth Demons can be slow, they are as intelligent as any other Demon. Standing close to eight feet in height, their bodies resemble rock piles, which they use to their advantage. Earth Demons are cunning; they use the prejudices others have about them against their opponents, which often gives them the advantage.

# Demon, Fire

Brawn 5 Quickness 10 Toughness 10 Wits 11 Will 12

Resolve 55 Taint 60

**Skills:** Resist [+12], Spell — Produce Element [+11], Spell — Ball, Fire [+13], Spell - Burn [+11]

**Traits:**

- *Breath — Fire*: Successful Quickness Test to hit their target. The range of the Demon's flames is 50 feet, and the fires have a Damage Value of 2(30)]
- *Fear -4*: Able to cause Fear in its targets. The Fear modifier is applied to a target's Will Test when they make a Fear Test.
- I*nfernal*: This ability is usually found in creatures that originate from otherworldly realms, called Infernal Realms, and confers to the creature an aura of evil that requires all within 10 feet of it to make a Fear Test. Upon failing this Test, the person feels uncomfortable, as well as having a desire to get away as quickly as possible. Infernal creatures are immune to normal weapons, but weapons that have been blessed by a religious figure cause them double damage.
- *Insubstantial*: Insubstantial is the ability that allows the creature to shift its body from a solid state to a gaseous state. In this state, all physical attacks pass through the creature harmlessly, causing no damage. In addition, while in this state, the creature is unable to make any physical attacks.
- *Manifest*: The creature is able to enter into the physical world and allows insubstantial creatures to make physical attacks.
- *Spellcaster*: The creature is able to work magic, and has at least one Spell it is able to perform. Creatures fuel their spells with Taint and Arcane Spells, creatures fuel the Sanity cost with Resolve.
- *Taint:* Infernal creatures have Taint, which is the evil of the creature that seeps into the natural world. Taint fuels the Infernal creatures when they manifest in the physical world. Taint fuels Infernal creatures as well as acting as their Vitality. Once the creature runs out of Taint, they are forced to leave the physical world and return to their native plane where they must "rest" for a number of days equal to their Will. In addition, it costs Taint to stay in the physical world, and every minute an Infernal creature must expend 1 Taint to stay fixed in the physical world.

Fire Demons are the least refined Demons. They burn with rage and delight in causing as much harm as they possibly can. These Demons resemble flames, and never assume a human appearance.

## Demon, Water

Brawn 8 Quickness 11 Toughness 10 Wits 7 Will 10

Resolve 50 Taint 50

**Skills:** Brawl [+10], Sense [+9], Spell — Bolt, Water [+9], Spell — Produce Element [+8], Stealth [+12]

**Traits:**

- *Fear -4*: Able to cause Fear in its targets. The Fear modifier is applied to a target's Will Test when she makes a Fear Test.
- Hug: This ability allows a creature to damage an opponent by squeezing or hugging them (either by enfolding the Hero in its arms, coiling around them with its body, or any other physical means it can use to Squeeze them). In order to use this ability, the creature must make a successful Brawl Test to grab its opponent. Those trapped can try to break out by making a successful Brawn Test. For every round trapped in the hug of the creature, the opponent suffers a cumulative -1 to the Test. For example, if the opponent has been in the hug for 3 Rounds he would suffer a -3 to the Test. The damage from this ability is equal to the creature's Brawn + Toughness.
- I*nfernal*: This ability is usually found in creatures that originate from otherworldly realms, called Infernal Realms, and confers to the creature an aura of evil that requires all within 10 feet of it to make a Fear Test. Upon failing this Test, the person feels uncomfortable, as well as having a desire to get away as quickly as possible. Infernal creatures are immune to normal weapons, but weapons that have been blessed by a religious figure cause them double damage. Sense [+9],
- *Insubstantial*: Insubstantial is the ability that allows the creature to shift its body from a solid state to a gaseous state. In this state, all physical attacks pass through the creature harmlessly, causing no damage. In addition, while in this state, the creature is unable to make any physical attacks.
- *Manifest*: The creature is able to enter into the physical world and allows insubstantial creatures to make physical attacks.

- *Spellcaster*: The creature is able to work magic, and has at least one Spell it is able to perform. Creatures fuel their spells with Taint and Arcane Spells, creatures fuel the Sanity cost with Resolve.
- *Taint:* Infernal creatures have Taint, which is the evil of the creature that seeps into the natural world. Taint fuels the Infernal creatures when they manifest in the physical world. Taint fuels Infernal creatures as well as acting as their Vitality. Once the creature runs out of Taint, they are forced to leave the physical world and return to their native plane where they must "rest" for a number of days equal to their Will. In addition, it costs Taint to stay in the physical world, and every minute an Infernal creature must expend 1 Taint to stay fixed in the physical world.

Water Demons have been relegated to the lowest rungs of the Demonic hierarchy. Having been pushed so low angers them, and they want nothing more than to overthrow the current social order and place themselves at the top. Water Demons resemble waves in form, and have no human-like features.

# Devil

The enemies of demons, devils are tempters and take pleasure in bringing harm to all.

## Flock of Death

Brawn 5 Quickness 13 Toughness 5 Wits 10 Will 11
Resolve 55 Vitality 55

**Skills:** Brawl [+8], Dodge [+13], Observe [+11], Sense [+13], Track [+12]

**Traits:**

- *Claws*: The Flock of Death has nasty claws, that are what they imply; they cause damage. The damage Claws cause is d12+Quickness.
- *Damage Reduction*: The Flock of Death takes half damage from all attacks involving heat and fire.
- *Fear -2*: Able to cause Fear in its targets. The Fear modifier is applied to a target's Will Test when they make a Fear Test.
- *Flight*: The Flock of Death is able to fly, due to having wings.
- I*nfernal*: This ability is usually found in creatures that originate from otherworldly realms, called Infernal Realms, and confers to the creature an aura of evil that requires all within 10 feet of it to make a Fear Test. Upon failing this Test, the person feels uncomfortable, as well as having a desire to get away as quickly as possible. Infernal creatures are immune to normal weapons, but weapons that have been blessed by a religious figure cause them double damage.
- *Manifest*: The creature is able to enter into the physical world and allows insubstantial creatures to make physical attacks. [See the changes for this as per the Air Demon, and incorporate them.
- *Scent*: The Flock of Death possesses an acute sense of smell, allowing it to track its prey with ease. The Flock can smell an opponent within an 80-foot range. If upwind, the distance is 160 – feet, and if downwind, the range is 40 feet.
- *Shift:* Through magical means, or by creating a rift the Flock of Death is able to shift its position by 5 feet as an Action. This Shift requires a Will Test, with success allowing the Flock of Death to shift. Dramatic Success allows it to shift 10 feet. Failing the Test means the Flock does not shift, and a Dramatic Failure causes the Flock to lose 5 Taint.
- *Taint:* Infernal creatures have Taint, which is the evil of the creature that seeps into the natural world. Taint fuels the Infernal creatures

when they manifest in the physical world. Taint fuels Infernal creatures as well as acting as their Vitality. Once the creature runs out of Taint, they are forced to leave the physical world and return to their native plane where they must "rest" for a number of days equal to their Will. In addition, it costs Taint to stay in the physical world, and every minute an Infernal creature must expend 1 Taint to stay fixed in the physical world.

The hunters and trackers of Hell, the Flock of Death are creatures that resemble hairless eagles. Averaging about 5-feet in width, their wingspan typically measures 14-feet in length.

## Horned One

| Brawn 13 | Quickness 10 | Toughness 13 | Wits 6 | Will 12 |
|---|---|---|---|---|
| Resolve 60 | Vitality 60 | | | |

**Skills:** Brawl [+14], Defend [+11], Intimidation [+10], Resist [+10], Sense [+9]

**Traits:**

- *Bite*: The Bite of a Horned One causes damage. The damage inflicted is d12+Brawn.
- *Claws*: The Claws of a Horned One cause damage. The damage inflicted is d12+Quickness.
- *Damage Reduction*: Horned Ones takes half damage from all attacks involving heat and fire.
- *Fear -2*: Able to cause Fear in its targets. The Fear modifier is applied to a target's Will Test when she makes a Fear Test.
- *Fierce*: Horned One's are naturally aggressive or becomes angry when threatened. Creatures with this ability must make a Will Test once they takes damage. If the Test is failed, the chimaera becomes enraged. As a result, its Brawn and Toughness are temporarily raised by 2 points each, and its Vitality is temporarily

increased by 15 Points. In addition, both its Will and Wits are temporarily reduced by 2 points each. Fierce lasts for 1d12 Rounds, and while in this state, Horned One's are immune to all Fear Tests and ignores any modifiers associated with lost Vitality. As soon as the Fierce state passes, Horned One's Abilities return to normal, and the boosted Vitality disappears.

- *Gore*: The Horned One is able to use its horns to attack an opponent, and does Brawn+1 in damage.
- *Horns*: The Horned One has a set of horns that it is able to use as a weapon. The damage caused by its Horns is Brawn+1.
- I*nfernal*: This ability is usually found in creatures that originate from otherworldly realms, called Infernal Realms, and confers to the creature an aura of evil that requires all within 10 feet of it to make a Fear Test. Upon failing this Test, the person feels uncomfortable, as well as having a desire to get away as quickly as possible. Infernal creatures are immune to normal weapons, but weapons that have been blessed by a religious figure cause them double damage.
- *Manifest*: The creature is able to enter into the physical world and allows insubstantial creatures to make physical attacks.
- *Natural Armor*: The Horned One possesses natural armor giving it AV 10.
- *Taint:* Infernal creatures have Taint, which is the evil of the creature that seeps into the natural world. Taint fuels the Infernal creatures when they manifest in the physical world. Taint fuels Infernal creatures as well as acting as their Vitality. Once the creature runs out of Taint, they are forced to leave the physical world and return to their native plane where they must "rest" for a number of days equal to their Will. In addition, it costs Taint to stay in the physical world, and every minute an Infernal creature must expend 1 Taint to stay fixed in the physical world.

These devils are the foot soldiers of Hell. They are vicious and enjoy fighting. Standing at just 6' in height, their bodies are covered with bony plates and their heads resemble those of a ram.

# Tormentor

Brawn 13 Quickness 9 Toughness 13 Wits 11 Will 13

Resolve 65 Vitality 65

**Skills:** Brawl [+14], Defend [+11], Intimidation [+14], Melee [+14], Tactics [+14]

**Traits:**

- *Fear -5*: Able to cause Fear in its targets. The Fear modifier is applied to a target's Will Test when they make a Fear Test.
- *Fierce*: Tormentor's are naturally aggressive or becomes angry when threatened. Creatures with this ability must make a Will Test once they takes damage. If the Test is failed, the chimaera becomes enraged. As a result, its Brawn and Toughness are temporarily raised by 2 points each, and its Vitality is temporarily increased by 15 Points. In addition, both its Will and Wits are temporarily reduced by 2 points each. Fierce lasts for 1d12 Rounds, and while in this state, Tormentor's are immune to all Fear Tests and ignores any modifiers associated with lost Vitality. As soon as the Fierce state passes, Tormentor's Abilities return to normal, and the boosted Vitality disappears.

- *Horrific Visage:* The Tormentor has a terrifying appearance, and those looking upon it are struck with fear that shakes their resolve. This Trait is always "on", meaning that whenever your Hero comes into contact with the Tormentor, she is affected by the creature's appearance. The effect of this Horrific Visage is such that the target must make a Will Test, with Failure causing her to lose 1 Sanity (4 Sanity on a Dramatic Failure).
- I*nfernal*: This ability is usually found in creatures that originate from otherworldly realms, called Infernal Realms, and confers to the creature an aura of evil that requires all within 10 feet of it to make a Fear Test. Upon failing this Test, the person feels uncomfortable, as well as having a desire to get away as quickly as possible. Infernal creatures are immune to normal weapons, but weapons that have been blessed by a religious figure cause them double damage.
- *Kick:* Tormentors cause damage by kicking. The damage is equal to Brawn +2.
- *Manifest*: The creature is able to enter into the physical world and allows insubstantial creatures to make physical attacks.
- Second Wind: Tormentors can shrug off minor wounds with ease. Once per day, the Tormentor can heal itself of a number of points of Vitality damage equal to its Toughness score.
- *Size (3)*: Tormentors average 12 feet in height.
- *Taint:* Infernal creatures have Taint, which is the evil of the creature that seeps into the natural world. Taint fuels the Infernal creatures when they manifest in the physical world. Taint fuels Infernal creatures as well as acting as their Vitality. Once the creature runs out of Taint, they are forced to leave the physical world and return to their native plane where they must "rest" for a number of days equal to their Will. In addition, it costs Taint to stay in the physical world, and every minute an Infernal creature must expend 1 Taint to stay fixed in the physical world.

These tall, powerfully built devils lead the warriors of Hell in war. To some, they are known as the Sergeants of Hell. The lower half of a Tormentor resembles that of a bull, while its upper half is that of a man, and the head resembles that of a boar.

# Dinosaur, Small – Raptor

Brawn 4 Quickness 10 Toughness 4 Wits 2 Will 2

Resolve 20 Vitality 20

**Skills:** Athletics — Running [+6], Brawl [+10], Tactics [+10]

**Traits:**

- *Bite*: The Bite of a Small Dinosaur does d12+Brawn damage.
- *Claws*: The Claws of a Small Dinosaur do d12+Quickness damage.
- *Scent*: Small Dinosaurs possess an acute sense of smell, allowing them to track prey with ease. These creatures are able to smell an opponent within an 80-foot range. If upwind, the distance is 160 feet, and if downwind, the distance is 40 feet.
- *Size (1)*: The Small Dinosaurs average 7 feet in length.
- *Unfathomable - Pack Hunting*: When 3 or more Raptors hunt together, they all gain a bonus to their attacks due to their ability to hunt in packs. This bonus depends on the number of Raptors; for every three Raptors, there is a +1 cumulative bonus to the TN. Thus, if there are 9 Raptors hunting together, they gain a +3 TN bonus to attacks.

Standing at just 2 feet in height, Raptors are 7 feet long. Smaller dinosaurs, they are covered in feathers that range in color from deep brown to pale green. More cunning then most dinosaurs, Raptors are often found in packs of three or more.

# Dinosaur, Medium – Pterodactyl

Brawn 6 Quickness 10 Toughness 4 Wits 3 Will 5
Resolve 20 Vitality 25

**Skills:** Brawl [+8], Dodge [+10]

**Traits:**

- *Bite*: The Bite of a Medium Dinosaur causes d12+Brawn damage.
- Claws: The Claws of a Medium Dinosaur cause d12 +Quickness damage.
- *Brittle Bones*: The Pterodactyl's bones are so weak that they cannot withstand hard or sudden impacts (falling, being struck by blunt weapons and the like). The creature also takes an additional 1d12 points of damage from any fall greater than 10 feet in height.
- *Glider*: The Pterodactyl has fleshy flaps that allow it to glide on wind currents. The creature may glide through the air as though flying, but only while descending in altitude. For every 20 feet in altitude that it descends, the Pterodactyl may move 80 feet horizontally. Thus, if it leaps off a 40-foot tall structure, it may glide horizontally for 240 feet.
- *Size (1)*: Standing at 6 feet in height, but has a 25-foot wingspan.

Their long bills are filled with sharp teeth, and they are one of the few dinosaurs that are able to fly. Though they fly, it is more a process of gliding on wind currents. Because they are more like gliders, they tend to dwell on cliffs and other high places.

# Dinosaur, Large – Stegosaurus

Brawn 7 Quickness 4 Toughness 10 Wits 4 Will 6
Resolve 30 Vitality 40

**Skills:** Brawl [+11], Defend [+10], Observe [+9]

**Traits:**

- *Bite*: The Bite of a Large Dinosaur causes d12+Brawn damage.
- *Bony Spurs:* Bony spikes protrude from the Stegosaurus's joints, giving it a jagged profile and making it dangerous to grapple. The spurs can do 1 DV attack to anyone the creature is grappling with.
- *Fierce*: The Stegosaurus is naturally aggressive, or becomes angry when threatened. Creatures with this ability must make a Will Test once they takes damage. If the Test is failed, the creature becomes enraged. As a result, its Brawn and Toughness are temporarily raised

by 2 points each, and its Vitality is temporarily increased by 15 Points. In addition, both its Will and Wits are temporarily lowered by 2 points each. Fierce lasts for 1d12 Rounds, and while in this state, the creature is immune to all Fear and ignores any modifiers associated with lost Vitality. As soon as the Fierce state passes, the creature's Abilities return to normal, and the boosted Vitality disappears.

- *Horns*: The Stegosaurus has a set of horns that it can use as a weapon. The damage caused by these Horns is Brawn+1.
- Natural Armor: The Stegosaurus has a tough hide, with an AV of 4.
- *Size* (3): The Stegosaurus stands 14 feet in height, and averages about 30 feet in length.

Standing 14 feet tall and 30 feet long, the Stegosaurus is covered in bony armor, as well as having spurs that race down its spine. A short, squat dinosaur,that despite its fierce nature, is slow to anger and very docile.

# Dinosaur, Large – Tyrannosaurs

Brawn 12 Quickness 12 Toughness 11 Wits 4 Will 10

Resolve 50 Vitality 55

**Skills:** Athletics – Running [+12/+13], Brawl [+15], Intimidation [+11]

**Traits:**

- *Bite*: The Bite of a Large Dinosaur causes d12+Brawn damage.
- *Fierce*: The creature is naturally aggressive, or becomes angry when threatened. Creatures with this ability must make a Will Test once they takes damage. If the Test is failed, the creature becomes enraged. As a result, its Brawn and Toughness are temporarily raised by 2 points each, and its Vitality is temporarily increased by 15 Points. In addition, both its Will and Wits are temporarily lowered by 2 points each. Fierce lasts for 1d12 Rounds, and while in this state, the creature is immune to all Fear and ignores any modifiers associated with lost Vitality. As soon as the Fierce state passes, the creature's Abilities return to normal, and the boosted Vitality disappears.
- *Scent*: The Tyrannosaurus possesses an acute sense of smell, allowing it to track prey with ease. The Tyrannosaurus can smell an opponent within a 90-foot range. If upwind, the distance is 180 feet, and if downwind, the distance is 45 feet.
- *Second Wind*: The Tyrannosaur can shrug off minor wounds with impunity. Once per day, the creature can heal itself of a number of points of Vitality damage equal to its Toughness score.

- *Size* (3): The Tyrannosaur stands 14 feet in height and averages about 30 feet in length.

Standing at 13 feet tall, the Tyrannosaur is 42 feet long from the tip of its nose to tail. Extremely aggressive creatures, Tyrannosaurs are powerful in both jaws and legs, and can easily run down their prey, and then grab it in their powerful jaws. Though with a poor sense of vision, they have a great sense of smell.

# Dinosaur, Giant – Apatosaurus

| | | | | |
|---|---|---|---|---|
| Brawn 16 | Quickness 3 | Toughness 16 | Wits 2 | Will 10 |
| Resolve 30 | Vitality 80 | | | |

**Skills:** Brawl [+16], Intimidation [+10]

**Traits:**

- *Bite*: The Bite of a Giant Dinosaur causes d12+Brawn damage.
- *Kick*: The Apatosaurus causes damage by kicking. The damage is equal to its Brawn +2.
- *Size (4)*: Though 15 feet in height, these dinosaurs average close to 85 feet in length.

- *Stomp:* The Apatosaurus is able to stomp creatures smaller then itself, and causes damage equal to its Toughness x 5 due to their immense size. In addition, this Trait can only be used against creatures that are at least 2 Size scores smaller than itself.

Though only 15 feet tall, the Apatosaurus is one of the longest dinosaurs known, measuring in at 85 feet in length. Large and slow, they are herbivores that live near lakes and swamps, where their long necks allow them to feed on the water bottom as well as grass along the water's edge.

# Elders

| Brawn 10 | Quickness 8 | Toughness 10 | Wits 15 | Will 15 |
|---|---|---|---|---|
| Resolve 75 | Vitality 50 | | | |

**Skills:** Lore [+15], Empathy [+15], Observe [+15], Resist [+18], Sense [+18], Spell —Awake [+15], Spell - Eldritch Tendril [+15], and Spell - Floating Disc [+15]

**Traits:**

- *Fear -4*: Able to cause Fear in its targets. The Fear modifier is applied to a target's Will Test when they make a Fear Test.
- *Fierce*: Elder's are naturally aggressive or becomes angry when threatened. Creatures with this ability must make a Will Test once they takes damage. If the Test is failed, the chimaera becomes enraged. As a result, its Brawn and Toughness are temporarily raised by 2 points each, and its Vitality is temporarily increased by 15 Points. In addition, both its Will and Wits are temporarily reduced by 2 points each. Fierce lasts for 1d12 Rounds, and while in this state, Elder's are immune to all Fear Tests and ignores any modifiers associated with lost Vitality. As soon as the Fierce state passes, Elder's Abilities return to normal, and the boosted Vitality disappears.
- *Flight*: Elders are able to fly using their wings.
- *Horrific Visage*: The Elder has a terrifying appearance, and those looking upon it are struck with fear that shakes their resolve. This Trait is always "on", meaning that whenever your Hero comes into contact with an Elder, she is affected by the creature's appearance. The effect of this Horrific Visage is such that the target must make a Will Test, with Failure causing her to lose 1 Sanity (4 Sanity on a Dramatic Failure).
- N*ight Vision*: The Elder is able to see in the dark as easily as it sees in full daylight, and ignores all penalties while fighting in the dark.

- *Spellcaster*: The creature is able to work magic, and has at least one Spell it is able to perform.
- *Telekinesis*: The Elder is able to move objects without touching them, using the power of its mind. The Elder can move a number of objects equal to its Will, and furthermore, it can move up to (Will times 10) lbs. in weight. This weight can either be one object or a number of objects that equal this total weight. Objects can also be moved a number of feet equal to Toughness+d12; if used as a weapon, an object does damage equal to the Elder's Will.

Found mentioned in the *Necronomicon* as well as other esoteric works, Elders are very suspect in terms of their existence. Though some sages and scholars argue and theorize that these creatures are a lost race, no one has seen them, and if they have, have not survived the experience. If they do indeed exist, they might exist in Atlantis, Mū or even the Wastes of Mictlan. It was the scholar E'ch-Pi-El who first wrote about them, in his work *Dissertations of the Past*, in which he wrote:

> *Six feet end to end, there and five-tenths feet central diameter, tapering to one foot at each end. Like a barrel with five bulging ridges in place of staves. Lateral breakages, as of thinnish stalks, are at equator in middle of these ridges. In furrows between ridges are curious growths - combs or wings that fold up and spread out like fans...*

# Elementals

Most of the inhabitants of The World do not realize that life is made up of a combination of elements. All life is a balance between these five elements, and all life is made up of them. Wizards, especially those who live in the decaying and decadent Atlantis, know the means of summoning Elementals, which are the physical embodiment of the elements. Elementals are not native to the physical world, as they are spirits native to different dimensions.

## Air Elemental — Sylph

Brawn 7 Quickness 15 Toughness 7 Wits 7 Will 12

Resolve 60 Plasm 60

**Skills:** Brawl [+9], Dodge [+17}, Resist [+13], Sense [+13]

**Traits:**

- *Flight*: Sylphs are able to fly through the use of their wings.

- *Immunity — Earth*: Sylphs suffer no damage when they come into contact with the element of earth. .
- *Insubstantial*: Insubstantial is the ability that allows the creature to shift its body from a solid state to a gaseous state. In this state, all physical attacks pass through the creature harmlessly, causing no damage. In addition, while in this state, the creature is unable to make any physical attacks.
- *Invisibility*: Sylphs have the ability to become Invisible, and gain a +2 to their Initiative and are at a -4 TN to be Hit. They can stay Invisible a number of Rounds equal their Will.
- *Manifest*: The creature is able to enter into the physical world and allows insubstantial creatures to make physical attacks.
- *Plasm*: The Sylph is able to tap into a source of power outside the scope of men, that fuels its abilities. This power, once drained, ends the Sylph's hold and ties to the physical world, and it must rest to regain more Plasm. When Sylphs manifest in the physical world, they expend Plasm. Every Round the Sylph is in the physical realm, it costs them 1 Plasm. Once the Sylph's Plasm is reduced to 0, they are forced to leave the physical realm and return to their home realm, and must rest while they regain their Plasm. Sylphs regain Plasm in a number of Rounds equal to their Will.
- *Shift*: By creating a rift, the Sylph is able to Shift its position by 5 feet as an Action. Shifting requires a Will Test, with success allowing the Sylph to shift. Dramatic Success allows the it to shift 10 feet. Failing the Test means the Sylph does not Shift, and a Dramatic Failure causes the Sylph to lose 5 Plasm.
- *Speed*: The Sylph is extremely fast, giving it the ability to chase down an opponent, or allowing it to have quicker reaction times. Sylphs gain a +1 to their Initiative Tests, as well as double their movement.
- *Telekinesis*: The creature is able to move objects without touching them, using the power of its mind or personality. The creature is able to move a number of objects equal to its Will, and furthermore, the creature can move up to Will times 10 lbs. in weight. This weight can either be one object or a number of objects that equal this weight. Objects can also be moved a number of feet equal to Toughness+d12; if used as a weapon, an object does damage equal to the creature's Will.
- *Weakness — Fire*: The Sylph has a weakness against fire. When in contact with or exposed to fire , the Sylph suffers double damage.

No one, not even the most ancient of wizards, has ever seen a Sylph. They appear as shimmering forms in the air, and their touch, depending on their mood, is as soft as a summer breeze, or as violent as a winter storm.

## Earth Elemental — Gnome

| Brawn 10 | Quickness 7 | Toughness 15 | Wits 4 | Will 10 |
|---|---|---|---|---|
| Resolve 50 | Plasm 50 | | | |

**Skills:** Bargain [+10], Brawl [+11], Craft (Stonework) [+9], Empathy [+12]

**Traits:**

- *Fear -3*: Able to cause Fear in its targets. The Fear modifier is applied to a target's Will Test when they make a Fear Test.
- *Hug*: This ability allows a creature to damage an opponent by squeezing or hugging them (either by enfolding the Hero in its arms, coiling around them with its body, or any other physical means it can use to Squeeze them). In order to use this ability, the creature must make a successful Brawl Test to grab its opponent. Those trapped can try to break out by making a successful Brawn Test. For every round trapped in the hug of the creature, the opponent suffers a cumulative -1 to the Test. For example, if the opponent has been in the hug for 3 Rounds he would suffer a -3 to the Test. The damage from this ability is equal to the creature's Brawn + Toughness.
- *Immunity — Fire and Heat*: Gnomes suffer no damage when they come into contact with fire, flames and/or heat.
- *Manifest*: The creature is able to enter into the physical world and allows insubstantial creatures to make physical attacks.
- *Natural Armor* [AV10]: Gnome's skin resembles rock.
- *Plasm*: The creature is able to tap into a source of power outside the scope of men, that fuels its abilities. This power, once drained, ends the creature's hold and ties to the physical world, and it must rest to regain more Plasm. When creatures with Plasm manifest in the physical world, they expend Plasm. Every round the creature is in the physical realm, it costs them 1 Plasm. Once the creature's Plasm is reduced to 0, they leave the physical realm and return to their home realm, and must rest while they regain their Plasm. They regain plasm in a number of Rounds equal to their Will.
- *Size (-1)*
- *Weakness, Water and Cold*: Gnomes suffer double damage from water and cold.

- *Unfathomable (Elemental Movement):* Gnomes are able to move through earth as easily as a person moves on the ground.

Standing no more than 4' high, Gnomes are creatures made from stone and mud, who are able to move through earth as easily as a person moves on the ground. They view themselves as the protectors of the earth's treasures, and they jealously guard all precious metals and gems as if they were their own. Though they typically shun humans, Gnomes tend to be slow to anger. Once angered, or threatened, they seek a means to end the threat as quickly as possible.

## Fire Elemental — Salamander

Brawn 4 Quickness 18 Toughness 4 Wits 7 Will 12

Resolve 60 Plasm 60

**Skills:** Brawl [+10], Dodge [+18], Resist [+10], Sense [+10]

**Traits:**

- *Cold Susceptibility*: The Salamander's body does not react well to particularly cold temperatures. Salamanders take double damage from prolonged exposure to extreme cold, as well as weapons, spells and the like.
- *Control — Flames and Heat*: Salamanders are able to control flames and heat. To use this ability the Salamander must make a Will Test, with success indicating that the creature successfully controls the object. The number of objects the Salamander can control is equal to its Will stat. The duration of this Control is equal to half the Salamander's Will and the range is equal to its Will x 5 feet.
- *Immunity — Fire*: Salamanders suffer no damage when they come into contact with flames, fire, or heat. *Manifest*: The creature is able to enter into the physical world and allows insubstantial creatures to make physical attacks.
- *Poison*: The touch of a Salamander is very poisonous. Those who touch, or are attacked, by the creature need to make a Toughness Test. Failure has them suffer 10 damage, and an additional 5 damage for 10 Rounds (Dramatic Failure results in the damage being doubled).
- *Plasm*: The creature is able to tap into a source of power outside the scope of men, that fuels its abilities. This power, once drained, ends the creature's hold and ties to the physical world, and it must rest to regain more Plasm. When creatures with Plasm manifest in the physical world, they expend Plasm. Every round the creature is in the physical realm, it costs them 1 Plasm. Once the creature's Plasm is reduced to 0, they leave the physical realm and return to their home

realm, and must rest while they regain their Plasm. They regain plasm in a number of Rounds equal to their Will.

- *Size (-2)*
- *Unfathomable (Extinguish)*: The Salamander is able to extinguish any flames that they touch.
- *Weakness - Water*: The Salamander has a weakness to water. When in contact with or exposed to water, the Salamander suffers double damage.

No longer than 2 feet in length, Salamanders have the body of a lizard and the face of a bearded, old man.

## Magic Elemental — Will-o'-Wisp

Brawn 1 Quickness 17 Toughness 1 Wits 12 Will 12

Resolve 60 Plasm 60

**Skills:** Dodge [+17], Lore [+12], Resist [+10], Sense [+14]

**Traits:**

- *Breath*: Magic Energy [DV 6(90), R 50, ROF 1/1]
- *Drain*: Sanity (touching the target drains her 6 of Sanity/Round in contact).
- *Flight*: The Will-o'-Wisp is able to fly due to its being made out of energy.
- *Hypersensitivity*: The Will-o'-Wisp is particularly sensitive to its surroundings, and gains a +2 bonus on Investigation and Observe Tests.
- *Immunity — Air and Water:* Will-o'-Wisps suffer no damage when they come into contact with air and water, and are immune to attacks made with these two elements.
- *Insubstantial*: Insubstantial is the ability that allows the creature to shift its body from a solid state to a ghostly state. In this state, all physical attacks pass through the creature harmlessly, causing no damage. In addition, while in this state, the creature is unable to make any physical attacks.
- *Manifest*: The creature is able to enter into the physical world and allows insubstantial creatures to make physical attacks.
- *Plasm*: The creature is able to tap into a source of power outside the scope of men, that fuels its abilities. This power, once drained, ends the creature's hold and ties to the physical world, and it must rest to regain more Plasm. When creatures with Plasm manifest in the

physical world, they expend Plasm. Every round the creature is in the physical realm, it costs them 1 Plasm. Once the creature's Plasm is reduced to 0, they leave the physical realm and return to their home realm, and must rest while they regain their Plasm. They regain plasm in a number of Rounds equal to their Will.

- *Shift*: By creating a rift, the creature is able to shift its position by 5 feet as an Action. Shifting requires a Will Test, with success allowing the creature to shift. Dramatic Success allows the creature to shift 10 feet. Failing the Test means the creature does not shift, and a Dramatic Failure causes the creature to lose 5 Plasm.
- *Weakness — Earth and Fire*: The Will-o'-Wisps has a weakness to earth, as well as fire. When in contact with or exposed to its weaknesses, Will-o'-Wisps suffer double damage and might be unable to act.

Unknown to many, Magic is an element. It is as fundamental to life as earth, fire, air, and water. Though sorcerers are able to work magic, many do not realize how fundamental it is in nature. Will-o'-Wisps appear as balls of light that float in the air, and dart around in a rapid, seemingly haphazard way. Typically white, their colors change depending on their emotional state.

## Water Elemental — Undines

Brawn 5 Quickness 18 Toughness 4 Wits 9 Will 10

Resolve 50 Plasm 50

**Skills:** Athletics — Swim [/+8+9], Brawl [+6], Performance [+11], Socialize [+11]

**Traits:**

- *Control — Men*: The Undine is able to control men. To use this Trait, the Undine must make a Will Test, with success indicating that it successfully controls the person in question. The number of people the Undine can control is equal to its Will score. The duration is equal to half the Undine's Will, and the range is equal to the Undine's Will x 5 in feet.
- *Gills*: Undines possess a set of gills allowing them to draw oxygen out of water. The gills appear on the Undine's neck. Consequently, the Undine can breathe both in and out of water, and never has to worry about the possibility of drowning.
- *Immune — Fire*: Undines suffer no damage when they come into contact with fire, flames, and/or heat.

- *Insubstantial*: Insubstantial is the ability that allows the creature to shift its body from a solid state to a gaseous state. In this state, all physical attacks pass through the creature harmlessly, causing no damage. In addition, while in this state, the creature is unable to make any physical attacks.
- *Manifest*: The creature is able to enter into the physical world and allows insubstantial creatures to make physical attacks.
- *Plasm*: The creature is able to tap into a source of power outside the scope of men, that fuels its abilities. This power, once drained, ends the creature's hold and ties to the physical world, and it must rest to regain more Plasm. When creatures with Plasm manifest in the physical world, they expend Plasm. Every round the creature is in the physical realm, it costs them 1 Plasm. Once the creature's Plasm is reduced to 0, they leave the physical realm and return to their home realm, and must rest while they regain their Plasm. They regain plasm in a number of Rounds equal to their Will.
- *Weakness – Earth*: The Undine has a weakness, earth. When in contact with or exposed to their weakness, Undines suffer double damage and might be unable to act.

The beauties of the water, Undines are typically found in forest pools and waterfalls, but they are also sometimes found in tidal pools and the like. Possessing beautiful voices, which are sometimes heard over the sound of the water, Undines seek men to control as well as prey upon.

# Gargoyle

Brawn 10 Quickness 9 Toughness 9 Wits 10 Will 11

Resolve 55 Vitality 55

**Skills:** Brawl [+11], Dodge [+10], Observe [+11], Track [+10]

**Trait:**

- *Bite*: The Bite of the Gargoyle does d12+Brawn damage.
- *Claws*: The Claws of the Gargoyle inflict d12+Quickness damage.
- *Fear -3*: Able to cause Fear in its targets. The Fear modifier is applied to a target's Will Test when they make a Fear Test.
- *Fierce*: Gargoyle's are naturally aggressive or becomes angry when threatened. Creatures with this ability must make a Will Test once they takes damage. If the Test is failed, the Gargoyle becomes enraged. As a result, its Brawn and Toughness are temporarily raised by 2 points each, and its Vitality is temporarily increased by 15 Points. In addition, both its Will and Wits are temporarily reduced by 2 points each. Fierce lasts for 1d12 Rounds, and while in this state, Gargoyle's are immune to all Fear Tests and ignores any modifiers associated with lost Vitality. As soon as the Fierce state passes, Gargoyle's Abilities return to normal, and the boosted Vitality disappears.
- *Flight*: The Gargoyle is able to fly because it has wings. *Horrific Visage:* The Gargoyle has a terrifying appearance, and those looking upon it are struck with fear that shakes their resolve. This Trait is always "on", meaning that whenever your Hero comes into contact with a Gargoyle, she is affected by the creature's appearance. The effect of this Horrific Visage is such that the opponent must make a Will Test, with Failure causing them to lose 1 Sanity (4 Sanity on a Dramatic Failure).
- *Night Vision*: The Gargoyle is able to see in the dark as easily as it sees in full daylight, and ignores all penalties while fighting in the dark.

A vile creature, the Gargoyle is fierce as well as often being used by evil beings as mounts. These creatures prefer the night, as well as high places, and tend to be solitary, unless they choose to mate. The great scholar, E'ch-Pi-El, once described them as:

> *"...hybrid winged things, not altogether crows, nor moles, nor buzzards, not ants, nor decomposed human beings, but something I cannot and must not control."*

# Golem

| Brawn 12 | Quickness 3 | Toughness 6 | Wits 3 | Will 5 |
| --- | --- | --- | --- | --- |
| Resolve 25 | Vitality 45 | | | |

**Skills:** Brawl [+12], Defend [+8]

**Traits:**

- *Damage Reduction*: Golems take half damage from bladed weapons.
- *Fear -1*: Able to cause Fear in its targets. The Fear modifier is applied to a target's Will Test when they make a Fear Test.
- *Size (1)*
- *Unfathomable - Blend*: Golems can appear inanimate and blend in with rocky surroundings or darkness easily. When hiding in place, clay golems have an effective Subterfuge Skill of 10. This ability does not work when the Golem moves.
- *Unfathomable — Smash*: A Golem's fists do 5(60) damage.
- *Weakness*: Golems take double damage from clubs.

Created by Alchemists, Golems are man-like forms sculpted from clay and given life through the Alchemical Arts. Usually they are much larger than normal humans, ranging from six to ten feet in height. Golems obey the commands of their creator at all times. They are famously literal-minded, however, and so their creators must be very careful and specific in

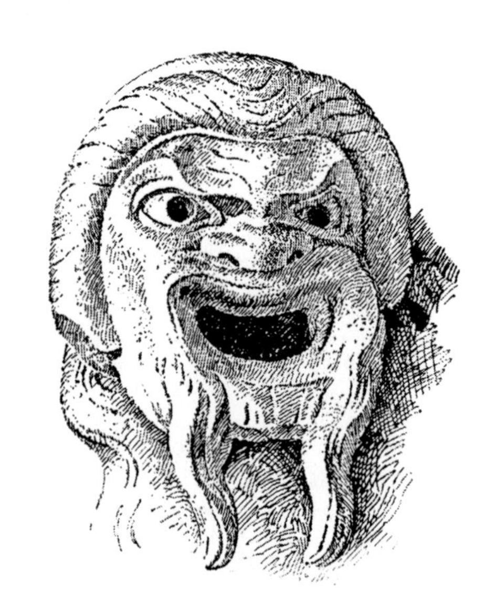

# Homunculus

Brawn 4 Quickness 10 Toughness 4 Wits 4 Will 7
Resolve 35 Vitality 20

**Skills:** Brawl [+7], Dodge [+11], Empathy [+8], Resist [+6], Sense [+6]

**Traits:**

- *Claws*: The Claws of the Homunculus cause d12+Quickness damage.
- *Drain*: The touch of the Homunculus drains Vitality equal to Will.
- *Fear -2*: Able to cause Fear in its targets. The Fear modifier is applied to a target's Will Test when they make a Fear Test.
- *Flight*: The Homunculus is able to fly because of its rather ugly wings.
- *Horrific Visage*: The Homunculus has a terrifying appearance, and those looking upon it are struck with fear that shakes their resolve. This Trait is always "on", meaning that whenever your Hero comes into contact with a Homunculus, she is affected by the creature's appearance. The effect of this Horrific Visage is such that the opponent must make a Will Test, with Failure causing them to lose 1 Sanity (4 Sanity on a Dramatic Failure).

- *Size (-2)*: Homunculi are no more than 2 feet tall.
- *Unfathomable (Transference)*: A Homunculus is able to give Vitality equal to its Will to the Alchemist who created it.

Resembling a small baby, with bat-like wings and a face that looks as if it was fashioned from melted wax, the Homunculus is an Alchemical creation, and can only comes to life via the skill of an Alchemist.

# Kraken

Brawn 15 Quickness 14 Toughness 17 Wits 5 Will 13

Resolve 65 Vitality 80

**Skills:** Athletics – Swim [+15/+16], Brawl [+17]

**Traits:**

- *Bite*: The Bite of a Kraken is quite terrible, and does d12+Brawn damage.
- *Extra Attacks*: Krakens have a total of 9 attacks, 1 for each Tentacle (see below), and 1 for its Bite.
- *Fear -4*: Able to cause Fear in its targets. The Fear modifier is applied to a target's Will Test when they make a Fear Test.
- *Horrific Visage*: The Kraken has a terrifying appearance, and those looking upon it are struck with fear that shakes their resolve. This Trait is always "on", meaning that whenever your Hero comes into contact with a Kraken, she is affected by the creature's appearance. The effect of this Horrific Visage is such that the opponent must make a Will Test, with Failure causing them to lose 1 Sanity (4 Sanity on a Dramatic Failure).
- *Hug*: This ability allows a creature to damage an opponent by squeezing or hugging them (either by enfolding the Hero in its arms, coiling around them with its body, or any other physical means it can use to Squeeze them). In order to use this ability, the creature must make a successful Brawl Test to grab its opponent. Those trapped can try to break out by making a successful Brawn Test. For every round trapped in the hug of the creature, the opponent suffers a cumulative -1 to the Test. For example, if the opponent has been in the hug for 3 Rounds he would suffer a -3 to the Test. The damage from this ability is equal to the creature's Brawn + Toughness.
- *Size (5)*: Krakens are said to be 20 feet in length, though some rumors state they can be as huge as 40 feet.
- *Unfathomable - Tentacles*: Kraken have a total of 8 tentacles measuring some 40 feet in length that inflict damage using the Hug (see above).

Krakens are considered to be a rumor or myth, but many sailors swear they have seen them. Krakens are monsters that live beneath the oceans' depths, and only rise when it is time to feed.

# Manticore

Brawn 11 Quickness 9 Toughness 10 Wits 4 Will 12
Resolve 60 Vitality 50

**Skills:** Brawl [+12], Dodge [+9], Intimidation [+12]

**Traits:**

- *Claws*: The Claws of the Manticore inflict d12+Quickness damage.
- *Fear -3*: Able to cause Fear in its targets. The Fear modifier is applied to a target's Will Test when they make a Fear Test.
- *Horrific Visage*: The Manticore has a terrifying appearance, and those looking upon it are struck with fear that shakes their resolve. This Trait is always "on", meaning that whenever your Hero comes into contact with the Manticore, she is affected by the creature's appearance. The effect of this Horrific Visage is such that the opponent must make a Will Test, with Failure causing them to lose 1 Sanity (4 Sanity on a Dramatic Failure).

- *Moan — Roar*: Anyone within a 50-foot radius of the Manticore must make a Will Test, with Failure causing them to lose Sanity equal to half of the Manticore's Resolve. Dramatic Failure causes them to lose all of their Sanity.
- *Night Vision*: The Manticore is able to see in the dark as easily as it sees in full daylight, and ignores all penalties while fighting in the dark.
- *Poison*: The Manticore's tail is poisonous, and does damage to any opponents struck by it. Anyone successfully hit by the Manticore's tail must make a successful Opposed Toughness Test or will be poisoned, suffering damage equal to the Degree of Success multiplied by 5.
- *Second Wind*: The Manticore can shrug off minor wounds with ease. Once per day the Manticore can heal itself of a number of points of Vitality damage equal to its Toughness score.
- *Tail*: The tail of the Manticore is tipped with a vicious stinger which secretes poison. Creature's struck by the tail suffer damage equal to the Manticore's Toughness x 2.

A Manticore has the body of a lion, the head of a man, and the tail of a scorpion. Manticores are furious beasts, that some argue are only possible due to the Alchemical Arts. However, some Manticores have been seen in the south that live naturally, and are not the products of Alchemy.

# Pegasus

Brawn 10 Quickness 10 Toughness 10 Wits 4 Will 11

Resolve 35 Vitality 50

**Skills:** Brawl [+11], Dodge [+11], Observe [+14], Resist [+9], Sense [+9]

**Traits:**

- *Flight*: The Pegasus is able to fly because of its wondrous wings.
- *Hypersensitivity*: The Pegasus is particularly sensitive to its surroundings, and gains a +2 bonus on Investigation and Observe Tests.
- *Night Vision*: The Pegasus is able to see in the dark as easily as it sees in full daylight, and ignores all penalties while fighting in the dark.
- *Spirit Animal*: The Pegasus gain a +1 bonus to all of its Abilities (which reflect this bonus). In addition, Pegasi are immune to Fear, and will aid all creatures within 10 feet of them by granting a +1 Bonus to all Fear Tests.

Created via Alchemical means, though some speculate that they can be found in the East, these creatures look like horses but have the wings of an eagle. Pegasus are the size of a regular horse, and their wings typically measure 20 feet

# Shark

Brawn 8 Quickness 11 Toughness 8 Wits 4 Will 11

Resolve 55 Vitality 40

**Skills:** Athletics – Swim [+7/+9], Brawl [+9]

**Traits:**

- *Bite*: The Bite of a Shark causes d12+Brawn damage.
- *Fear -1*: Able to cause Fear in its targets. The Fear modifier is applied to a target's Will Test when they make a Fear Test.
- *Fierce*: Shark's are naturally aggressive or becomes angry when threatened. Creatures with this ability must make a Will Test once they takes damage. If the Test is failed, the chimaera becomes enraged. As a result, its Brawn and Toughness are temporarily raised by 2 points each, and its Vitality is temporarily increased by 15 Points. In addition, both its Will and Wits are temporarily reduced by 2 points each. Fierce lasts for 1d12 Rounds, and while in this state, Shark's are

immune to all Fear Tests and ignores any modifiers associated with lost Vitality. As soon as the Fierce state passes, Shark's Abilities return to normal, and the boosted Vitality disappears.

- *Scent*: The Shark possesses an acute sense of smell, allowing it to track prey with ease. Sharks are able to smell an opponent within a 90-foot range. If "upwind," the distance is 180 feet, and if "downwind," the distance is 45 feet. This range can be increased for each additional point spent.
- *Size (2)*

The fiercest of all the ocean's predators, Sharks can be found in all oceans of The World. Though there are smaller sharks, the one's most sailors know are known as The Great White and average close to 20 feet in length.

# Shoggoth

Brawn 11 Quickness 12 Toughness 11 Wits 7 Will 12

Resolve 60 Vitality 55

**Skills:** Brawl [+11], Observe [+10], Resist [+9], Sense [+9]

**Traits:**

- *Elasticity*: The Shoggoth is able to bend and twist its body in unnatural ways, allowing it to squeeze into and through very tight spaces. Consequently, the Shoggoth can squeeze through an opening or passage one-fifth as wide and tall as its height, in inches, although it does so very slowly compared to its normal movement rate.
- *Fear -4*: Able to cause Fear in its targets. The Fear modifier is applied to a target's Will Test when they make a Fear Test.
- *Horrific Visage*: The Shoggoth has a terrifying appearance, and those looking upon it are struck with fear that shakes their resolve. This Trait is always "on", meaning that whenever your Hero comes into contact with a Shoggoth, she is affected by the creature's appearance. The effect of this Horrific Visage is such that the opponent must make a Will Test, with Failure causing them to lose 1 Sanity (4 Sanity on a Dramatic Failure).
- *Immunity - Physical Attacks:* The Shoggoth is immune to physical attacks, and suffers no damage when they are physically attacked.
- *Size (3)*: Shoggoth's measure close to 12 feet in length.
- *Speed*: The Shoggoth is extremely fast, giving it the ability to chase down an opponent, or allowing it to have quicker reaction times.

Shoggoths gain a +1 to their Initiative Tests, as well as doubling their movement.

- *Squeeze*: This ability allows a creature to damage an opponent by squeezing or hugging them (either by enfolding the Hero in its arms, coiling around them with its body, or any other physical means it can use to Squeeze them). In order to use this ability, the creature must make a successful Brawl Test to grab its opponent. Those trapped can try to break out by making a successful Brawn Test. For every round trapped in the hug of the creature, the opponent suffers a cumulative -1 to the Test. For example, if the opponent has been in the hug for 3 Rounds he would suffer a -3 to the Test. The damage from this ability is equal to the creature's Brawn + Toughness.

A very rare creature, the Shoggoth is one that no has survived to tell tales about. This creature was created by the Elders for reasons unknown. Only one person has ever lived to describe what Shoggoth look like. It was E'ch-Pi-El who described them as:

> *"It was a terrible, indescribable thing vaster than any... —a shapeless congeries of protoplasmic bubbles, faintly self-luminous, and with myriads of temporary eyes forming and un-forming as pustules of greenish light all over the tunnel-filling front that bore down upon us, crushing the frantic penguins and slithering over the glistening floor that it and its kind had swept so evilly free of all litter."*

# Unicorn

Brawn 10 Quickness 10 Toughness 10 Wits 4 Will 13
Resolve 65 Vitality 40

**Skills:** Brawl [+11], Resist [+9], Sense [+9]

**Traits:**

- *Gore*: The Unicorn is able to use its Horn to attack an opponent, and does Quickness+1 damage.
- *Horn*: The Unicorn has a single horn that it is able to use as a weapon. The damage caused by Horns is Brawn+1.
- *Hypersensitivity*: Unicorns are particularly sensitive to their surroundings, and gain a +2 bonus on Investigation and Observe Tests.
- *Night Vision*: The Unicorn is able to see in the dark as easily as it sees in full daylight, and ignores all penalties while fighting in the dark.
- *Spirit Animal*: The Unicorn gains a +1 bonus to all Abilities (abilities reflect this bonus). In addition, Unicorns are immune to Fear, and will aid all creatures within 10 feet of them by granting a +1 Bonus to all Fear Tests.

Created via Alchemy, some so-called experts have speculated that Unicorns can be found in the West. These creatures look like horses, but have a horn atop their heads.

# Whale

Brawn 14 Quickness 10 Toughness 14 Wits 8 Will 15

Resolve 65 Vitality 50

**Skills:** Athletics – Swim [+14/+16], Brawl [+14]

**Traits:**

- *Bite*: The Bite of a While causes d12+Brawn damage.
- *Fear -3*: Able to cause Fear in its targets. The Fear modifier is applied to a target's Will Test when they make a Fear Test.
- *Fierce*: Shark's are naturally aggressive or becomes angry when threatened. Creatures with this ability must make a Will Test once they takes damage. If the Test is failed, the chimaera becomes enraged. As a result, its Brawn and Toughness are temporarily raised by 2 points each, and its Vitality is temporarily increased by 15 Points. In addition, both its Will and Wits are temporarily reduced by 2 points each. Fierce lasts for 1d12 Rounds, and while in this state, Shark's are immune to all Fear Tests and ignores any modifiers associated with lost Vitality. As soon as the Fierce state passes, Shark's Abilities return to normal, and the boosted Vitality disappears.

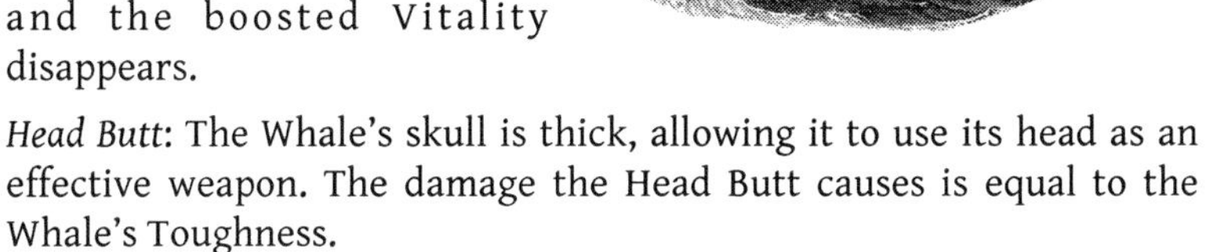

- *Head Butt*: The Whale's skull is thick, allowing it to use its head as an effective weapon. The damage the Head Butt causes is equal to the Whale's Toughness.
- *Natural Armor* AV 10: Due to the whale's blubbery hide, it is very tough to penetrate their hide.
- *Size (4):* Whale's range in length, but the typical size is 16 feet.
- *Unfathomable – Tail Buff:* Can use its Tail to slap, and this causes (Brawn + Toughness) damage.

Whales are large creatures native to the seas; Whales are found throughout The World. There are numerous types of whale ranging in color and size.

CPSIA information can be obtained at www.ICGtesting.com
224547LV00002B/6/P

9 780979 636196